The Good, the Bad
and the Little Bit Stupid

The Good, the Bad and the Little Bit Stupid

MARINA LEWYCKA

PENGUIN BOOKS

PENGUIN BOOKS

UK | USA | Canada | Ireland | Australia
India | New Zealand | South Africa

Penguin Books is part of the Penguin Random House group of companies
whose addresses can be found at global.penguinrandomhouse.com.

First published by Fig Tree 2020
Published in Penguin Books 2021
001

Copyright © Marina Lewycka, 2020

The moral right of the author has been asserted

Typeset by Jouve (UK), Milton Keynes
Printed and bound in Great Britain by Clays Ltd, Elcograf S.p.A.

The authorized representative in the EEA is Penguin Random House Ireland,
Morrison Chambers, 32 Nassau Street, Dublin D02 YH68

A CIP catalogue record for this book is available from the British Library

ISBN: 978-0-241-43032-3

www.greenpenguin.co.uk

MIX
Paper from
responsible sources
FSC® C018179

Penguin Random House is committed to a
sustainable future for our business, our readers
and our planet. This book is made from Forest
Stewardship Council® certified paper.

This book is dedicated to the World's
Greatest Living Historian, who also
cooks a mean rack of lamb.

Each year over £2 billion is lost to financial fraud in the UK, and often this money is ploughed right back into other criminal enterprises, from drug trafficking to people smuggling to organ harvesting. This is a story about one family's modest contribution to that sum – how George gets caught up in it, and how his son Sid, his wife Rosie and his . . . er . . . mistress Brenda join forces to rescue him.

If you want to read a warm-hearted story, about how villains get their just rewards, and the good guys find happiness in the end, this is not the right book for you; in fact there are no good guys in this book, unless you count George and Rosie Pantis who, like most people, are both good and bad and a little bit stupid. They're both quite embarrassed at how they behaved and they've each got their own version of the truth. George believes it is essentially a story about how passion never dies (*his* passion of course). Rosie believes it is a story about how easily people (apart from herself) can be conned, politically as well as financially. But to Sid the overall message is utterly clear: never trust *anybody* with your banking password. Sid will guide you through the quagmire of his family and their story about marriage, money and kidney theft.

Sid sees financial fraud as a flat-out game played out on a global pitch between the financial industry, who are busily developing new fraud-prevention technologies, and the criminals, who are discovering increasingly creative new ways to steal from us. In this view, his father George is just another innocent punter, waiting to be fleeced, and the beginning of this story is when he gets an excited phone call from George one evening in July saying he has won a billion lek in a foreign lottery that he never entered. Or perhaps, Sid reflects, it really all started three weeks before that, in the bitter aftermath of the 2016 referendum in June, when the wheels finally came off his parents' increasingly rickety marriage and they went their separate ways, setting his 79-year-old father free to chase after his dubious dreams.

Sid's parents, George and Rosie Pantis, have always been an oddly matched couple, so different in age they belong to different generations, and it is a wonder, he thinks, that they have managed to stay married for more than thirty years. George was born in 1936 into a world perched on the abyss of war, a world of all-pervasive brownness that you can still see in the photographs that have survived from that era: muddy home-grown football squads, beige hand-knitted cardigans, taupe trilby hats, and puddings browned in the oven. Its musical accompaniments were big band, jazz and those classic crooner songs which Sid has tried to imitate and add to his repertoire. It believed in old-fashioned codes of masculinity and class deference. Rosie was born in 1956, just in time for the sixties to shower their bounty of colour, fabulous music and egalitarian attitudes upon her while she was growing up. No wonder, Sid thinks, that Rosie and George argue a lot, often in public, in embarrassingly loud voices. When the split finally happened, on 23rd June 2016, Sid and his sister Cassie were not particularly surprised. George voted for Brexit for reasons Rosie never understood.

'Take back control!' George shouted, before he nipped outside for the fateful cigarette.

Sid has perhaps reacted to all the politics that surrounded him as he was growing up, by steering clear of argument and expressing himself mainly through music. He plays a mixture of old and contemporary music on the acoustic guitar, as well as some of his own compositions.

He is nicknamed Sensible Sid.

SID: Panties

One Friday in mid-July 2016, a miserable summer's day with an early, misty drizzle of rain turning into a warm, steady downpour as the day wears on, Sid leaves work late, so the traffic has already built up. Somewhere up ahead, according to the radio, a van destined for one of Sheffield's sex shops has skidded out of control, smashed into a lorry and shed its load of kinky videos and sex toys across both lanes of the Ring Road. There is a note of glee in the announcer's voice as he describes the looting.

Sid needs something to cheer him up. There's something particularly deadening about the combination of evening, rain, Yorkshire and traffic jams that could bring down the most buoyant of personalities, which he guesses don't include him. Stuck in his car on the Ring Road, listening to the news on the radio, and watching his windscreen wipers flick uselessly backwards and forwards, spreading a film of grease across the glass, he has plenty of time to imagine the scene of the crash and to replay scenes from his parents' car crash of a marriage in his mind, each time focusing on different details. Suddenly his phone rings. It is his father, his voice breathless with emotion.

'Listen, Sid, do you know what?'

'What is it, Dad?' One of his favourite songs is on the radio. 'Save the Last Dance for Me'. He hums along beneath his breath, humouring his father, thinking of Jacquie, imagining dancing cheek to cheek with her and the dance going on forever, hoping she'll be there when he gets back.

5

'I just had a phone call of congratulations from the Kosovan State Lottery. They told me I have won a billion lek. Of course an Albanian lek is worth quite a bit less than a pound, but when I worked it out it comes to seven million, three hundred thousand, three hundred and twenty-one pounds and thirty-three pence.'

In front of Sid, a small blue van brakes abruptly and he almost goes into the back of it.

'Thirty-three pence? Are you sure?'

'Sure I'm sure. Do you think I'm stupid?'

'Hold on, Dad.' Sid tries to bring his father back down to earth gently, knowing he is sometimes given to flights of fancy. 'Did you actually buy a ticket for this lottery?'

'Possibly. I may have done.' Pause. 'I can't remember, Sid. I do vaguely remember filling in an online form ages ago. They wanted all kinds of personal information and contact details, and in exchange they entered me in the lottery. And I must have won. I won the lottery.'

Sid feels both irritated and at the same time protective towards his father. He guesses that George hasn't bought a ticket at all, and somebody is trying to scam him, poor befuddled old codger that he is, hailing from his brown pre-technological world.

'It's probably a scam, so just ignore it. And I suppose they asked you for your bank details, so they could deposit the money?'

'How did you know?'

'They need an account number and sort code, but they don't need your password or PIN to deposit money, just to take it out. These people, they specially target the confused and elderly. Listen, Dad, the best thing is if you go into your branch in person. Set up a new password to the account you keep your money in.'

6

'Elderly? Confused? Who exactly are you talking about?'

'You know what I mean, Dad. You can even do it online, if you can get to grips with the technology. And don't use something obvious like your birthday. Or mine. Or Cassie's. Choose something random. Make up a memorable sentence like, "I am George Pantis and I am seventy-nine years old." You won't forget that. Then use the first letters for your password, IAGPAIA79YO. A combination of upper case, lower case and numerals.'

'Can you say that again slowly?' George says.

'No, Dad. Make up your own sentence. Do it now. It's probably just a scam, but they may try to infect your computer with malware. So don't click on any links in the email. And whatever you do, don't share your new password with anybody, not even the staff at the bank.'

'Thanks, Sid. I knew you'd have some sensible advice.'

'Then you can just forget about the money. It's not worth getting excited about.'

Sid thinks he detects a very quiet click on the line as he says this, as though a phone extension has just been replaced. Has Brenda been listening? Ah well, it is probably all nonsense anyway. But his father is clearly hooked on the idea.

'I can get a sports car now, top of the range, like I've always wanted. We can get life membership of Sheffield United. Whatever you set your heart on, if money can buy it, we can have it,' he burbles happily.

'Forget it. It's not your money, is it, Dad?'

'Why not? It might be.'

'But it isn't, is it? What are you thinking of?' His father's intransigence can be infuriating. 'Dad, I can't talk now, I'm driving.'

It is not for nothing they call him Sensible Sid.

The blue van is still in front of him, and it is braking and accelerating erratically. A logo on the back reads 'Pattie's Mobile Pet Parlour', with a sprinkling of paw prints. The rain is coming down fast now, and his windscreen wipers can barely keep up. A small black Mini pulls up alongside him, and in the back seat a teenage girl yanks her top up and presses her bare boobs against the side window. He attempts to ignore them and focus on the road ahead. When he takes a quick sideways glance, they are still there. He tries to recall Euler's equation about the nature of spheres. $(T+N) - (E+N) + (V+1) = 2$, that's it. As the equation forms itself in his mind, he smacks into the back of the blue van. Clunk!

Pattie, it must be her, gets out of the driver's seat of the blue van and raps on his window. She is blonde, with dark roots, her hair cut short at the sides but high on top, which makes her look a few inches taller than her actual height – at least five foot nine, he guesses – and solid with it. A sort of female version of Donald Trump, with a round aggressive mouth and professionally whitened teeth. She is holding a big wriggling dog – an ugly creature with short pale fur and slitty eyes – in her muscular arms. Water is streaming in rivulets out of her stiff blonde hair on to her orange square jaw. He winds the window down and smiles.

'Who is naughty boy? I will have to put you back in cage.'

It isn't clear whether she is talking to him or the dog. He notices there is a damp patch spreading on the lap of her pale blue trousers. Cage? What cage? The word registers at the back of his mind. The dog wasn't in a cage, and it should have been.

'Sorry. It wasn't my fault.'

'Who else's could it be? What you thinking of? You not paying attention to driving.' She has a slight guttural accent,

8

or maybe it is just the aggression in her voice which confuses him.

'I was distracted. There was this girl . . .'

He looks around for the black Mini but it has gone. The traffic is moving again, apart from them.

'Is this your typical response? Always find somebody else to take blame? Pathetic!' A raindrop trickles down her nose and the pooch leaps up to catch it with its tongue.

'Look, I said I'm sorry,' he mumbles, suddenly not feeling sorry at all. 'I'll get a picture on my phone of the damage.'

'Ow! Ow! Whaaah!' Pattie suddenly screams and doubles over. The dog wriggles, but she grips it tightly to her chest.

'What's that about?' he asks, alarmed. Her apparent agony is unexpected and frightening.

'Whiplash, you idiot.' She clutches her neck and moans through gritted teeth. 'I hope you fully insured. Ow! Whaaah!'

'Whiplash? You're putting it on. You were perfectly okay a minute ago.'

'Now I no longer okay.'

It is obvious to him that she is faking it.

'Here's my name and the name of my insurance company, madam,' he says with exaggerated politeness, scribbling it on a piece of paper and taking a few more photos.

She looks at the paper. 'Panties? Your name is Sid Panties?' she mocks.

'Pantis,' he corrects her pronunciation, putting the emphasis on the last syllable.

She mutters something under her breath that sounds suspiciously like 'another bloody foreigner' as she gets into her van with the dog and drives off.

He gets back into his car and rests his hands on the steering wheel because they are shaking. Then he rests his head on his hands. He tries to phone Jacquie but she doesn't pick up the phone. He tries to ring his mother, but her phone is switched off so he leaves a message that mentions both his car accident and his father's unexpected news.

It is already dark when he gets home. Jacquie is lying on the sofa in front of the TV, which is blathering at full blast to nobody. She's fallen asleep. She jumps up as he comes in, her neat black brows furrowed with concern.

'What's happened, love? Why are you so late? You look awful.'

He leans forward and kisses her almond-scented hair. 'I went into a mobile pet parlour on the Ring Road.'

The absurdity of it makes them both laugh.

'Oops!' Jacquie claps her hand over her mouth, relishing the drama. 'Was it serious? Are you okay? Was anybody hurt?'

'No. Well, the driver said she had whiplash, but I reckon she was faking it. You can fake anything these days.'

'Yes, we get loads of people in the Infirmary wanting to make fake insurance claims.'

'I did go into the back of her, but it was a very minor bump. It was raining, and I got distracted. Dad phoned to say he had won seven million quid on some dodgy foreign lottery.'

'Seven million quid? Are you sure, Sid?'

'I'm not sure. In fact I think it's highly unlikely.'

'Because it would come in handy right now,' she sighs, nursing a little smile.

'What do you mean?'

'It would come in handy because I've got some great news for you.' She sits on the sofa and pulls him down beside her. 'Sid, I think I'm pregnant.'

A woozy, mystical feeling comes over him, like the sound of angel bells or the Callan-Symanzik equation sweeping through the firmament and children's voices singing in chorus. They have waited for this moment for so long. He pulls her close. Her hair smells of warm nut oil and her skin faintly of hospital disinfectant. Is now the right time to propose? He has intended for some time to ask her to marry him, but it is such a major decision . . . His throat is sticky with sweetness and he can only manage to blurt one word out: 'When . . . ?'

'I think I got pregnant towards the end of June, on referendum night. Remember, I stopped over? I missed my last period, but I didn't want to get your hopes up until I'd done a pregnancy test, so today I did it in a toilet at work, and it was positive. The baby should be due in March.'

Jacquie and Sid have been trying for a baby for what feels like ages, mainly at weekends and holidays. At last it has happened. His heart flaps its wings against his ribcage like a trapped songbird. Should they get married? he wonders. Maybe. But how does one go about it? He hesitates and searches in his mind for the right words. 'How about . . . ? Isn't it about time we . . . ? Jacquie, shall we . . . ? Jacquie, will you . . . ?'

Then just as he is going to pop the question the phone rings. It is his mother.

'Hi, Sid. Is this a good time to talk?'

'Well . . .'

'I just got a message from George. I'll ring you tomorrow if you prefer.'

'Whatever.'

'He had some garbled story about winning the jackpot on a lottery.'

'He rang me, too. I don't think he even entered the lottery, Mum, so don't get too excited.'

Jacquie kisses him on the cheek and goes upstairs, and he nods to indicate that he will join her soon.

'I've been trying to contact George but he's not answering his phone,' continues his mother, her voice faint and crackly down the line. 'In the end I had to ask Brenda, but she doesn't seem to know where he is either.'

'Don't worry, Mum. I spoke to Dad earlier today. He rang me in a state of great excitement while I was stuck on the Ring Road in a traffic jam. He told me the same story about how he'd won seven million quid on the Kosovan State Lottery. It's very likely not true, but it might explain his odd behaviour.'

'Seven million quid? It can't be true, can it? So what did you tell him, Sid?' Rosie's voice is sharp.

'I told him it was probably a scam.'

'Hmmmph!' she snorts. 'Is that all? I don't expect that the millions will last long, anyway, even if it's true. I expect he'll buy himself a red Ferrari, like he's always wanted, and go cruising with his elbow hanging out of the window, revving up the engine, trying to attract the attention of pretty girls. Or he'll just fritter it away on drugs and booze, expensive holidays and fancy women. We could do with that money, Sid, to see us through our old age. But George doesn't believe he'll ever grow old, even though he's already older than me.'

Sid dislikes the way his mother makes a habit of badmouthing his father, trying to wheedle him over, to get him to take her side against George.

'I think his old Mazda is burning oil, Mum. I don't think he does drugs. And I wouldn't begrudge him a spot of booze or a nice holiday.' He tries, as always with his parents, to keep things in balance. 'He's been quite depressed since he retired. And Brenda isn't exactly a fancy woman, is she?'

'You're telling me she isn't. With her bleached blonde hair and her kitten heels, parading around the Chamber of Commerce decked out in costume jewellery.'

'Listen, Mum, I've got some terrific news for you!' Sid says into the phone, then he waits a few seconds to build suspense. 'Jacquie's pregnant.'

'Aaaw!' Rosie shrieks. 'That's the good news I've been longing for!' Then she adds in a low voice, almost as an afterthought, 'You'd better not tell Brenda next door. It'll offend against her ideas of racial purity.'

'Mum . . .' But she isn't listening.

'Anyway, you try talking to him, Sid, and find out what's really going on with this money. He doesn't pick up the phone. I don't know if it's just me he's avoiding. If he *has* won all this money in a lottery, he should put it aside and get some proper investment advice so I can retire from work now, we can have a comfortable old age and still give something to you and Cassie now that you need it. I'm sure Sunil would advise him.' Sunil is Rosie's new beau, who used to be her financial adviser. 'And if he hasn't won it, he should watch his back. Whoever it belongs to is going to want it back, aren't they? Listen, Sid, I can't get through to him. His answering machine is always on. And it has this weird message: "Due to circumstances beyond my control, I cannot take your call." Something like that.'

Hm. That *does* seem weird. Circumstances beyond his control? His dad went on and on about sovereignty and taking back control during the referendum campaign, but this seems to be something different.

'I tell you what, I'll ring you back tomorrow,' his mother says, 'and have a chat with Jacquie. Give her my love.'

'Of course I will,' says Sid, thinking to himself, the Kosovan State Lottery? It sounds highly irregular.

His laptop is open on his desk, tempting him to do a spot of silent googling. Kosovo – in the Balkans. The first thing he

13

discovers is that Kosovo is not exactly a state at all. It is not recognized as such by the UN, which is still divided over recognition: Russia, India and China do not recognize it, though it is recognized by the US and several European countries, including the UK. And yes, it does have a lottery. Though when he tries to google this, a warning flashes up: 'This site is not secure.' When he googles 'Kosovo' and 'crime' Wikipedia informs him that 'since the 1990s Kosovo War, Kosovo has become a significant center [sic] of organized crime, drug trafficking, human trafficking and organ theft'.

There are quite a few results for this search, but none of them seem to prove anything conclusive. He checks the references at the bottom of the wiki page – most are references to books or journal articles, but one is available online and it sticks in his mind. It is a paper dated 2012 by someone blessed with the name Angus Aberdeen; having been christened Poseidon Pantis, Sid feels a twinge of fellow feeling. The guy is talking about new frontiers in crime, including organ theft, and links between the Kosovan mafia and the Italian Mafia. It makes his hair stand on end.

Organ theft? What has his dad got himself embroiled in now?

By the time he's eaten the gone-cold couscous Jacquie has left for him, cleared up and got upstairs, Jacquie is already asleep. He puts his laptop away and cuddles up beside her, not too worried – for, as far as he can tell, organ theft cannot yet be carried out online – feeling her warmth and sweetness, and thinking, so long as we are together, surely everything will be alright, won't it?

ROSIE: *Take back control*

Rosie Pantis, née Harvey, wife of George Pantis, mother of Poseidon Pantis and Cassiopeia Pantis, aka Sid and Cassie, often phones her son Sid and Sid's partner Jacquie on a Saturday morning while they are still in bed. Jacquie is such a sympathetic listener that Rosie prefers talking to her, rather than to Sid, whom she thinks of as a bit of a cold fish, and she regrets that she has so easily slipped into venting her rage about Brexit to Jacquie, rather than expressing what she regards as perfectly legitimate grievances against her husband and her neighbour, not to mention her son Sid.

Sid, despite being named Poseidon, has turned out so nauseatingly sensible, sometimes she thinks she must have overdone his toilet training. She doesn't tell Jacquie this. Jacquie, his girlfriend, is a French citizen, though she hails from Martinique in the French Caribbean, and she probably has a very French and no-nonsense approach to toilet training, as to most things. She is a no-nonsense kind of girl, with a warm heart underneath her brisk exterior, and she is deeply committed to the NHS, which to Rosie is one of the wonders of the world.

Rosie loves Sid, of course. He is a truly wonderful young man, but in her opinion he is a long way over on the spectrum; in other words, he is great at maths and solving puzzles, but he has no idea at all what makes people tick. She still doesn't know what Jacquie saw in him when she first set them up on that blind date three years ago. Sid was no Apollo even then, being a bit on the pudgy side with distinct love handles and big round owly specs. But whatever it was, Rosie is overjoyed that Sid and Jacquie have fallen in love: and now they are going to make her a grandmother.

Sid's lack of interest in politics irritates her. Still, he is quite good on the acoustic guitar and she likes the songs that he sings. 'Is It All Over Now?' by Donald and Kim and the Bigger Rockettes. 'Never' by Harvey and the Me-Toos. 'Oy Vey' by Jezza and the Jews, with its frantic strumming and its wailing chorus. She has no idea where he gets them all from. Sometimes she thinks he just makes them up himself, although he is not really the creative type.

His attitude to Brenda next door also annoys Rosie – even before George's defection. Sid used to say of the UKIP poster in her window that she was entitled to express her views. Rosie knows this is wrong. She has studied philosophy.

She confides in Jacquie on Saturday morning over the phone. 'People are so easily duped these days, Jacquie, you never know whom you can trust. Not even the BBC.' She falls silent for a moment, in contemplation of the awful upsurge in mendacity that, in her view, characterizes modern life. There is silence and a rustling of bedclothes on the other end of the phone, which Rosie takes as an invitation to continue.

'I can understand that Sid still hero-worships his dad,' she tells Jacquie. 'In my student days George had the aura of a legend about him, but I sometimes think that nowadays he has lost the plot.'

She herself used to really look up to George when they first met, over thirty years ago. He was a stunningly good-looking guy, with long wavy chestnut-brown hair, a Che Guevara moustache and twinkling eyes. And he had gravitas, unlike the other guys she knew; he even knew how to tango. He was a lecturer while Rosie was still a student, and she would be the first to admit that, in a way, he taught her everything she knows. He still has those twinkling eyes, even though much of his hair has fallen out, especially on the crown.

'Advancing age takes no prisoners. In the end it kills all of us,' she sighs. 'I still love my husband, of course, Jacquie, but recently, since I started to think for myself, I've started to question him more than I used to. Recently, in fact, I've begun to think his grip on reality is slipping. First it was the Brexit vote, then it was Brenda, now it's his financial immaturity, as evidenced in his obsession with red sports cars.'

'Red sports cars?' enquires Jacquie in a hypnotic voice.

She must take back control of their marriage, before it ends in disaster, thinks Rosie, a moth of panic fluttering in her chest.

'Take, for example, what went wrong on referendum night,' she continues. 'You can ask Cassie. Cassie was at home that night, so she witnessed her father's peculiar behaviour. She had come over for a late takeout pizza and all three of us settled down afterwards in our pyjamas and dressing gowns to watch the results on the telly. We asked Sid, too, because it was meant to be a family bonding occasion, but he said he wanted to stay at home with you, Jacquie. And anyway, it wasn't a family bonding occasion, it was our family's bonfire.'

She remembers how late it was, how the tension rose as the results trickled in slowly, and they were all tired. Every time a result came through for Leave, George leapt up shouting 'Yes!' and punching the air.

'I told him to calm down. Well, maybe I did call him an old idiot. Then, during a lull in the results, George – who doesn't usually partake of tobacco – nipped out into the dark garden in his pyjamas for a cigarette. And I turned the key on him. Snap! George didn't hang about outside, he went next door to

Brenda's. He said he just wanted to get indoors, but they ended up in bed together. That bitch and George!' Rosie moans to Jacquie.

'Mmhm,' murmurs Jacquie.

In the background Rosie thinks she can hear the faint tinkle of a teacup being stirred. Maybe Jacquie isn't listening. Undeterred, she ploughs on.

'It didn't take her long to get her manicured claws into poor George, he was so aroused by the emancipatory promise of Brexit. It went straight into his veins like a drug! It was all so childish – a ruined relationship piled on top of national ruin,' she says.

'Tinkle, tinkle,' says the teacup.

'Mhm,' says Jacquie.

'Okay, so I shouldn't have locked him out in the garden in his pyjamas; but he shouldn't have called me a "self-righteous, privileged, *Guardian*-reading liberal"!'

'Oh dear,' murmurs Jacquie.

Then Rosie tells Jacquie about the conversation they had before the referendum. '"Pride, Rosie!" George said to me as the three of us tucked into the pre-referendum pizza. "You've got to have pride in your country! Without pride, we're just dry leaves blown about on the winds of history!" So I said to him, "You're so bloody naive, George! You believe everything those charlatans tell you. Do you think they give a fig about this country? All they think about is themselves." George goes on about sovereignty and taking back control from faceless bureaucrats. Does he really think the bureaucrats in Brussels are more faceless and less elected than the ones in Sheffield City Council Planning Department?

'Do you know what George said? He said, "Rosie, light of my life, as Hegel said, we are all guilty of innocence. It's the tragedy of our age." So I shouted at him, I said, "Come down to earth, George. Stop spouting pretentious nonsense! Get a grip! I have a degree in philosophy too, you know." I sometimes wonder how I put up with him for thirty-five years,' she confides to Jacquie. 'But I was madly in love.'

'Mmhm,' murmurs Jacquie.

'George is just like the brainless squirrel that lives in the tree at the bottom of our garden, driven by blind instinct. Every autumn, without fail, it steals the bread that I put out for the birds and buries it all around the garden, digging up the lawn with its beastly little claws. It doesn't ever seem to learn from experience or have any idea of forward planning, just like George.'

Rosie holds back from telling Jacquie that after the referendum, when George moved in next door with their neighbour, whom she has dubbed 'Brexit Brenda', part of her died inside. But she puts on a special show of civility for both of them, with exaggerated smiles and hugs for George and doorstep air-kisses for the Bitch. She is sure that after a while George will return. As it is, he frequently comes back for lunch or a coffee during the day while Brenda is out at work, to take Heidi, their ex-RSPCA golden Labrador, out for a walk, or to leaf through his tattered poetry tomes. How that must annoy the Bitch!

'I wonder what he and the Bitch talk about together. Maybe they don't.'

'Mmhm,' Jacquie murmurs.

SID: Symmetry and beauty

After Rosie rings off on Saturday morning, Jacquie and Sid finish their breakfasts, then Sid totters down the stairs with the dirty breakfast things on a tray, while Jacquie yawns, rolls over and tries for another nap. To Sid, she looks deliciously edible with her shiny, shapely limbs stretching out from under the cream duvet, and he still can't quite believe she is his. What does she see in him? He isn't good-looking (as his mother often hints). Jacquie once said, with a quiet laugh, that she found him and his family *'amusant'*. She speaks English with an increasingly slight but still adorable French accent; but what exactly did she mean by *'amusant'*? Who would have guessed, when they eyed each other hopefully on that nerve-racking blind date, set up by a mutual friend – for which Rosie persists in claiming the credit – that they would still be together after three years? Her stunning good looks still make Sid feel slightly unworthy.

Okay, so they don't actually live together, because of their different work patterns. Sid has his own little two-up-two-down terraced house at Hunters Bar, not far from his parents, where Jacquie stays at weekends; Jacquie, who works as a radiographer at Leeds General Infirmary, stays over in Leeds midweek in a big Victorian house she shares with a woman called Annabel, who has long yellow hair, parted in the middle, and works from home. Sid has no idea what she does.

Sid teaches maths at one of the Sheffield College campuses, having failed to secure a job at one of the two universities when he decided to move back to Sheffield. The teaching is rather basic and boring, with no opportunity for research, and this sense of failure, of unfulfilled potential, leaches into his daily life, making him generally quiet and careful. But Sid has found in the maths itself an unexpected consolation, a symmetry and beauty that lifts his days out of mind-numbing tedium. In the interests of survival, he has fallen into an early-start-early-finish routine this term, so he is usually in the staffroom before 8.00 a.m. and home by 5 p.m.

Jacquie and Sid have been trying for a baby for two years. Often during those two years Sid has thought that he should ask her to marry him, but he has somehow never managed it. Jacquie has always seemed to him to exist on a higher plane where only angels dwell. Now he cannot stop himself thinking about that tiny fertilized egg of the baby – *his* baby – growing inside her. Is it just his imagination, or is she already growing rounded and lush? She is only just four weeks gone, and he knows, objectively speaking, she must look exactly the same. Now with the baby on the way they will finally be able to live together properly: all three of them in his little terraced house within earshot of the Blades stadium, and at weekends they will go to the match – which Jacquie will soon learn to love.

He deposits the breakfast things in the dishwasher, and he is just about to rejoin Jacquie in bed when the phone rings again. It is his father.

'Hi, Dad, are you alright? Everyone's been worried about you.'

'Who do you mean, everyone?' His father's speech comes out in short, jerky bursts.

'Mum just phoned Jacquie.' He puts on a world-weary voice. 'I spoke to her yesterday and she says she's been trying to contact you. She says she keeps getting a weird answering message.'

'Ah! Her fragrant ladyship! Tell her that's not weird. Tell her that's the new normal. Now I've come into some money, I don't want people bothering me all the time.' His father's voice is prickly, ending in a little triumphant snort. 'I suppose she wants a share of my winnings. Well, she can stuff that. TELL HER TO STUFF IT IN HER PANTIES!'

'Calm down, Dad. She doesn't want your money. She thought you might need some investment advice, that's all.'

'I suppose she means from that creep Sunil. Well, tell her I'd rather suck slug-slime through my teeth than listen to that CRAWLY GASTROPOD lecturing me about how to maximize my returns. I'd rather crunch a slug between my teeth and suck out the slime than listen to him oozing out all that FOETID MENDACIOUS DRIVEL that passes for wisdom among the NEW ELITE of the finance industry that has almost ruined our ONCE-GREAT NATION! It's my money, and I'll spend it how I like! And if her fragrant ladyship doesn't like it, she KNOWS WHERE TO STUFF IT!'

'Shhh. It's okay, Dad. No need to shout. I'll pass on your message.'

Sid replaces the phone and, to calm himself down, he takes the guitar off its stand and checks it is still in tune from yesterday. He strums his fingers across the strings, and riffs into 'Your Funny Kind of Love' from his favourite band, Ee-You and the Ramonas. It's one that Jacquie likes, but he plays it quietly, so as not to wake her.

Then the phone rings again. This time, it is his sister Cassie.

'Listen, Sid. I've just had this really weird voicemail from Dad.'

In Sid's opinion, Cassie is the most dysfunctional member of the dysfunctional Pantis family, but she is closer to their parents because she stayed at home when he left for uni. Perhaps that's why she's so dysfunctional, he surmises. They agree to meet one day later that week for an after-work drink in the Fat Cat on Alma Street.

ROSIE: Cut and colour

Rosie tries hard to avoid being snobbish in relation to Brexit Brenda, aka the Bitch, who used to be her hairdresser. She is one of those slightly overweight blonde women, a bit younger than Rosie, who always wears high heels and full make-up, even to go to the shops, Rosie observes with an inner sneer. But she censors her sneers, and puts on a pious, respectful air whenever they meet. After all, Brenda is her neighbour.

There was once a bloke in Brenda's life during the time she has lived next door, whom she referred to as 'Sniffer', but he departed four or five years ago. Maybe he was her husband or maybe a lover. He was a bulky, ugly guy with a scar on his face and a fondness for fierce dogs with studded collars. He was always very polite when Rosie encountered him on the shared path, as though he was determined to dispel any preconceptions she might have about men with scarred faces and fierce dogs. Since then, there's been no one in Brenda's life, as far as Rosie can tell; no one, that is, until she managed to snare poor deluded George.

Brenda owns a hairdressing salon in town called Lovely Locks. Since Sniffer's departure, she has acquired another salon in Crookes, and now calls herself a businesswoman rather than just a hairdresser. In fact, Brenda has become a big cheese in the Chamber of Commerce. Rosie thinks she doesn't do much hair-trimming herself any more, and now prefers swanning around in costume jewellery and 'networking', as she calls it. Through the window of the Lovely Locks salon, whenever Rosie passes, she sees a few bored middle-aged ladies wielding sharp scissors, and a flock of trainees with fake tans and high-concept haircuts, scurrying around carrying cups of tea, sweeping the floors. She probably gets some government training grant to teach them how to do it, thinks Rosie.

She has gone in there for a trim, from time to time, and over the years Rosie and Brenda have developed the kind of intermittent intimacy that women sometimes have with their hairdressers, talking about men, holidays, recent purchases, that kind of thing.

Then something happens that will fracture their relationship forever.

In mid-July, more than three weeks after the referendum and George's desertion, Rosie books in to Lovely Locks for her usual cut and colour. She knows it is a bad idea, that she should go somewhere else, but she is in a hurry, the other local hairdresser has moved out to Middlewood, and she surmises that in any case Brenda probably won't be there – she'll be 'networking' at the Chamber of Commerce – and she'll be done by one of the trainees. Anyway, it is a massive mistake. Brenda is there, cutting hair in person, and she takes one look at Rosie's hair and shrieks, as hairdressers do, 'Whoever cut your hair last time, Rosie? It looks like an old armchair with the stuffing hanging out!'

'It was you, Brenda,' Rosie replies, barely concealing her irritation. It is too late to leave now. 'It was you that cut it. Don't you remember?'

Her eye falls on a folded copy of the *Daily Mail* resting on the counter. Boris Johnson has called for the Royal Yacht *Britannia* to be recommissioned as a floating embassy to drum up post-Brexit trade. Hm, she sneers inwardly, I might have guessed.

'It can't have been me!' Brenda raises her perfectly plucked eyebrows and shakes her head, with a look that implies that Rosie has behaved irresponsibly in relation to her appearance. 'Or if it was, it was over three months ago. You shaggy types need regular maintenance. Wait here, love. I'll just finish with my lady here, then I'll sort it out for you.'

A shaggy type? Rosie? What an unfortunate turn of phrase. She feels another hot flush creeping up her cheeks. Her hormones are on the loose again. She flicks open the newspaper at a page that shows a leggy female 'celeb' in a 'naughty nurse' outfit and sparkly suspenders who has just got off with another bare-chested male 'celeb'. She has never heard of either of them, but she picks up the paper, rolls it up into a baton and slaps it down on the counter in front of Brenda.

'Were you wearing your naughty nurse outfit that night? Or did he fall for the sparkly suspenders?' she hisses, loudly enough for all the other customers and the trainees to hear and turn their heads.

'I don't know what you're talking about, pet.' Brenda rolls her eyes. 'What are you on? I think you need to sober up. Would you like a cup of tea while you wait? I'll just finish this lady off.'

In the chair next to Rosie sits a middle-aged Asian woman with a straight black bob, lightly dusted with silver. Rosie stares. It is Sunil's mother, a formidable Indian widow whom Sunil speaks of as 'Mataji'. Rosie gives Mataji a cheery smile and nod of recognition, and she smiles back, faintly embarrassed, as though she doesn't really want to admit that she knows this gobby Englishwoman. Mataji is turning her head and gazing at a reflection of the back of her hair in a mirror that Brenda is holding up for her.

The hot flush reaches Rosie's brain. She leans across and

whispers, 'She's cut it crooked! It looks ridiculous! Look, that side's far too long! You can't go out looking like that, Mataji!'

Mataji shuffles in the chair and cranes her head from left to right, peering harder, trying to see the back of her head.

'Are you sure it doesn't need little bit straightening up?' she says to Brenda.

'It looks nice!' says Brenda.

'It looks like a drunken gardener's been at it with a pair of blunt shears,' Rosie blurts.

Mataji looks agitated.

'Take no notice. I'll even it out for you,' says Brenda. She pulls down the hair, holding it between two fingers, and snips a bit more off one side. She has pulled too hard. When she lets go and the hair springs back, it is visibly unbalanced. Even the customer can see it. So then Brenda over-corrects on the other side. Soon the hair is both crooked and too short, swooping in two jagged wings above the cheekbones. It looks awful.

'It looks awful!' Rosie says in a loud whisper. 'A proper mess.'

'Yes, it looks wrong!' repeats Mataji. 'I cannot go outside looking like this.'

'Well, all it needs is just a little teeny bit trimming off on the left, sweetheart,' says Brenda, in a thick crooning voice like a broody pigeon.

'Not a teeny bit. At least an inch,' Rosie butts in. She can feel a hot pulse beating in her temples. 'You can't see straight, Brenda, for all the off-piste shagging you've been doing with other people's husbands!'

'Whatever are you talking about? Off? Pissed? I think that's you, darling. Shut your big gob, Rosie Panties.' Brenda's voice resounds like a slap. 'Let me cut this lady's hair.'

'Let's face it, Brenda! You've taken your mind off hair-cutting, now you've got involved in politics. I've seen the UKIP poster up in your window.'

'What's that got to do with anything? Look, we're not here to discuss bloody politics, so keep your opinions to yourself, and let me do my job.'

'Don't you remember when the Ali family moved in next door to you, you pinched your nose and said the area was starting to smell of chicken curry? You said, "It's going down-hill, because the likes of the Alis just want to come here to live off child benefits." Now look at you, taking this good lady's money and sending her out looking ridiculous.'

Although Rosie is still hissing, her voice has risen. The temperature in the little salon has risen too. There is a smell of scorching hair from the hairdryer.

Brenda responds in a fiery screech. 'I'm not making her look ridiculous. That's just your warped imagination. Anyway, you never said nowt about Mrs Ali at the time. You managed to keep your big gob shut, for once.'

To Rosie's mind, the street started to go downhill when the likes of Brenda and Sniffer moved in with their fierce dogs and their 4x4s. But she censored her judgement and welcomed them with frosty politeness.

'Yes, I regret not speaking out at the time. But I'm saying it now!'

'And I'm just saying what I think. That's what you can't stand, isn't it? Anyone else speaking out about their beliefs, if they're different than yours? You with your daft "Hope not Hate" poster? It's not about hate, it's about hairdressing!' She pats Mataji's shoulder reassuringly and snarls at Rosie. 'At least your hubby's got more sense than you!'

'At least George is not a racist like you!' Rosie retorts.

'What is going on, Brenda? Why is it so much shouting?' Mataji interrupts. 'You do not like Indian people?'

'Course I do, pet,' croons Brenda. 'Take no notice of her. She's just jealous.'

'Don't lie!' Rosie snaps. 'You can't tell the difference between Indians and Pakistanis, you think they're all the same. You said they smell of curry, I've clocked the way you wrinkle your nose when you pass Sunil on the front path.'

'Where you been getting these bad ideas about my boy? He is not a Paki,' cries Mataji, close to tears, snatching the scissors from the counter and hurling them across the room. They spin in a low arc through the air, coming to rest when the points embed themselves in the shin of a middle-aged woman who is sitting under the old-fashioned hairdryer with rollers in. She screams and jumps up. Her head collides with the hood of the dryer. The hairdryer overbalances and smacks into the wall mirror, making a jagged crack. The woman faints. Blood is gushing from the wound in her leg. A pair of customers, a mother and daughter who have just walked into Lovely Locks, turn tail and flee, knocking into one of the young apprentices, who is balancing a cup of tea in one hand and a palette of mixed colour in the other. She slips in the pool of blood on the floor and spills the hot tea all over the bleeding woman. The bleeding woman screams and shoves her aside. Mataji gets out her phone and calls for an ambulance.

After that, everything calms down. The apprentice girl who has spilt the tea goes and makes five more cups. The woman with the bleeding shin turns out to have a St John Ambulance first-aid certificate; she drags herself up on to the couch and raises her bleeding limb above the level of her heart. Mataji purses her lips as she drinks the hot tea, then puts her cup down calmly and walks out without paying.

Brenda turns to Rosie and says in a steely voice, 'You'd better go home now, Rosie, you mad old cow. You've heard of mad cow disease? That's what you've got, Rosie Panties. You'd better see a doctor. And don't come in here again.'

'That's no great loss,' Rosie snaps back. 'You're a rubbish hairdresser anyway!'

Rosie stomps out of the salon, banging the door behind her. She runs down the street towards the town centre, breathing in the pollen-laden scent of summer, feeling vaguely exhilarated. In the opposite direction an ambulance is wow-wowing up the street.

By the time she reaches home, the exhilaration has evaporated to be replaced by a gnawing unease. What has got into her? Is she really a mad old cow? Soon it will be her birthday, the big six-zero. It will be the first birthday since she met George that she will be spending without him. As their birthdays are a couple of months apart, they usually have a joint party round about the beginning of September. What will happen this year? Rosie wonders.

She senses a febrile atmosphere in the country as her birthday approaches, and her own brain is febrile, prone to sudden ups and downs that rise and fall with the news, to which she listens obsessively. Nigel Farage is often on the television or the radio, explaining how soon the British people will have their country back, will throw off the shackles and no longer be a vassal state. She wrinkles her nose with contempt. Democracy has triumphed – so why does it not feel like a triumph, but a festering swamp of hatred? Every day the newspapers ooze stories about feckless scroungers claiming thousands of pounds in benefits, or audacious immigrants taking advantage of the British people's tolerance. 'Enemies of the People' are everywhere.

Rosie sees the headlines screaming in chorus from the newspaper racks in the supermarket when she goes to do her shopping, while politicians tighten the thumbscrews of austerity, slashing benefits, closing day-care centres and the local library.

She finds herself turning her back on the newspaper racks and smiling ostentatiously at dark-skinned people she encounters in the street, as though to dissociate herself from any 'hostile environment' they might be experiencing. It is only a few weeks since the referendum and her bust-up with George, but already she is learning to navigate the changed terrain.

Later that evening, Brenda appears on her doorstep with an enormous tube of Hollywood Glamour Hair Balm in her hands.

'Peace offering. Free sample. You have to rub it into towel-dried hair, and leave it for two or three minutes, then rinse it off,' she says, holding it out to Rosie with a saccharine smile. 'I didn't mean all those mean things I said, sweetheart. We shouldn't fall out, being as we're neighbours.'

Rosie reaches out her hands and accepts her neighbour's peace offering. 'Thank you so much.' She gives her two little pecks on the cheeks. 'No hard feelings. I'm sorry I misbehaved, Bren,' she says. 'Please, won't you come inside for a cuppa?'

BRENDA: *Faking it*

Brenda hesitates, and then steps over the threshold. Is she letting herself in for a grilling? You'd think that someone who talks posh, and put on airs and graces, like Rosie, would live in a posh house. But Rosie's house is scruffy and old-fashioned, and, let's be honest, slightly smelly. She follows Rosie through to the kitchen at the back of the house. It is one of those farmhouse-style kitchens that used to be popular thirty years ago, with polished pine units and integrated appliances, and a rustic pine table flanked by a pine bench on one side and two matching pine chairs on the other. The pine is grey with fingerprints, especially around the doors and the drawer handles of the units. There is a vase of russet and gold dahlias on the table, which provides a vibrant contrast to the grubby kitchen units and the food-splashed flowery wallpaper.

'Sit down. I think we need to talk,' says Rosie, pulling out a chair in front of the table for her neighbour. 'I'm a bit worried about George.'

Just a bit worried? Brenda wonders. Or very worried? If she was married to George, she'd be extremely worried.

'Yes, me too. He seems to have all sorts of funny ideas.'

'Sports cars. Does he go on about red sports cars?'

'Well, he did say something about needing a new lawn mower. I don't know if it was meant to be red.'

'Oh, that again! He's always going on about that sodding lawn mower. I'm hoping he'll calm down a bit, now that there's a baby on the horizon.'

'What horizon?' asks Brenda, a shrill note of alarm in her voice. All her suspicions about George's continuing relationship with his wife are heightened.

'Well, it isn't actually due until March.'

What a bastard, thinks Brenda, fuming inwardly. He must have been sneaking back for sex all the time during the day while sleeping with Brenda at night. It just confirms her idea that, underneath, all men are untrustworthy. Was he going to tell her, or was he going to let her find out the hard way?

'How lovely,' she says aloud to Rosie in a sugary tone of voice. 'I expect you're over the moon.'

'Yes, of course I am. It's what I've been waiting for. But with the country in the mess it's in, not to mention my relationship with George, it's not the best time to be bringing a baby into the world.'

'There's never a best time, sweetheart,' she murmurs, 'you just have to go along with it as best you can.'

Rosie frowns and says, 'I was hoping . . .' Her voice trails off, as if she is hoping Brenda will help her out with articulating her hopes.

Well, sod that, thinks Brenda. Pregnancy is a game two can play. 'He's quite something, your George.'

'Yes,' Rosie agrees. 'He's a one-off.'

'Yes, not many men in their seventies can make a woman pregnant.'

'Erm . . . aren't you a bit old for that, Brenda?' There is a catch in Rosie's voice.

'I'm younger than you, Rosie Frillies,' retorts Brenda quickly. 'And with a little help from modern science, it's amazing what can be done these days, especially if you can catch the man's sperm and freeze it at once – I read recently in the

Daily Mail that in Italy a woman has become pregnant at the age of sixty-one.'

'How do you catch it? In a fishing net?' Rosie's face is a picture.

'In a condom, silly.'

Brenda has it on the tip of her tongue to say, 'I know you're faking it, you Mad Cow. But you can't fool me.' But she thinks it will be amusing to spin Rosie along. After all, she has won George, and Rosie has lost him. It is time the Mad Cow came to terms with that. And besides, what if it is true that he has won some money in a lottery? Her mind flips back to the brief conversation she overheard. She has forgotten how much money is meant to be involved, but she owes it to herself to get her hands on some of it, or at least have a good holiday or two, before it is too late. But how?

All the while another suspicion is pricking at the back of her mind. How old is Rosie, anyway? Her hair is turning grey at the roots, and the wrinkles on her neck make her look about sixty. Isn't that a bit too old for pregnancy? But no one is ever too old to fake a pregnancy, depending on how gullible the so-called father is.

SID: Yorkshire Blonde

Sid is a few minutes late. When he arrives at the Fat Cat on Alma Street, Cassie is already sitting at a table by the window cradling her usual half of shandy. She is wearing tight jeans with high heels. Her long red-gold hair is swept over to one side and held in place by an ivory flower-clip. Sid will never say this to her, of course, but it does strike him what a very attractive woman his little sis has become. Yet she never seems to have any luck with men. Maybe it is that overly intense and slightly crazed stare she has inherited from Rosie. Maybe it is her voice, with its flat Yorkshire vowels and its querulous upward inflection, like an annoying little kid asking endless questions. Maybe it is because she is too serious about her job in an environmental NGO, and she is inclined to go on about composting a bit too much. Or maybe it is just because Ivor keeps the other men away. Ivor is one of her former lecturers and she is besotted with him, even though he keeps her dangling on a string, swearing he loves her but refusing to leave his wife Barbara. The same thing has happened to another girl he knows who is in her forties now and still single.

'Hi, Sid. You're late? As usual?'

'Hi, Cassie. Can I get you another?'

'No, it's alright? One's plenty? I have to drive?'

Sid orders a Yorkshire Blonde and a bag of crisps. It has been a stressful day and he feels as if he deserves a reward – well, if truth be told, every day he spends teaching maths to those kids, he feels like he deserves a reward. He tries to explain to Cassie what he hates about teaching maths. It isn't the maths or the kids he hates – but the kids' attitude towards it.

'What do they think is behind all those tablets and iPhones they seem so obsessed with? Exactly!' he grumbles to Cassie. 'Without computability, without the cool logic of numbers, none of it would work.'

'Don't be so Aspergic, Sid?' she says, rolling her eyes.

Sid is used to his family writing him off as Aspergic but he doesn't let it bother him; he knows it is not true, and he doubts that it is politically correct anyway.

'So, what was Dad's message?' He bites on a mouthful of crisps and washes them down with the cool beer. He starts to relax. The froth clumps on his upper lip as the coolness slides down his throat.

Cassie fumbles a piece of paper out of her bag. 'I wrote down exactly what he said? Because I don't want you telling me I made it up? Alright, Sid?' She is really in a full-on whiney today. 'Dad said, "I've moved in next door with Brenda. We've fallen in love. Don't try and stop us."' She crumples up the piece of paper. 'Poor Mum. I bet he said that bit about "fallen in love" just to spite her.'

'I don't think she'll care. Now she's got Sunil.'

Sid likes Sunil, with his dry sense of humour, his chunky hand-knitted cardigans and his permanent look of surprise. He's just what Rosie needs now to cheer her up and steady her down, he thinks. He hopes she will make a go of it with him. True, she is a bit opinionated, but not about things Sunil knows about.

'Don't you believe it. She still misses Dad. She says she regrets what she did?' Cassie giggles and puts her hand over her mouth. 'Oh, our insane parents! I keep thinking of the pathetic look on his face pressed up against the glass door when she locked him out in the garden. In his pyjamas. In the pouring rain?'

'Don't you think they're both equally to blame over what happened that night?' Sid insists. 'Sometimes, when Mum gets a bee in her bonnet about something, you're just forced to react negatively. For example now, thanks to Mum's constant moralizing and pressure, I feel vaguely hostile towards the EU. As well as kombucha, yoga and refugees.'

'Kombucha? Yoga? Refugees? Really, Sid! That's pathetic!'

'Well, Mum is always trying to ram them down our throats.'

'I guess when things go wrong in life you can always blame your mother?' snaps Cassie. 'Poor Mum. When I think of all she's had to put up with. Dad's philandering. His weird opinions. Their weird sex life?'

'What do you mean, weird?' Sid doesn't like to think about his parents doing anything weird, especially in bed.

'Well, she once told me that when they were having sex Dad would suddenly go as rigid as a plank and shout out at the top of his voice, "Caustic soda!"'

'She told you that?'

He tries to picture his parents having sex, George's thin jerky limbs grappling with Rosie's more pneumatic upholstery. The thought makes him feel slightly queasy. Or maybe it is just the over-salted crisps and the Yorkshire Blonde, which fizz on contact. A bit like caustic soda.

'Why would he shout caustic soda? It's not very romantic, is it?' Cassie complains. 'I told Ivor, and he said it was a case of delusional psychosis.'

Sid feels an instinctive mistrust of Ivor and everything he says, even though he has only met the guy once, but he can't say this to Cassie, who worships him irrationally.

'Anyway, Cassie, whatever Ivor says, he's still our dad.' Sid tries to sound decisive. 'So we have to stand by him, don't we?'

'Not necessarily.'

Cassie shakes her head so forcefully that the ivory hair clip falls out of her hair and plops into her shandy.

GEORGE: Quite something

From George's point of view this is primarily a story about passion. Rosie thinks that he is a bit old for passion at seventy-nine, but George firmly believes he has life in him yet. Oh yes.

He still loves Rosie, but look, he tells himself, when a bloke gets to seventy-nine, with eighty and old age looming around the corner, and he's been with the same woman for thirty-five years, he starts to get a bit restless. He wonders what he's missing out on. When you've done the romantic thing (several times, in George's case) and the husband thing (twice, in his case) and the dad thing (twice again) and the career thing (mixed), you ask yourself, is that it then? Is that Life? Isn't there anything else? That's the point George had reached when Brenda barged into his life.

In George's opinion, Rosie has always been a bit unhinged, in a lovable sort of way, long before the sodding referendum. But it's got worse as she's got older and has started to have rather fixed opinions of her own. When she was young she was not much interested in politics and was content to be guided by him in matters political. She's lately become stridently feminist and pro-Europe. When we were first married, thinks George wistfully, she was just a lovely kid with bare feet and flowers in her hair, and she was fantastic in bed.

He is not trying to make excuses for himself. In fact, if Rosie hadn't locked him out that night, he probably wouldn't have done anything about it. Inertia is a powerful force among elderly males, he has observed. He guesses Rosie still loves him but she doesn't seem to respect him any more. She thinks he's an old fool who has to be kept under control. George resents that. He has always thought he had the upper hand in their relationship, but lately he has doubts. Anyway, when Brenda saw him standing there on the doorstep, dripping wet, his pyjamas clinging to his skin, he saw something in her eyes that he hadn't seen for years in Rosie's. Something raw and elemental.

'Come in, my pet,' she said, 'did you get yourself locked out?' Her eyes flickered over him, green and curious, and it seemed to him that they lingered for a moment on the mound where his pyjama pants bunched over his damp, rain-shrivelled manhood. The thought crossed his mind that he must look to her like Colin Firth emerging from the lake at Pemberley in a clinging wet T-shirt, in that TV adaptation of *Pride and Prejudice* beloved of Rosie.

'Sort of,' he replied. 'Well, Rosie locked me out. We were watching the referendum results, and we didn't quite see eye to eye. She's all for the EU, you see, and she got upset that I voted for Leave.'

George had noticed the UKIP poster in the next-door window, and he guessed he would get a sympathetic ear if he played his cards right, maybe even a cup of tea. He was quite unprepared for what came next.

'You poor pet. Victimized for your beliefs. So she's a bit intolerant, is she?' Brenda moistened her lips with a quick pink tongue.

'Mmm. Just a bit.' George nodded glumly, feeling guilty at his betrayal. It was one thing to disagree with Rosie himself, quite another to hear her being disparaged by a third party.

'Typical member of the politically correct brigade, your Rosie. Here, love,' Brenda passed him a tumbler and poured a

40

generous measure of Scotch into it, 'that'll soon warm you up.' Her tongue flicked across her lips again.

On top of the wine he had already drunk, the whisky went through him like rocket fuel. He can't clearly remember the steps by which Brenda got him into bed, but he will fully admit that he did not exactly protest or have to be tied down. Her breasts were plump, round and white, like two iced buns with glacé cherries on top. He was so fired up he even had to use the old caustic soda trick to cool himself down at the crucial moment.

Afterwards, she rested her head on his chest. George stroked her hair, which was stiff and an unnatural-looking yellow colour, like a shop-bought sponge cake, and wondered what he had done.

'I really needed that,' she sighed. 'You're quite something, Mr Panties.'

What bloke can resist such an encomium? George felt a momentary glow of pride, followed by searing guilt. He had been with Rosie for thirty-five years, and he knew she loved him. This could not end well – he was bound to end up hurting one or both of them.

He wanted to behave like a gentleman, but Rosie did not make it easy for him. Next day, when he went home, she was still unrepentant; the moment he appeared at the back door she started to harangue him about *that* bus, about the NHS, about Nigel Farage, about their children's future, now blighted thanks to his idiocy. Or words to that effect. He shut off his attention, and batted off her interrogation about where he had spent the night. She got quite wild and started throwing her breakfast around. George sneaked off upstairs and packed a holdall.

As he mounted the stairs on the worn red carpet with its

familiar pattern of orange swirls, he couldn't help noticing how grotty and neglected their place was compared with the house next door. There was a smell of burnt toast lingering in the hallway, and the pile of old shoes and hats seemed to be spreading like a skin disease from under the stairs into the rest of the house. There was his old red bobble hat that he hadn't worn since the kids were young. There were the smelly trainers he had discarded when he started his last job. Why were they still here, taking up space? It was just another sign of the way that everything seemed to be slipping out of control: the house, the town, the whole country. Crowds of people from who-knows-where congregating in the city centre, speaking in languages he didn't understand; the bus service rerouted away from his home; ever-increasing traffic; inconvenient one-way traffic systems; nowhere to park your car in town; the disappearance of familiar landmarks, including two of his favourite pubs, to be replaced by a nightclub and a coffee shop; queues at the Post Office; graffiti everywhere; rudeness; public peeing; a makeshift encampment of homeless men in Ecclesall Woods; new ugly buildings sprouting up like toadstools overnight, no doubt to house more bureaucrats. Even his bladder seemed to be malfunctioning recently, forcing him to find a lavatory urgently or risk humiliation. Of course, all the public lavatories in town were closed to stop vagrants using them.

He didn't expect Rosie to be so hostile. After all, he never stopped loving her, just as there is still a part of him that keeps a little flame going for Eugenie, his first wife. You don't just suddenly stop loving people, do you? When he had gathered together a few necessaries, he told Rosie he had to go out for a bit to see someone, and he hot-footed it back next door. He only wanted a change.

Brenda was certainly a change. It is hard to imagine someone more different from Rosie, in temperament as well as in appearance. She was groomed and fragrant, whereas Rosie was scruffy and her hands usually smelled of onions from cooking. Brenda didn't cook at all; she was forever on a diet, or she ate out, or she ordered takeouts, or she kept a freezer full of elaborate pre-prepared meals with the word 'Luxury' embossed in swirly gold script on the packaging. Her dislike of all things foreign does not extend to food, or holidays.

When he first met Rosie, their sex was frequent, raw and elemental, but over the years it has become occasional and domesticated. With Brenda, that first night, he recaptured the newness that made all his senses more alert, colours more vibrant, sounds more musical, smells more intense. But after he moved in with her their sex soon went down to once a week, if he was lucky, and it quickly became cuddly and cosy rather than raw and elemental. And she never again told him that he was 'quite something'.

She started addressing him in a squeaky little-girl voice that was meant to be endearing, but that he found irritating, asking him to bring her cups of tea in bed and massage her feet, and help her do the crossword, and hang out the washing, and put out the bins, and change the light bulbs, and go down into the basement to reset the boiler, just as Rosie had, and . . . oh, Lordy, he mutters under his breath, is there ever any limit to what women want?

And Brenda's personal philosophy, which at first seemed patriotic, robust, down-to-earth and wise – in fact, it seemed to rather chime with his – now sometimes seems somewhat basic. Despite her professed patriotism, she is oblivious to the charm of the England he has grown up loving: misty mornings; medieval church spires; clouded hills; great poetry. That sort of thing. At least Rosie, if you catch her in the right mood, can wax lyrical about landscapes or trees. Brenda waxes lyrical about hairspray.

After they have been together for just a few weeks, Brenda has started coming in after a hard day managing her hair salons, flinging off her kitten-heeled shoes in the hall, putting her feet up on the sofa, wiggling her misshapen varnished toes like little pink shrimps, and telling him about her day, which seems to him to be unrelievedly boring, occasionally enlivened by some new hair-care product she's recently discovered. She asks him in that squeaky voice to massage her feet and to bring her a cup of tea, or she will launch into a weary, rambling rant against whoever has crossed her that day: an unduly demanding customer, a careless employee, a hapless shop assistant.

One Saturday in mid-July she came home with a dramatic tale of how Rosie barged into the salon and smashed it up. George wouldn't put it past Rosie. He has seen her throw things around before, so he nods sympathetically.

'You see, George, she accused me of being an evil racialist, and wearing sparkly suspenders and a naughty nurse outfit – which I never did – just because I voted to leave the EU,' she shrills. 'I'm not an evil racialist, or a naughty nurse. I get on like a house on fire with your Sid's Jacquie. And with Mrs Ali next door. She's a really nice lady. It's not personal. But when all these immigrants came over from the West Indies and India and Pakistan, and then the so-called refugees started coming over from Kosovo and Afghanistan and Iraq, it was a big change in our country but we weren't allowed to express our feelings. They said we were racialist if we said anything.'

'But hold on a minute, Brenda, that's nothing at all to do with leaving or remaining in the EU,' he answers mildly.

'But it wasn't democratic, was it? We didn't get a vote on it, did we? But this time they gave us a democratic vote, and we voted to get back control of our country.'

George just sighs, which she takes as assent.

She takes a deep breath. 'There's people who believe there's a secret plot to take over Europe by flooding it with Muslims. I've seen pictures of the queues at the borders. I'm not saying it's true, but they have a point, don't they? There's only one man that can put a stop to this invasion. I've got his poster in the window upstairs.' She rolls her eyes upwards. 'Everybody laughs at him now, but you wait . . . he'll be proved right.'

George opens his mouth to say something, but can't get a word in.

'Why do they all want to come to Britain? You don't think it's for safety, do you, when they cross through all the safe countries of Europe to get here? We never went into their countries, did we? So why do they all want to come here? I'll tell you why – it's to claim our benefits. That's why the Health Service is collapsing. All these foreign women having babies.'

'Brenda, listen . . .' He tries once more to interrupt, but she is off again.

'Once they've got a foothold in the EU, they'll all make their way over here.' She pauses for breath, and moistens her lips with her tongue. 'It's all a German conspiracy, isn't it, to weaken us?'

George throws her a doubtful look but Brenda is on a roll.

'Well, you tell me, who won the World Cup in 1966? They want their revenge now, don't they? They want to be the master race in Europe. The last war was started by the Germans wanting more *Lebenskraut*.'

Her cheeks are flushed, her eyes bright, her whole manner animated.

'I think you mean *Lebensraum*.'

45

'Whatever. You know what I mean.'

It seems pointless to argue.

Anyway, nothing much seems to be happening on that front. As the summer deepens, the threatened disasters of Project Fear fail to materialize, one by one – as he guessed they would – despite so-called 'experts' threatening a collapse of civilization and imminent ruin.

George, whose grandfather was Greek, does not get a chance to explain to Brenda that his own reasons for voting Leave are to do with its treatment of Greece, and the excessively corporate nature of the EU – the way it seems to hand control to the transnational corporations, who are forever lobbying for this or that. Then there are all the rules, about free competition, free movement of people, cleaner beaches, GM foods, product safety, electricity consumption, working time, licensing of pharmaceuticals, mobile phone roaming charges. It goes on and on. Who needs all those rules? he thinks. Can't we British people make up our own rules? It's all a matter of sovereignty, isn't it? There is even a rumour that they tried to outlaw bendy bananas. How stupid and petty can you get?

George's own grandfather came to Britain as an immigrant, so he has nothing against immigrants. He finds Brenda's opinions increasingly intense and irrational. Far from regaining control of his life, he seems to be relinquishing it to another more unpredictable despot.

He might have gone back to Rosie at this point, but she's got herself a new man, a dapper little Asian gent. George sees him coming and going like he owns the place. He says hi to him when they pass each other on the front path, and the gent nods politely, as though he has no idea who he is. George recognizes him as Sunil, their former financial adviser, but he,

George, obviously did not make much of an impression on him at the time. Not as much of an impression as Sunil made on Rosie.

That's when he decides to seize back control from both Rosie and Brenda and get a place of his own. He will live independently, without frills and without clutter, as he did before his first marriage. He will have relationships with women, of course, but on his own terms. Who knows, someone new might even come along? He is not yet eighty. He will learn to cook. He will write poetry. He will get an open-top sports car and feel the wind in his hair. He will be free.

He signs a rental contract on a flat in a new development converted from a former mill on the edge of Totley, with spectacular views of the moors, out beyond the old village where he spent his childhood. Even then, Totley was more of a suburb than a village, with good bus and train links to Sheffield but within walking distance of the open countryside.

He is full of enthusiasm for his new life when he moves into the new flat. He signs up for evening classes in Greek at the university, intending to keep his brain supple, and he agrees to take Heidi to come and live with him for part of the time, Rosie being still at work during term time. Heidi greets his suggestion with a storm of enthusiastic tail-wagging. If only the women in his life were as amenable, he thinks.

After his move, Cassie comes around in the morning to inspect the new flat and make him a cup of tea, as though he is already an inmate in a geriatric institution. He hugs her tightly. Her body feels so warm and alive, despite her grumpy and slightly bossy manner. She glances briefly at the spectacular view from the bedroom window, where the heather is in full bloom, and complains about how let down she feels by the adults in her life. The way she says it hints that she means him.

Then Rosie comes in the afternoon and throws a jaundiced eye over the flat. She says the rent is too expensive and she hopes he can afford it, but she agrees to shorten the curtains he has bought – though she can't resist adding, 'Won't Brenda do it, then? Huh?'

Brenda refers to the new flat as a 'love nest', and persuades him to entrust her with a copy of the key, but she doesn't visit him there often, saying she is too busy, she finds it remote and gloomy and the open view too exposed, and she laughs off any suggestion that she might alter the curtains, saying it is 'not her thing'.

Sid comes and helps George to move his stuff discreetly out of the old house in Crookesmoor without upsetting Rosie, and they put up some bookshelves together. Once his books are in place the flat seems less dead and more home-like.

Sid questions him none too subtly about the phone call and the lottery win. George is non-committal in his replies, wishing he had not mentioned it. He should have known that his son would just treat him like an elderly incompetent. George tells Sid that he has changed his banking password, just to humour him, although of course he has done nothing of the sort. Sid can get overly obsessive about that sort of thing, thinks George.

SID: Caustic soda

On Friday night, a week after his little car accident, Sid gets home from the college just before five and he can hear the phone ringing in the hall as he walks in through the door.

He picks up the phone. It is someone from his car insurance company, informing him that a claim has been filed against him regarding an accident on the Parkway when he drove into the back of a van. The victim, who has suffered severe whiplash injuries, is submitting an insurance claim.

'Look,' Sid says to the bloke, 'it was a very minor bump. She can't have got bad whiplash. She's hopping around all over, trying to pull a fast one. Neither of the cars was damaged. I took photos. The woman braked sharply because her dog peed on her.'

'It peed on her? How can you know that?' He hears a suppressed laugh on the line.

'Her clothing had a wet stain. On her lap. I got a photo. And she was holding the dog in her arms, not tied up or in a cage. She must have been driving with it on her lap. She was driving erratically.'

He can tell from the voice that the insurance guy is intrigued.

'Could you forward the photos? We'll have to look into it.'

He grunts assent and puts the phone down.

Lately, because of his changed status in the hierarchy of life, Sid has in idle moments found himself speculating about what kind of dad he will turn out to be. Having a baby changes a woman's life: Jacquie is already changing visibly before his

49

eyes; her bump seems to get bigger every day. But becoming a dad changes a man's life too, thinks Sid. Is he prepared? Will he be the sort of coochy-coochy dad who is always changing nappies and wiping sour milk off his shoulder, flushed with paternal love, or will he be the sort of moochy-moochy dad, bitterly jealous of Jacquie breastfeeding and all that intimacy he'll be left out from? Only time will tell. These thoughts lead him to wonder about his own father, and how George was when he, Sid, was a baby. He didn't get much coochy-coochy from George, but then he didn't get much from Rosie either. Cassie coochy-coochied him a bit, but being three years his junior, and moody even then, she was just as liable to thump him or flush his Spiderman cloak down the toilet if he crossed her.

George really came into his own as a parent when Sid was in his teens, and just beginning to wonder how to navigate the choppy waters of adolescence into the safe harbour of Wendy Dalrymple's knickers. George must have been in his early fifties then, a mature handsome man with godlike legs, like a rock at the centre of Sid's life.

'Shoot for the moon, son. Even if you miss, you'll land among the stars,' he advised.

Then he gave Sid a weird bit of advice that he still remembers to this day. He said the first time you go to bed with a girl, it's so exciting that you come almost immediately. That's humiliating for you, and isn't much fun for the girl either. So when you feel you're going to come, the thing is to distract yourself by thinking about something totally mundane and unsexy, like how to unblock a blocked drain. That'll soon take you off the boil.

Sid never got the chance to find out whether it would have worked with Wendy Dalrymple, who was the new probationary

PE teacher at his school, and much lusted after by all the boys on account of her blonde ponytail and her pert nipples, all too visible through the tight-fitting Lycra tops she wore. A few days later, he walked in on George and Wendy Dalrymple holding hands over an intimate pizza on London Road after a Blades home match.

'Sid! Come and join us!' George yelled after his departing back.

Next day, when George passed him on the stairs at home, he murmured, 'It wasn't what it looked like, son.'

He did not wait to find out. He dived off sideways, into his bedroom.

'But don't tell your mother – she's a bit puritanical!' George added in a whisper.

Sid has tried the caustic soda trick once or twice – when he was a student, in different relationships – but with Jacquie, their bodies work in such perfect sync, it really isn't necessary.

He has noticed George gazing lustfully at Jacquie from time to time. But to be fair, as far as Sid knows, his father has never tried anything with her.

When he came back up to Sheffield after university, he started meeting George for a drink in town or an outing to a Blades match, and those meetings have carried on after George left Rosie, moved in with Brenda, then into his own flat. Sometimes he has even gone out for a meal with George and Brenda. When Rosie found out, she got seriously upset, he doesn't know why.

Usually when he gets home after work he has a bottle or two of beer out in the back yard, but lately, because of impending life changes, he has started having a cup of coffee instead. As a soon-to-be family man he needs to steer clear of alcoholism, and anything that might lead to it. So he is fuelling up the espresso machine for a caffeine fix and idly running over Noether's theorem in his mind. Along with a coffee, he needs his maths fix after an afternoon with his hormone-fuelled students, as a reminder of the symmetry and orderliness of maths. It has been a hot afternoon, and even though the sun has gone down behind the houses, it is still pleasantly warm, so he takes his acoustic guitar out into the back yard and starts to strum.

A tune floats into his head, an Ee-You and the Ramonas number that has briefly become a hit in the summer of 2016, 'Phone Roaming Charges!' It reminds him, he should phone his father, listen to the latest instalment of his lottery story, reconnect him with reality. He holds the guitar between his knees and stabs the phone buttons with his bitten-down fingernails, and then he holds the phone up to his ear with his shoulder, but all he gets is an engaged tone. Beep, beep, beep, beep. He picks up the guitar and sings the song through again, all the verses, and he repeats the tricky bit about waiting by the telephone a couple of times until he gets it right. Then he phones George again. Beep, beep, beep, beep. Who the hell is he talking to for so long? Sid hangs up and tries once more. This time, he gets the same answering machine message.

He is just trying to decide what to do next when the door-bell rings. He puts the guitar down on its stand and goes to answer it. A bloke is standing there, a smiley curly-haired bloke in a tight blue suit and trainers. Looking like a dodgy car salesman or something.

'I em looking for Mr Pentiz.' The bloke has a foreign accent and he doesn't snigger as he says the name, as the locals usually do.

'Yes, that's me. What can I do for you?'

'I em from Northern Counties Bank. There is major problem with your account, Mr Pentiz. Somebody has cloned your card.'

He hands Sid a business card with the bank's logo, and the name Mr Sammy Cross, Fraud Investigator.

But I don't bank with Northern Counties, thinks Sid. Then he remembers that his parents do. He is just about to tell the man that, when the thought pops into his mind. Whoa. This doesn't look like a bloke from a bank. The trainers are the give-away, just like a spelling mistake on an otherwise perfect fake website. Sunil never wears trainers, thinks Sid. And besides, surely if he works for the bank he will have his parents' correct address.

'Can I come in?' says the bloke.

'I don't think so. No. I . . . I'm just going out for . . .'

Over the bloke's shoulder Sid can see a low-slung red sports car nosing its way into a parking space up the street. And there, to his amazement, is George, hunched over and gripping the steering wheel. His father sees Sid watching him, and Sid waves to him to go away. The bloke thinks he is waving *him* away.

'Do not be unfriendly, Mr Pentiz. I am try to be helpful. This is urgent matter demanding immediate resolution. Otherwise we will eff to suspend account. This means all direct debits, standing orders, credit card payments, all cancelled. It is very great inconvenience. It is much better if we can resolve quickly.' His voice speeds up as he races through the list of inconveniences.

At that moment, a small blue van appears around the corner, pulls up at speed behind the red car, and slams the brakes on. But not in time. Clunk! It is Pattie's Mobile Pet Parlour.

Pattie jumps out, holding her horrible dog on a lead. George gets out too, carefully stretching out one spindly leg at a time, to inspect the damage to his car that is still puffing out clouds of blue smoke from its exhaust. Heidi, the golden Labrador his parents adopted from the RSPCA when George retired, jumps down beside him, wagging her tail. Sid is fond of Heidi: she is perhaps the only normal member of the family, normal in the way that only a dog can be.

Pattie and George start yelling at each other. Sid thinks his father looks like a crazed daddy-long-legs, making wild, jerky hand and leg movements as he shouts. Pattie looks like a female version of Donald Trump, making emphatic downward gestures with her free hand. Then Pattie spots Sid standing on the doorstep watching them, and she rushes towards him, still yelling. Her neck looks perfectly okay to Sid, even though she is wearing one of those big pink whiplash collar things.

'You bastard. You told them I am liar!' She squares up to him. She is at least as tall as him, and much angrier. 'You accuse me of trying to commit fraud!'

The bloke from Northern Counties Bank spins round to face her.

'Be calm please, madam! I not accusing anyone for fraud. It is because there is irregularity –'

George butts in, his voice trembling with righteous anger. 'You should watch your driving, young lady. Have you any idea how much that car cost?'

'Have you any idea how pathetic you look in that big red sports car, you old baldie?' Pattie has gone red with rage. 'I suppose you think it will attract girls. Well, if you turn your deaf aid up, you will hear what they are saying about you!'

George splutters and shakes with fury. Pattie puts her hands on her hips, sticks her chin out and looks tough. Sid tries to get in between them. Heidi sticks her nose in Pattie's crotch and thrashes her strong stubby tail. Pattie's horrible dog starts thrashing its tail too.

'Dad, what are you doing here in that car?' Closer now, Sid can see it is not the Porsche or the red Ferrari of Rosie's fantasy, it is the same old banger of a Mazda, spray-painted red.

'So he is your father?' Pattie turns on Sid. 'I could have guessed. Terrible driver. Like father like son.'

'Can I come inside, son?' whines George. Then, gesturing at the man from Northern Counties Bank, 'Who is this bloke?'

'He says he's a fraud investigator.'

George turns pale, spins on his heel, and hot-foots it back towards the red car, dragging Heidi along behind him. Heidi follows somewhat reluctantly. She seems to have taken a shine to Pattie's horrible dog, in spite of their differences, and is making whimpering 'come hither' noises.

'Stop, Mr Pentiz! Come back!' yells the fraud investigator. 'I em trying to be of help! I em investigating irregularities.'

'Fraud investigator?' Pattie shoves Sid aside to confront the man. 'Yah! Go, Max!'

She lets the horrible dog off its leash. It lunges forward and sinks its pointy teeth into the man's ankle. He yowls in pain. Hopping on one foot, he tries to shake it off, kicking it at the same time with the other foot – an impossible manoeuvre which leaves him off balance. Heidi has broken free from George's grip on her leash and comes to the rescue, luring the vicious dog away into the bushes with more of her seductive whimpers. Pattie, who has the build of a rugby player, tackles the fraud investigator at the waist. Soon they are both rolling on the ground outside the door as she pummels him with her fists. The low-slung red car, meanwhile, reverses into Pattie's blue van, leaving a visible dent, does an irregular three-point turn and zooms away in a cloud of blue smoke, leaving Sid to surmise that the engine of the

Mazda sports car has had some rough use from a previous owner. He gives his father a quick wave, steps inside his house and bolts the door, and tidies up the kitchen and living room in preparation for Jacquie's homecoming later that evening.

Half an hour later, when he opens the door, they have all gone, Heidi included, but Pattie's horrible dog is still there, slumped on the doormat with a blissed-out look on his face. You can never tell with dogs, thinks Sid.

On the dot at ten o'clock next morning, Sid's mother Rosie phones, oblivious to the drama which has taken place the previous day at Sid's place. She often phones on Saturday mornings while he and Jacquie are still in bed. Sid finds this particularly annoying because they work in different cities, so they only get two lie-ins together in a week, and his mother is taking over one of them.

She is still tearful and upset about George's exit, though it is now over four weeks ago, and it comes up nearly every Saturday morning in her confessionals with Jacquie. Jacquie is super-soothing and does not let her boredom show – she is used to dealing with distressed people in her job.

'How are you feeling, Jacquie?' Rosie says, when Sid passes over the phone to Jacquie. 'I had morning sickness when I was pregnant with Sid. It was awful.'

Jacquie mumbles something vague, so Rosie continues. 'I'm so happy for you both. And for myself. I've been longing to be a granny. Sid's a wonderful young man, you know, the way I brought him up. Not given to straying, like George, who is always on the lookout for women he can charm. Did I tell you how George went next door to Brenda's on referendum night, just because we had a bit of a disagreement about Brexit?' Rosie complains.

'Mhm,' murmurs Jacquie.

'Before I let him back in, I extracted a promise that he'd write personally to Nigel Farage about the three hundred and fifty million pounds a week for the NHS. That's fair enough, isn't it? I scribbled it on a sheet of paper and held it up against the glass door. At first he just laughed and wiggled his eyebrows, as he always does when he wants to put on the charm, then when he realized I was dead serious, finally he nodded. Then as soon as I opened the door, he tried to go back on his word. He said the exact sum didn't matter; it was the thought that counted, he said. The people had voted with their hearts, not with their calculators, he said. What tosh! I got so angry I threw a triangle of toast with marmalade at him that stuck in his hair. He just shrugged. Then he removed the toast from his hair and ate it. He said he was just a patriot saving his country. Chomp, chomp, chomp. From rule by an alien culture. Chomp, chomp, chomp.'

'Your poor mum. I can hear the distress in her voice,' whispers Jacquie to Sid.

'You can't blame him, can you?' Sid says, overhearing Rosie's diatribe because Jacquie is holding the phone away from her ear while she drinks her tea. 'Not after Mum locked him out in the rain?'

'Was it raining? She didn't say that. But all the same . . .' Jacquie's eyes narrow as she wrinkles her nose thoughtfully.

Sid lays a hand on hers.

He had the same argument with his parents the day before the referendum. George said he was thinking about voting Leave, because the England he grew up in had been colonized by the EU, and its officialdom and its sovereignty were compromised. George said you only had to look at Greece to realize that the EU was not all benign. Rosie burst into tears and read something aloud in an actressy voice from a library book lying on the kitchen table.

'Listen to this!' She read that morbid symptoms become apparent when the old world dies, and the new world is not yet born. 'Gramsci,' she said. 'Don't forget, Sid, I know about philosophical thought.'

Somehow the immense shock that has been rattling the country is reverberating through Sid's own family.

GEORGE: *No room at the inn*

George in his prime years has been a dab hand at juggling two women at a time, but this time it is more difficult and the women, he finds, are more demanding. It all comes to a head over Rosie's birthday, when his two-women juggling act finally collapses.

One Saturday afternoon in August, George goes out shopping in the town centre, determined to buy a birthday present for Rosie's sixtieth birthday, but with no ideas about what she would like. Brenda, as the supposed expert on feminine desires, comes along to advise.

Without its temporary occupation by students, who swoop down on the city in late September and fly away in the summer months to warmer climes, Sheffield now reveals itself as a declining industrial town with an increasingly impoverished population. In autumn, he knows, the students will return like a noisy, brightly coloured flock of birds, covering the town with their crap of discarded beer cans and takeout cartons, livening up the city with their partying and loud music, annoying the hell out of the locals.

Although it is usually temperate in Sheffield in the summer months, a thing George likes about the city, this year a heavy moisture-laden heat hangs in the air, creating an air of listlessness and suffocation. Brenda is wearing a stylish sleeveless dress with a geometric pattern in yellow and sky blue. She quivers and grips his hand.

'I love the summer, George. Don't you? A chance to let your

skin take in the sunshine. I feel sorry for these Muslim women who have to cover themselves up. All those veils and shawls. I suppose showing a bit of skin is against their religion. Funny, isn't it?'

'But showing off your suntan is a recent idea,' he ripostes. 'In my young days, women used to wear hats and gloves to keep their skin white. It was an ideal of beauty, not religion, that lay behind it.'

He remembers beautiful Eugenie's spectral whiteness. Rosie, by contrast, used to sunbathe nude in the back garden. But there is so little sun in Yorkshire, it didn't make much difference.

'Keeping the sun off you is nothing to do with being a Muslim, Brenda, it's a fact of life in a hot climate. In Greece the people cover themselves up and prefer to stay indoors, or in the shade, in the summer. It's nothing to do with religion.'

She catches the inflamed look in his eye and misinterprets it. 'I don't mean you, George. You're one of us. Your parents didn't just come here to live off benefits, did they?'

For the first time in his life, George finds himself questioning his Britishness. He isn't sure he belongs in this island with these insular people. What does he have in common with them? At least Rosie, with her part-Jewish ancestry, has a wider perspective, a whiff of faraway lands about her. But if this is not his home, where is?

'Of course, all that's changed now.' Brenda's voice takes on a grumpy tone. 'Nowadays we're not even allowed to have a proper Christmas any more, with Baby Jesus and the manger and all that, in case Muslims get offended.'

'Do you think anyone was really offended? I think that's just a made-up story. Everybody enjoys Christmas. I've never met anyone who was offended.'

'That's what they told us, the politically correct brigade. It was in all the papers.' She clutches his hand. 'Christmas always reminds me of when I was little. I lived in Hillsborough with my Mam and Dad and my two younger sisters, and Dad used to get dressed up as Father Christmas, but we knew it was him because of his crooked nose, and we'd seen the real Father Christmas at Atkinsons. At school in assembly we used to sing, "While shepherds washed their socks by night . . ."'

George laughs. 'I remember that. When I was in primary school in Totley, I was the innkeeper in the nativity play, dressed up in my mother's dressing gown, with a tea towel on my head. When Mary and Joseph arrived, I had to bar their way and say, "No room at the inn."' He growls in a deep voice and puts up his hand.

Brenda quivers with suppressed excitement and moistens her lips. 'That's right. That's what we should be saying to all the immigrants now. No room. This island's full. Go somewhere else. Anyway, pet, let's keep off politics. We'll only fall out.' Changing the subject, she points at a display in a window. 'Look at that new Gwyneth Paltrow perfume and body lotion set! Do you think Rosie would like that?' She sucks in air through her teeth. 'Not cheap, is it? At that price you'd think it must have got gold filings in it!'

'Maybe it smells expensively nice,' he says, thinking about Eugenie, who wore Lancôme and always smelled expensively nice. Is Brenda perhaps hinting at the birthday gift she would like for herself? When *is* her birthday? Before he can ask her, she changes the subject.

'Shall we go away somewhere this August Bank Holiday, pet? On the twenty-ninth? It usually rains in Sheffield. We could go somewhere warm. By the sea,' Brenda says. 'I've heard they do lots of last-minute travel offers at the Co-op.'

'Let's think about it.'

Rosie has already asked him, and in a moment of absent-minded nostalgia he has agreed, to have a joint birthday dinner with her and the kids, like they did in the old days. The Asian gent, he assumes, will not be involved. The date has been fixed for the 4th of September, when both Cassie and Sid will be free. If he goes away with Brenda, he may not be back in time. Pleasant memories beset him as he remembers his old pre-Brenda life. They will be together as a family, as they have been for thirty-five years, opening presents, getting a bit tipsy, then demolishing a roast and sliding into a stupor around the table. The trouble is, he hasn't told Brenda yet. He is waiting for the right moment to break the news.

'I was thinking we could drive out to a country pub in the Peak District for the August Bank Holiday,' he says, wiggling his eyebrows and putting on his most romantic voice. 'Have a moonlit dinner in a pub garden. Then come back into Sheffield for all the excitement in the streets. Wouldn't you like that?'

'Mmm. Sounds alright. But what about going away somewhere, now you don't have kids to worry about?'

'But in August it'll be over-booked and expensive, and full of noisy kids. We could go away later.' He can see in her eyes that she is weighing up the idea. Then her mouth turns down. 'And,' he continues quickly, 'I've sort of promised Rosie I'll have a birthday dinner with her and the kids . . .'

As far as he is concerned, he's being fair to both of them, keeping everybody happy. But Brenda punches his arm with her fists and starts to howl.

'You've just been using me for sex, then running back to Rosie now she says she's pregnant and you think you're going to have another baby with her.'

'What?' he exclaims. Can Rosie be pregnant by Sunil? Is that possible? He is far from an expert on female anatomy, but surely she is too old by now? He remembers with a shudder her prolonged and tempestuous menopause, finally tamed by massive doses of HRT. Maybe she has undergone some procedure?

Before he can marshal his thoughts, Brenda adds, 'And you still call them kids! They're in their bloody thirties! They don't still believe in Father Christmas, do they?'

Although George sometimes thinks much the same of Cassie and Sid, he doesn't think it is Brenda's place to say so. She turns her back on him and storms off into the perfume store, without looking round to see if he is following.

Outside the shop a different kind of fracas is taking place. A big group of lads, out on the town with cans of beer in their hands, have surrounded three women who are out shopping, two in full niqabs, only their terrified eyes showing, one wearing an elaborate black flounced hijab pinned to her head. The lads start jostling and shouldering them, grabbing at their shopping bags. One of the bags spills open, and a bright red lacy bra falls out on to the pavement. They laugh and make loud, sexy kissing noises. The woman bends low to pick it up, but one of the lads grabs it before she can reach it, and another steps forward and casually treads on the end of her niqab as it trails on the ground, so that when she straightens up, it is pulled back, revealing her hair. The woman reaches up and tugs the niqab, trying to keep her head covered with her other hand. The lads laugh.

'Gone all shy now, have we?' mocks the first lad, dangling the bra in front of her.

'We voted for you to get out!' shouts another, burping so loudly that the others laugh. 'So why are you still here? Go back to where you come from!'

A crowd of passers-by have stopped to watch, but nobody

intervenes. A couple of young people start videoing the scene on their phones. George looks around. Where are the police when you need them? He steps forward, putting on what he hopes is a deep, authoritative voice – though, truth to say, he is scared.

'There's no need for that, lads. Get yourselves off home.'

Then the girl wearing the black hijab shoves her way forward, and lets forth a torrent of abuse at the lads in the broadest Yorkshire.

'Fuck off, you fuckers! We're here because we're here! Now fuck off back to the cave you crawled out off-of!'

George recognizes her from when he had taught at the college, where she had been a hairdressing trainee, a pretty girl. He is impressed at her manifest assimilation, her ability to straddle two cultures. He wiggles his eyebrows in appreciation. Her eyes are sparkling with fury and her cheeks are bright pink with rage. The lads looked cowed. There is a little patter of applause from the onlookers. This is Sheffield, after all, not so long ago the Socialist Republic of South Yorkshire.

Then a lone voice from the crowd shouts, 'You bugger off home your sen, Mr Panties. We know where you come from with that naughty name. And we know where you live,' the voice adds with a hint of menace. He scans the group and recognizes a couple of regular Blades supporters he has exchanged chit-chat with, among the gaggle of baseball-capped males.

'Don't you remember, you said the Greeks invented democracy? Ha bloody ha! It was us British invented the Magnet Carter! And we just had a democratic vote on getting immigrants out of our country!' the voice mocks. 'And we won!'

Above the heads of the crowd, George can see two police caps weaving slowly towards them. He breathes a sigh of relief.

At that moment, Brenda emerges from the store with an elaborately wrapped parcel. She pushes through the throng to stand beside him and, holding up her palms at the young men, she says in a firm tone, 'Enough's enough, lads. The cops are coming. You'll get into trouble. We're not racialists, are we?'

The lads mumble something and start to shuffle away. As soon as their circle is broken, the women they have surrounded dart into the perfume shop giggling.

Brenda turns on him. 'Why did you want to pick a fight with that lot? D'you want to get your face slashed?' Her cheeks are flushed, her lips tight.

Later that evening, he rings Rosie to see whether they can fine-tune their birthday dinner arrangement. He doesn't mention the pregnancy. But it turns out that Rosie has already invited the kids over for 4th September and bought a massive frozen beef Wellington that will feed an army; and Brenda, without consulting him, has gone ahead and booked a luxury spa break for two in the Canaries.

The 'joint birthday dinner' with Rosie and the 'kids' turns out not to be the jolly family occasion of his memories, but a stiff, awkward affair of tough, dry beef moistened with salty gravy, accompanied by lurid, emerald-coloured frozen asparagus.

Rosie has her hair wound up in a pink towel-turban with a Minnie Mouse headband stuck on top, for some reason.

As she bends over to lift the hot beef Wellington out of the oven, George dives forward to help her, saying, 'Careful now, Rosie!'

'What do you mean, "careful now"? Stop trying to infantilize me, George!'

'Aren't you expecting Sunil's baby?'

'Ha ha! Whatever gave you that idea?' She throws back her head and laughs.

Chastised, George glues himself to his chair and never mentions the supposed pregnancy again.

Instead of a jolly flow of family banter there are awkward silences as they pick their way around the conversational landmines, avoiding talking about her supposed pregnancy, his new car, his new flat, Brenda, and all topics that might lead on to Brexit – but which inevitably do.

ROSIE: Minnie Mouse

Rosie finds that her kids react in different ways to the Pantis family break-up. Sid, typically, obsesses about the logistics of who will live where, including the dog Heidi, whom they agree to share. Cassie, who already has an over-developed sense of victimhood that she must have learnt from her father, says she's suffered all her childhood from inconsistent and erratic parenting, of which this is just the latest example. It is why her life has been a disaster which she is still trying to get under control with therapy, pilates, a gluten-free diet, and advice from Ivor. Despite all that negativity, she's a good kid, thinks Rosie, but soon to reach thirty-two, a dangerous age, and still single, with no boyfriend on the horizon, apart from that pompous commitment-phobic prick Ivor, that failed-philosopher parasite, that useless leeching lump of self-regard. So no prospect of grandchildren there, alas.

Neither Cassie nor Sid are as frequent visitors home as she hoped after the break-up, so she is grateful to Heidi and Sunil for filling the void in her life.

When George went off with Brenda, Rosie went to Sunil for some financial advice about dividing and investing the pension before George squandered it all, and she ended up blubbing all over his lever-arch files. He whipped out a box of tissues. He had plenty of those. It turned out he had recently lost his wife to breast cancer. That's how it all started. But Rosie has explained emphatically, more than once, to both the kids that this fling with Sunil is only a fling – in her heart she still belongs to George. She just wants to teach him a lesson.

She doesn't tell them that, a few weeks after coming off HRT, her hot flushes have returned and her hormones seem to be waging war on her. She doesn't tell them about George's on-off relationship with his ex-wife, the ever-youthful Eugenie, or his infidelity with a married colleague, back in 2001, which was traumatic at the time but later forgotten in the happy years that followed. Apart from those summer clouds, her married life with George had been, on the whole, as joyful and fulfilling as a Jane Austen novel, a merry romp – which is what she tells them, and that seems to keep them happy – until the Bitch came along and lured George away with her naughty nurse outfit and sparkly suspenders.

George is, however, coming home for a joint birthday dinner on the 4th of September. Rosie has made a detailed plan for her birthday celebration; George will come round at seven o'clock for an early dinner, and Sid and Cassie will be there already, and they will all have a big birthday meal together, just like old times, with a few drinks in the garden afterwards, weather permitting. Maybe he will apologize for his folly, and all will be back to normal. He will have a change of heart about the EU, dump the Bitch, and move back into their marital home, she hopes.

On the morning of the birthday dinner, Rosie looks in the mirror and notices how grey and straggly her hair has become. Since George has moved out, she has let herself go. If she washes and colours it now, it will be dry, bouncy, silky and sweet-smelling by the time George and the kids come round for dinner. The beef Wellington is already cooking slowly in the oven, the frozen asparagus spears are thawing, the potatoes are ready to go in. Now it is time to look after herself.

In the bathroom, she turns on the shower to let it run hot, filling the chilly bathroom with a warm steamy fug, and reaches for the herb-perfumed shampoo. After the shampoo she applies dye to the grey roots. Then she remembers Brenda's gift of Hollywood Glamour Hair Balm and she realizes she hasn't yet tried it out – this is her chance. She feels for the tube in the under-basin cupboard. Her eyes are stinging with soapy shampoo, and she squeezes them tight to stop it leaching in, so she can't actually see the tube, but she can feel it, plump and squishy in her hand. She unscrews it and gives it a big squeeze. The hair balm has an unusual cloying smell, but that, she guesses, must be the glamour ingredient. She works it into her towel-dried hair and leaves it for about three minutes (yes, that's what the Bitch said, didn't she?). Then she rinses it off under the shower.

As she rinses, she observes that she is shedding an unusual amount of hair. A very unusual amount. Her newly dyed auburn curls swirl down into the outlet hole, almost blocking it up. She has to empty it out four times. As she reaches up her hand, she can tell there is more hair swirling into the shower than is left on her head. What has the Bitch put in that conditioner tube? Then she wipes the soap from her eyes and realizes it isn't Brenda's Hair Balm she has applied – it is depilatory cream, from an old tube which was lurking among the clutter under the basin.

Then the doorbell rings. George has arrived.

She quickly turbans up her hair in a greying pink towel, and runs down to open the door and give him a kiss.

During the birthday dinner she sits stiffly with her hair twisted in a turban which she brightens up with a Minnie Mouse headband that once belonged to Cassie, stuck on top.

'What have you done with your hair, Mum?' asks Cassie suspiciously. 'Why are you wearing that thing on your head?'

'That bitch next door gave me a tube of hair remover and told me it was hair conditioner,' Rosie says.

'No! I would have killed her!' exclaims Cassie.

'Why did she do that?' asks Sid.

'I've no idea. You'd better be careful!' Rosie warns George. 'It could happen to you.'

He reaches up and pats his thinning hair with a look of alarm. He doesn't spring to Brenda's defence, which Rosie reckons is a good sign.

No one enjoys the birthday dinner. The beef Wellington is dry and tough; the gravy is salty; the asparagus tips are mushy; the conversation is stiff. They just keep their heads down, chew hard, and get through it as fast as they can. Everybody is desperate for it to be over.

It's not easy, Rosie reflects with hindsight, to make a frozen beef Wellington from a discount supermarket chain taste yummy; or to make a frozen heart seem gay just by putting a Minnie Mouse headband on top of your turban. Recalling the evening makes her shudder.

Next day, Rosie goes to the hairdresser at Middlewood and has what is left of her hair cut close to her head.

She tries to disguise her shorn hair with scarves and hats, until her colleagues at work ask whether she has undergone cancer treatment.

By mid-September her hair will have grown back, short and curly like a ginger lamb. Sunil says he likes it like that. When she looks in the mirror she sees a different person, neater, more subdued.

GEORGE: The Great Poem

The day after Rosie's birthday party, George and Brenda fly straight out to the Canaries from Manchester. Apart from the weather, which is rather warm, the Canaries are not much fun. Brenda spends hours having manicures and pedicures, waxings, hot stone treatments, mud masks, peelings, Botox injections and massages, while he stays in the shade and reads a novel – something about a young woman being murdered – by the hotel pool which, despite it being term time, is still full of boisterous, splashy English kids. In the cooler evenings he and Brenda walk along the still-warm beach to watch locals taking a dip, then stuff themselves on deep-fried food in the fuggy over-crowded dining room at the hotel. At the end of the holiday, they catch a taxi back to Sheffield from Manchester Airport. George watches the speeding clouds above the open moorland that is still covered in purple-flowering heather as they cross the Snake Pass, through a sudden violent shower that blurs the view. It is good to be back, he thinks.

When George returns to his flat that night, it is not the open, creative space he imagined and yearned for, it is more like a trap. When he closes the door and turns the key, the cool, bare echoing walls seem to clamp tight around him like a pair of jaws. He shuffles around in his slippers and unpacks his case.

He finds he does not sleep well in this flat. Somehow, it is too quiet. He has adapted to a certain level of background noise during his thirty-five years with Rosie: her unpredictable outbursts of raucous laughter; her sudden bad-mouthing of politicians on the television; her singing in the shower; her grunts as she does her yoga exercises; her melodious snoring. All he can hear in his new flat, if he really listens hard, is the burble of the television of his upstairs neighbour, a quiet elderly widow called Mrs Timms who welcomed him with tea and home-made flapjacks when he arrived, and who eyes him hopefully whenever their paths cross. But she is far too old for him, in her seventies at least – almost as old as he is – and not his type. George never invites her back. She is not at all what he has in mind. No.

For some reason, he has started waking two or three times in the night to go for a pee. He tiptoes to the bathroom along the unfamiliar corridor, trying not to wake Heidi, but she is always alert and inevitably jumps up, thrashing her tail and sticking her moist nose into his pyjama pants. Afterwards, it takes him ages to get back to sleep. He lies awake, worrying that this excessive night-time peeing is a sign of prostate cancer – but not actually going as far as making an appointment with Dr Khan to have it investigated. Worrying that old age and his own mortality are creeping up on him before he has written that Great Poem he was planning, the Great Poem that will secure his place in literary history. He sits at the window and stares at the weather galloping down over the hills, his brow furrowed with concentration, but nothing will come. He is glad, in a way, that neither Rosie nor Brenda are there to witness his disintegration.

SID: Red Ferraris

Cassie phones Sid early one Tuesday morning in mid-September, shortly after George's return from the Canaries.

'Hi, Sid. Why does nobody ever ring me?' she accuses.

He finds that his sister can be quite hard work first thing in the morning, so he mumbles, 'I was just about to ring you, Cass.'

'Listen, Sid, I'm a bit worried about Dad. I spoke to Mum yesterday. She thinks he's gone a bit bonkers since winning twenty million quid on the Albanian lottery. She said he's been parading around town in a red Ferrari. Did you know about that?'

'Yeah, sort of. He came out with the same story a while ago, but I don't suppose there's any truth in it. Anyway, it's not twenty million. More like seven and a bit. And it's not Albania, it's Kosovo. And I don't think it's a Ferrari, it's an old Mazda. The whole thing is probably a scam.'

'Well, if she and Dad are not actually divorced, she must be entitled to some of that lottery money? But knowing how unreliable Dad is, he'll just squander it on red Ferraris and suchlike?' Cassie says.

She sounds distressed, like a child who's dropped her ice cream in a puddle.

'I don't think there *is* any lottery money to squander, Cass. Anyway, where did you get the idea he wanted a red Ferrari? They're quite rare, you know. I don't think he could even find one in Sheffield.'

'Mum told me he wanted a Ferrari? But she doesn't know anything about cars?'

'I don't know why Mum's so upset at Dad coming into some money.' Sid tries to stay neutral between his parents, and it irritates him that Cassie is so definitely a mother loyalist.

'I don't think she's upset about the money? I think she's still upset about Brenda?'

That is Sid's thought exactly, but he wants his sister to take a balanced view of their parents, as he believes he does.

'I don't think she's so bothered about Brenda now she's with Sunil.'

It's the fact that she went on living with their parents longer than he did, and Rosie used to confide in her – that's probably why she always takes Mum's side, thinks Sid.

'Can you blame her?' Cassie continues. 'They're not actually divorced, so some of that money, if he has really won it, must be hers by rights, but she thinks Brenda will persuade him to spend it all on glitz and bling. He's already squandering it on red Ferraris and suchlike? The thing is, Sid, I tried to ring him at his flat in Totley, and I couldn't get a reply? I kept getting this answering machine message?'

There is a distraught edge to her voice that makes Sid prick up his ears. Perhaps something is really wrong with his father, he thinks. Or perhaps his sister is just being typically unreliable.

SID: Red bobble hat

Later that same afternoon, while he is out getting a set of new strings for his guitar, Rosie calls Sid on his mobile, asking him if he wants to come round for supper on his way home. She has something to discuss with him, she says. When he drops in on her a couple of hours later she is fuming about George's lack of communication, but mainly because he's left her to look after the dog.

'Wherever he is, he's left Heidi here when he knows it's his turn to have her. He knows Sunil's allergic to dogs, but he just doesn't care. He's like a spoilt brat – never thinks of anyone or anything beyond his immediate wants. Me, me, me.'

Sid mumbles some soothing words while he tries to stay loyal to his father. He has sweeter memories from his childhood of his father playing football with him and Cassie in Endcliffe Park, wearing a red bobble hat and fingerless gloves, jerking his skinny legs out to kick the ball, or scuttling across the pitch with his knees up like a demented stick insect. They were both keen Sheffield United fans, and a lot of bonding took place in the Blades stadium.

Those memories played a large part in Sid's decision to return to Sheffield after university, and they've kept up the tradition of going to matches and getting sillily drunk together once in a while. Even though he now thinks of himself as an independent adult, he does not want to listen to his mother bad-mouthing his father.

'I thought you were happy with Sunil.'

'But I can't have Sunil and Heidi at home at the same time, can I? Anyway, Sid, this fling with Sunil is just that – a fling. In my heart I still belong to George, but I want to teach him a lesson.'

'So maybe he is having a last fling too. Maybe this crisis is just Dad's way of dealing with the approach of old age. His way of coming to terms with mortality. Just hang in there, Mum,' he says with a bounce of optimism in his voice that he does not actually feel.

His mother sits down slowly and replies, 'That's what I hope, Sid. That's what I hope. Maybe this moment of delirium will pass, maybe the stars will realign themselves and things will once again be as before. Poor George. He can't help it, any more than the crazy squirrel can help stealing the birds' bread and burying the bread in the garden. He follows his desires just like a tomcat, but he means no harm. He wants everyone to be happy all the time. But you can't always have that, can you?'

'So let's try to be constructive, Mum. Let's work out why he's lying low. It could be to do with all this money he thinks he's won.'

'I told Sunil the lottery money story, and he said it was an everyday scam whereby someone tries to take control of your bank account. Either that, or it was probably just a typo – somebody had just keyed in a wrong digit. No doubt the bank will soon be in touch. Or maybe someone could be using George's account for money laundering. Sunil said there's no end of crime involving banks these days. Apparently, they just need to deposit money for a very short time in a legitimate account, to hide the trail of where it has really come from. If George changed the password they wouldn't be able to get it back out. You did tell him to change the password, didn't you? Only the person who has the password can get money out, and knowing how forgetful he's become lately . . .'

'He might have written it down, even though they advise you not to.'

'Sunil says it's potty expecting elderly people to remember lots of different passwords without writing them down. The banks are looking for a different technological solution.'

Sid bows to Sunil's greater knowledge about that sort of thing. Sunil used to work in a bank, and he became Rosie and George's financial adviser when George retired and took his pension. George once referred to him as a 'member of the new financial elite that's bleeding the country dry', but Rosie trusts his advice.

Rosie continues. 'After he retired, your dad started talking wistfully of withdrawing part of our pension and buying a new sports car. I persuaded him it was a waste of money. And it would be harmful for the environment, as well. No doubt Brenda has been encouraging him now – favouring, as she does, displays of conspicuous consumption.'

Sid ignores the provocation and replies in a neutral tone. 'I think he needs a new car, his old car is burning oil. That's not good for the environment either, is it, Mum?'

Rosie shakes her head absently and reaches for a prawn curry out of the freezer, shoves it brutally into the microwave, sits down at the kitchen table, and goes on talking. Sid thinks at first she is talking to him, but then he realizes that she is, in fact, talking to herself, going over old stuff from their marriage.

'The way George was carrying on about the referendum, you'd think he'd become an overnight Greek Nationalist. He never used to be like that, never even talked about being Greek, but recently something's got into him. I don't know what it is. It's like a cloud of poison gas drifting across the world, making everybody mad who comes into contact with it. Hungary. Turkey. America. Germany. France. Even here in Crookesmoor. Even your own father, Sid.'

Her voice drops to a conspiratorial tone, and she wiggles her fingers in front of her face to suggest the rising cloud of poison gas.

'Mmm. Mum, it could be poison gas, but it's more likely to be poison money. When someone unexpectedly acquires that amount of money, the world's full of people who want to part him from it. He could be in trouble.'

'Drowned in the spa pool at some fancy hotel, no doubt! With the Bitch shedding crocodile tears over him all the way to the bank. Ha ha!' She grins spitefully.

'Like you said, Mum, there's two sides to every story.' But sometimes, he might have added, the 'his and hers' versions of the story don't match up. He doesn't want to arbitrate in this dispute between his parents; he just wants it to be over, and for things to be stable once more. He wants to be loyal to his father while supporting his mother, but it is harder than he thought to get the balance right.

From where he is sitting, he can see the usual jumble of old coats and shoes in the hall that has been there since his childhood, and a subtle but pervasive smell of humanity touches his nostrils, musty and very faintly sickly, which he recognizes as the sad lingering smell of their family life together, a life that has been flung so recklessly on to this angry national bonfire by his enraged parents.

He bends down and picks out George's old red bobble hat, from the jumble under the stairs, and puts it on his head.

His mother says, 'You've lost weight, Sid. You look so like George used to look when I first knew him.'

78

She leans forward across the kitchen table, cupping her face in her hands. She is wearing nail polish in a subtle sea-green shade. When Sid lived at home, he never, ever saw her wear nail polish. He thinks this must be Sunil's influence. She seems much happier since she's been with Sunil.

While they are talking, the phone rings in the hall. Rosie goes to answer it, but he can't hear the conversation, all he can hear is her voice saying, 'Yes . . . okay . . . yes . . . I get it.' Heidi ambles into the kitchen, wagging her tail, and presses her nose against his knee. The dog looks pleased to see him, but when his mother comes back she gives Heidi a hard slap on the rump.

'Get out! You know you're not supposed to be in here.' Then she sits down opposite him again, and a tear leaks out of her left eye. 'That was Sunil. He said he's going back to live with his mother, because of the dog.' There is a sob that catches in her throat. She can't talk properly. She whispers, 'Can't you take her, Sid?'

'I would, Mum, but Jacquie is scared of dogs. She got bitten when she was a kid.'

'Heidi wouldn't bite a thing. She's the most good-natured dog anyone can imagine. That's how she can put up with your dad.' Rosie sighs. 'Cassie can't have her for more than a few days, her flat's too small and it's on the fourth floor. You've got to persuade your dad to come back, Sid. There's no other way.'

'I can't sort out your relationship with Dad, Mum. That's up to you two. I have to concentrate on my relationship with Jacquie now. Our baby is due next March.'

Rosie snorts. 'You were always so conventional, Sid. I don't know where you got that from. Not from me, and definitely not from *him*. The baby isn't due for another six months. Jacquie will be perfectly okay. She's a strong girl.'

'You could always give Heidi back to the RSPCA.'

In the silence that follows, they can hear scratching and the soft whimpering let-me-in sound from behind the door. Their eyes meet. A tear trickles out of Rosie's right eye, and Sid can feel his eyes watering up too.

'Okay. I'll do what I can, Mum.'

ROSIE: *Tesco's own-brand taramasalata*

After Sid has left, Rosie gazes out of the back window into the dark rain-battered garden and swirls hot water into the sink, while random thoughts swirl through her head. You never stop worrying about your kids, do you, however adult they seem to be? She has always tried to do her best for Sid and Cassie, to bring them up to know right from wrong, to control their tantrums, to share with others and not to stick their fingers in electric sockets, but it's harder than you think to get your kids to turn out the way you want them to. She feels it's up to her to make up for George's neglect, now he's gone off with the Bitch. Who's going to make sure they're happily married? Who's going to babysit the grandchildren while their parents pursue their busy careers? Who's going to buy them those little extras? Who's going to help them put a deposit down on a home of their own? It's not that George doesn't love Sid and Cassie, but he just doesn't think that way. Now he thinks he's got a bit of money, he just wants to indulge himself, she fulminates silently as she stamps around in the kitchen washing up the plates she and Sid have dirtied and scraping the remnants into the brown compost caddy that Cassie has badgered her into adopting.

Sid and Jacquie seem to be well settled, with a baby on the way, she thinks. Sid is sensible and will work things out for the best, and Jacquie has registered for UK residence, so Brexit won't affect her. Now she, Rosie, just needs to keep Brenda and her malign 'I am not a racialist' schtick out of this new extension to her family – or else, in the wink of an eye, Brenda will be telling them how much she adores 'coloured' people, knitting bonnets and bootees for the 'Referendum Baby', as she insists on calling it. Or buying them in designer stores, more likely. Bitch.

Most of all Rosie worries about Cassie, who still doesn't have a permanent man in her life at thirty-one. She's an attractive girl with a responsible job, muses Rosie. She's been on plenty of dates, but Cassie seems to be locked into a dead-end relationship with a middle-aged man called Ivor, her former philosophy lecturer at university, twenty years older than her, with a shadowy wife called Barbara, an incipient paunch and bloodshot eyes and, according to Cassie, a powerful personality. Ivor keeps Cassie dangling on a string, refusing to let her go, yet still refusing to leave Barbara, while Cassie's biological clock ticks away. Surely Cassie deserves better?

Rosie has even arranged a couple of blind dates for Cassie herself – with Brad, her dentist, with Tim, the geography teacher at her school. Perfectly nice men, both of them, but Cassie said they weren't her type. Who is she saving herself for? George bloody Clooney, for God's sake? Cassie needs to get a move on, as Rosie frequently reminds her. All her colleagues at school have grandchildren already, and they are never shy about flashing their baby pictures around in the staffroom. She can't help but ask herself, where did she go wrong?

And George, even though he has taken himself off to Totley, still occupies her mind. He still thinks of himself as a victim of the burdens that family life puts on creative men – geniuses like himself, ha ha. He calls it the 'pram in the hall' syndrome, but she's the one still sitting in the daily traffic jam, while he took early retirement from his job, saying he wanted to give himself more time to write poetry. If he actually wrote any damn poetry, she'd be more sympathetic, but he spends his days surfing the internet in his underpants, googling Greek recipes and mooching through his old poetry collection from his student days, while she still has to slog out another six years teaching RE and general studies to fifth formers, even though she has the same qualifications as her husband.

Rosie is subject to that unfortunate EU ruling which equalized retirement ages between men and women. When you think about it, she's the one who has reason to be anti-EU, but she is in fact an EU enthusiast because she looks forward to a better future for Sid and Cassie, whereas George, who is twenty years her senior, still lives in a past when Britain had an empire. Hm!

Recently he claims to have rediscovered his 'Greek identity'. For heaven's sake. He's about as Greek as Tesco's own-brand taramasalata, thinks Rosie, furiously squirting a blast of washing-up liquid into the bowl, and watching with satisfaction as it foams up, shrouding all the residue of their meal in bubbles.

She knows a bit about George's family history – more than he does, in fact. George's grandfather was a Greek Cypriot who moved to England from Cyprus in the 1920s with George's dad, then just a toddler, who kept his Greek surname, Pantis (what a mistake that was!), and passed it on to his son when he married an English schoolteacher called Sarah. So George grew up speaking English and thinking of himself as English. Until the day he saw that poster of a queue of immigrants from somewhere waiting at the border, supposedly desperate to get into the UK, *his* UK, just as his grandparents had done. He was going through a post-retirement depression, and that awakened a sense of victimhood in him. And what is national identity but victimhood with boots on?

There's a black-and-white picture of those grandparents, looking stiff and formal, beside a rakishly informal wedding photo of herself and George on top of the piano that nobody plays, in the sitting room that nobody sits in. They were both better looking in those days: 45-year-old George, recently divorced from the beautiful Eugenie, looking magisterial with dense cascades of wavy dark hair and a curving moustache; Rosie just turned twenty-five, wearing a long hippyish dress that barely conceals her pregnancy bump (Sid) with her bare feet poking out under the hem, a crown of daisies on her hair. Their expressions are carefree and hopeful, their hands entwined, their eyes fixed on the future.

Rosie feels a pang of sorrow like a sharp stab in her soul, to see how age has marked both of them. Her thick auburn curls, legacy of a Jewish grandmother, are now streaked with grey, which she keeps at bay with a little help from Brenda. George's dark cascades of hair have long since turned silver and have thinned considerably, so that they cling in a straggly semi-circle around the bare dome of his distinguished-looking skull. Or used to cling. Until the Bitch got rid of that – like she couldn't wait to make her mark on him – substituting the fashionable shaven-headed baldie look, which in Rosie's humble opinion makes him look like a neo-Nazi, or an escapee from an asylum.

He let his imagination range free in choosing the kids' names, naming them after Greek mythological figures, which was the vogue at the time, even though they lived in a very mundane environment in a semi in Crookesmoor. Sid was called Poseidon, after the sea god, because he was conceived in a B&B overlooking the stormy moonlit North Sea just outside Whitby in 1981. And Cassie's full name is Cassiopeia, after the constellation that guided their steps as they walked along the same clifftop towards Robin Hood's Bay three years later. Snuggled up in the creaky double bed back at the B&B, he'd related the legends in his deep romantic voice, before making love. Nowadays the kids usually shorten their names – Poseidon has become Sid and Cassiopeia calls herself Cassie – but they're stuck with the family surname, and they can't escape having their full names on official documents: Poseidon Pantis, Cassiopeia Pantis.

She blames herself for having gone along with it. She should have nipped his nonsense in the bud, but she was so young and so in love with George and his deep romantic voice, his worldly charm and his animated eyebrows. Oh, how gullible she was in those days. Life has hardened her. After their break-up she has gone back to using her maiden name: Rosie Harvey.

She hasn't heard from George since their disastrous birthday dinner, and whenever she tries to ring him she always gets that same annoying message; maybe he is still in the Canaries, she thinks, as she stamps around in the silent kitchen. Suddenly the phone rings. It is Cassie, ringing her to report receiving a 'weird' voicemail message from George.

'Darling, why don't we go out for a coffee on Eccy Road tomorrow, and have a good heart to heart?' Rosie says to her.

The phone goes silent at the other end, as though Cassie is ticking off a mental list of potential drawbacks.

'Okay?'

Rosie can't blame George for Cassie's troubles, much as she would like to. When Sid and Cassie were little, George was an exemplary father – she has no complaints on that score. He used to play football with them in the park, the kids tearing after him, their cheeks bright pink, their hair wind-tousled. Those were happy days.

When Sid turned fourteen, George took him aside for the

birds and bees talk – which, of course, Sid knew already – so they went to the pub and he bought Sid a pint. Sid came back with a pink face and glazed eyes, and a knowing smirk.

'Hi, Mum,' he smirked, eyeing Rosie knowingly.

But it had worn off by the next day. He sidled up to her while she was in the kitchen with a puzzled look on his face. 'Mum, does Dad ever talk to you about unblocking the drains?'

'No. Why?'

'He said it's what you have to think about when you're having sex, to stop yourself coming too soon. It's how you control yourself.'

'He said that?'

Her mind raced down the avenue of years of their lovemaking and came to a sudden halt on a puzzling incident early in their relationship. Ah yes. They were in bed, making love in her room in college, when all of a sudden George went as rigid as a plank and shouted out at the top of his voice, 'Caustic soda!'

She was a virgin when she went to university, so she didn't quite know what to expect, but that was unexpected.

'Is it true, Mum?' Sid asked.

'I wouldn't know. It's different for women. Ask your dad. He's the expert.'

Her heart tightens now, remembering *that* George.

GEORGE: PASSWORD

After splitting up with both Rosie and then Brenda, George is finding life tougher than he imagined it would be, living on his own in Totley. It is the first time in his life that he has been on his own so much – eating on his own, going out on his own, doing his own housework. It gets a bit lonely, just him and the silent view and sometimes sane, lovable Heidi. Then late one night, as darkness gathers outside and he listens to the rain beating its insistent rhythm on his windows in the deafening silence of his flat, suddenly the phone rings.

He picks it up and barks, 'Yes?'

A young woman with a husky, sexy voice says, 'Mr Pantis? This is Miss Arilla from the Kosovan State Lottery, reminding you that you have not yet given us the information we need in order to process your prize.'

His heart pounds against his ribs. This must be the same Miss Arilla who called him ages ago, when he was still with Brenda, congratulating him on his prize. It was worth one billion lek, she said, which worked out at an astonishing seven million, three hundred thousand, three hundred and twenty-one pounds and thirty-three pence. All he has to do is give her his bank details. Seven million quid: it will open doors into a quite different world. It is more than he has earned before in his entire life as an educator, let alone as a poet.

He phoned Sid straightaway when he got that first phone call from her, of course, and Sid advised caution, saying it was most likely a scam by someone trying to get control of his bank account. Sid said he should never give anyone even a few digits of his password, especially if it was one he used for a number of different accounts, which he denied, though of course it was – how the hell can anyone remember more than one password?

Sid told him to set up a new password and even suggested one that George would find easy to remember: I am George Pantis and I am seventy-nine years old. George knows that his existing password, PASSWORD, is easy to guess, and he knows he must change it, but has never got around to it. Sid even hinted that he might not have entered the lottery at all, which was grossly unfair – he vaguely remembers having filled in an online entry form many months ago, long before the referendum was any more than a twinkle in a politician's eye, giving his name, date of birth, address, phone number and some other personal details that they said they needed in order to enter him in the lottery, and to contact him in case he won. Sid snorted and told him to forget all about the lottery prize, and so he has, preoccupied as he is with balancing the two women in his life.

So Miss Arilla's second phone call unnerves him. In a husky, breathy urgent voice she tells him she needs his account details at once to process his prize. She says the money is there, waiting for him, but she needs to deposit it in an account. He hesitates for a moment and then gives her the details of an old dormant savings account, and since that account only has about £4.50 in it, he isn't too worried.

He telephones Sid again but Sid doesn't answer the phone, so he leaves a message. Sid gets back to him a couple of hours later and tells him he has been for dinner with Rosie, who is coping well without him. He doesn't share his father's excitement about the money, and calls him a pre-digital bumpkin, which in George's opinion is rather unfair. George does not tell Sid he has given Miss Arilla the account details.

'But when I told you before to change your password, Dad, you did, didn't you?' says Sid. 'You should really change it regularly, every few months.'

'Of course I did!' he lies, and crosses his fingers to remind himself he must do it now, as soon as he puts the phone down.

But then something mysterious happens. Fifteen minutes later, when he logs on to change his password – using his old password, PASSWORD, which he set up twenty years ago because it was easy to remember – he discovers that the sum of seven million, three hundred thousand, three hundred and twenty-one pounds and thirty-three pence has suddenly appeared in his account. So Miss Arilla must have been telling the truth all along – he has won the money in a lottery. There can be no other explanation. To keep Sid quiet he changes the password to the one Sid suggested: IaGPaIa79yo. He scribbles it down on a Post-it note, and sticks it on his computer monitor so he won't forget.

Although George is not the materialistic type, and reckons you cannot afford to be materialistic if you have dedicated your life to poetry, seeing that money sitting so snugly in his account starts to have an unsettling effect on him. What if it is really his? He starts to dream.

ROSIE: Not Ivor

On a rainy Wednesday in mid-September, Cassie and Rosie meet up to compare notes and enjoy an afternoon coffee in a café on Ecclesall Road.

Rosie is a bit late and when she arrives, she shakes out her umbrella and deposits it in a stand beside the door. Cassie is already sitting at a table by the window, nursing her cappuccino, wearing a tight green dress and sheer black stockings with black patent high heels. Her long, reddish curly hair is swept over to one side and held in place by an ivory clip carved with an exotic flower. Seeing her like this, not in her usual pyjamas and slippers, which she wears at home, she is struck by what a very attractive young woman Cassie is, and she wonders yet again why she doesn't have a full-time lover in her life. Surely any normal man would snap her up, put her on a pedestal and cover her with roses? Or a woman – she isn't fussed, and surrogacy or adoption are popular offspring options nowadays.

Perhaps it is that intense, slightly crazy stare Cassie has inherited from George that puts men off. Or her voice, which takes on a plaintive upward bleat at the end of every sentence, as she goes on about the joy of compost.

'Hi, Cassie.' Mwah! Mwah! (They air-kiss.) 'Can I get you another coffee?'

Cassie shakes her head, loosening the flower-clip, which slides down over her ear. 'No, it's alright, Mum? One's plenty for me? I'm sensitive to caffeine?'

Ivor has persuaded her she is sensitive to everything, thinks Rosie, with an inner sigh. She orders a latte and a slice of chocolate cake. The cake, when it arrives, is deliciously squishy. She passes Cassie a mouthful on a teaspoon, but her daughter shakes her head.

'I'm avoiding gluten?'

Surely all this self-denial cannot be good for her, Rosie thinks.

'Your hair looks nice, Mum?' says Cassie. 'It suits you short at your age?'

'Yes, I thought it was about time. Sunil suggested it,' she lies and changes the subject. 'That's a pretty clip you're wearing in your hair, Cassie. Isn't it ivory? I thought that was supposed to be a no-no nowadays.'

'It's plastic? Fake ivory, Mum?'

'Oh, I see. It reminds me of one your granddad brought back for your grandmother from Hong Kong. It wasn't banned in those days.'

'I think I remember seeing her wearing it once? When she got all dolled up on Granddad's eightieth birthday? It was so romantic, seeing them still so in love after all those years?'

Romantic is not a word Rosie associates with her elderly and slightly frumpy parents.

'Sid said it's unlikely Dad has bought a red Ferrari. Mum, are you sure it's a Ferrari? You don't know anything about cars?'

Cassie's tone is accusatory, as though she hasn't yet decided who is to blame for the state of the world, but she is not ruling out her parents and their flaky attitude towards composting.

'I didn't say he *has* bought a Ferrari, darling. I just said he *wants* to. I am aware there is a philosophical difference.'

A red Ferrari indeed! She wouldn't put it past him! No doubt it is the Bitch's idea.

'Whatever. I don't know what's going on in this family?' Cassie complains. 'Nobody ever tells me anything? The thing is, listen, Mum, I've been trying to ring Dad, and I can't get a reply? Yesterday I just got this weird voicemail message?'

Cassie has a tendency to bleat like a lost sheep when she feels hard-done-by, which is most of the time. Rosie is struck with guilt whenever Cassie opens her mouth, regretting that she has failed as a parent to make her daughter happy and resilient. Sid is okay, she tells herself, but he's not exactly going to set the world alight, is he? And Cassie looks as though she's not even going to move on to the next stage, i.e. parenthood.

'So, Cassie, darling, how's your romantic life blossoming?' Rosie asks. 'Is Ivor still on the scene?'

'Mum? Please. Don't go on about it?'

'Sorry, darling. I just wondered.'

There is the same age difference between Cassie and Ivor as there is between Rosie and George. Like Cassie, Rosie was once besotted with an older married man, so she knows that feeling of hopeless, dragging attraction, that pit-of-the-stomach churning, that waiting for hours beside the silent phone. But George did the decent thing, he ditched his wife and married her – he didn't just keep her dangling. Decent? Of course it was not very nice for Eugenie, his wife, but Rosie was young and governed by uncontrollable emotion, and Eugenie was old (at that time forty seemed old) and shouldn't expect too much.

In those days George didn't go on about control – as far as she was concerned, control was just something you did with your core muscles in yoga.

When Rosie got together with Sunil, neither of them made a bid for control in that relationship, though he seems happy enough to have his life still controlled by his mother Mataji, and Rosie does not care. Fortunately, the kids adore Sunil, with his dry sense of humour and his eyebrows raised in a permanent air of surprise. Probably Cassie and Sid are relieved that Sunil saved her from going to pieces when George left. She has even started to varnish her nails a subtle shade of sea green that matches his hand-knitted cardigan, which he likes.

'Hmm, I wonder what Brenda makes of it,' she continues. 'Last I heard, they were supposed to be in love. Now it looks like he's dumped her too. He must be going through a delayed mid-life crisis. Loss of virility. Sorry, darling, does that sound bitchy?'

Cassie shrugs. 'Just a bit.' She wipes a finger inside the rim of her cup, then sucks it, licking off the last remnants of frothy milk. 'But probably true. That's what Ivor says. I keep thinking of the pathetic look on Dad's face, pressed up against the glass door, when you locked him out in the garden. The night of the referendum. In the rainstorm. Do you remember, Mum?'

'Of course I remember. He called me a typical self-righteous privileged *Guardian* reader,' Rosie says.

'And you called him a *Daily Mail* throwback? Which he is,' adds Cassie loyally.

'Did I? Maybe that's a bit harsh.' Rosie sucks the remnants of the chocolate cake off the spoon she offered to Cassie, curling her tongue into its curve to get every last bit. 'Anyway,' she continues in a more decisive tone, 'he seems to be lying low. What are we going to do, Cassie?'

'I've got no idea?' Cassie shakes her head. 'Anyway,' she glances down at her watch, 'I've got to go now?' She stands up.

'Meeting someone?'

'Give over, Mum.'

Cassie rises to her feet and moves towards the exit. Through the steamed-up glass door of the café Rosie can see a male figure lurking, a dumpy figure in a red raincoat. Cassie looks around at the same time. Rosie jumps up too, snatches her umbrella from the stand, and races her daughter to the door. She pulls it open, revealing a small fat man with a completely shaved head and a bushy brown beard and moustache, from which his pale face peers, pudgy and vulnerable. She stares at the face. It can only be Ivor.

'You stinking piece of shit!' She spits the words out, grabbing his arm and tugging at his raincoat. 'You pompous, pretentious little prick!'

Cassie pulls her other arm. 'Mum! Stop it!'

'You think it's okay to kill a young woman's happiness, to thwart her hopes of parenthood!'

'Mum . . . !'

'To sacrifice her dreams on the altar of some pseudo-liberated philosophy, which is really just the same old patriarchal crap!' She whacks him with her umbrella.

'Mum, stop it! Stop! It's not Ivor!'

The man in the red raincoat looks scared. Then he looks bewildered. Then he looks cross. Then he pulls himself free and faces her. He smiles pinkly through his bushy brown beard.

'I don't think it's me you want, duck,' he says.

Rosie stops, stares, and blushes.

'I'm frightfully sorry,' she says. 'A case of mistaken identity.'

'By 'eck, I'm glad I'm not Ivor.' He shakes his bald head.

A small crowd of passers-by have gathered around them. A tall woman with straggly hair is videoing it on a mobile phone.

'It's not my fault. You look just like Ivor,' blurts Rosie in a self-righteous voice. Then she adds, 'All you shaven-headed, bushy-bearded men look the same. There are so many of you around. It started off being cool and retro, but now it's become like a uniform.'

'Mum, shut up. Enough! Stop digging,' shouts Cassie. 'I've got to go now? I'm late as it is? Byeee! Don't get into any more fights, Mum?' She pecks her mother quickly on the cheek and dashes off down the rainy street.

'I'm frightfully sorry,' she says shamefacedly to the red-raincoat man.

'It's alright, duck. Nobody's perfect,' he says. 'Sometimes my own missus doesn't recognize me with this beard and moustache. I'm only growing it for prostate cancer. I'm shaving it off at the end of November.'

'But . . . !'

How can someone in this modern age harbour such delusional beliefs as to think growing a beard can have any effect whatsoever on his prostate cancer? She has it on the tip of her tongue to inform him, but Cassie's admonition rings in her ears.

When she gets home after her coffee, later that day, Brenda is waiting on the doorstep, wearing a strange mauve cloth head-dress with lumps sticking out under the cloth, presumably to conceal her hair, which must be undergoing some process. Normally, she would make some comment but, remembering Cassie's words, she keeps her mouth shut. Brenda comes over to her car and raps on the window until she winds it down.

'That dog that was running around on the loose this afternoon, Rosie, sniffing around your door, that ugly Staffie, do you know whose it is?' She watches Rosie's face for a reaction, but there is none, so she continues, 'It's a bloody public danger, don't you think? I think we should call the Council and get it put down.'

Rosie shrugs. 'I haven't seen any dog.'

She opens the door of her house and Heidi greets her in the

hall in an excitable mood; she hasn't been out all day, poor thing. Arming herself with a couple of poo-bags, Rosie clips Heidi's lead to her collar and takes her up to Ponderosa Park. Heidi trots beside her quietly and does her business neatly.

At the Ponderosa, she unclips the lead and lets Heidi run. At one point, as they are crossing the green, another dog, a sly-eyed ugly Staffie, comes bounding up to Heidi, sniffing her enthusiastically, and the two of them run off into the bushes, their tongues hanging out. Then someone on the far edge of the green whistles, and the Staffie leaps sideways and runs away, looking behind him to see whether Heidi is following. But she calls Heidi to heel, and she comes at once. Good dog.

She makes her way home, thinking about Sunil, his devotion to Mataji, and his newly discovered dog allergy, and she wonders whether she prefers Heidi. They both help to fill a George-shaped hole in her life.

After a couple of hours of bracing marking in front of the TV, she is worn out. She makes a cup of cocoa and takes it upstairs, to get herself ready for bed. First she cleans her teeth and takes off her make-up carefully, examining herself in the mirror. It is one of those magnifying mirrors that show up every wrinkle and red vein. She looks old. Somehow, being dumped by Sunil is much more of a blow to her self-confidence than being walked out on by George, whose desertion just seems like a cry of despair about the inexorable advance of old age. Poor George, she thinks, how will he manage to navigate old age on his own?

SID: Lucky escape

When Sid gets home from college, the phone is ringing. It is his father, his voice throbbing with excitement like a little kid.

'Sid, I checked my bank account last night and it was in there.'

Sid yields to his curiosity with a sigh. 'What was?'

'You'll never believe this, Sid. That money I won, a billion lek, in the Kosovan State Lottery that you said was a fraud. Well, it's not a fraud, it's real. Seven million, three hundred thousand, three hundred and twenty-one quid and thirty-three pence has suddenly appeared in my account.'

'Don't get excited, Dad, it's probably a scam of some kind.'

His father's voice splutters like he is choking on his own words.

'Why are you always so negative, Sid? You always say it's probably just a scam. Well, let me tell you again. It's sitting there IN MY ACCOUNT. It's not easy, you know, winning seven million quid. I admit I've still got to work out how to take it out and spend it. You think it's JUST A PIECE OF PISS, Sid? Wait till it happens to you! The phone NEVER STOPS RINGING,' his voice is building up to a crescendo, 'with people wanting to offer me UNBEATABLE INVEST-MENTS or UNBELIEVABLE DEALS. I don't know how they found out about it or got my number, but I seem to be in the cross hairs of every scammer from Beijing to Barnsley. I narrowly avoided getting scammed just today. I got a phone call from my bank telling me I needed to reset my password, because there'd been some suspicious activity . . .'

Uh oh. Despite himself, the hairs on the back of Sid's neck bristle. 'You need to be careful about phone calls at home, Dad. What did you do?'

'It's okay. I checked. They told me to phone the number on my bank card and confirm. I did it right away, and the lady at the bank was just helping me to reset my password when Heidi started barking at the postman. And by the time I calmed her down and got back to the bank, they'd rung off. So I don't know where that leaves me.'

'Listen, Dad, you had a lucky escape – that *was* the scam. You didn't get through to the bank. The scammers keep the line open at their end, so you think you're phoning the bank, but the person you talked to was another scammer.'

'It can't be. It was that young Russian woman who works at the main branch in town. That pretty girl. She said she was at school with Cassie.'

GEORGE: *Seduction*

From his silent flat in Totley, George starts logging in every night with his new password, just to have a look at the Money sitting there in his account before he goes to bed. It seems to be real enough. It doesn't suddenly disappear, as he thought it might. It winks at him once or twice, fluttering languorous eyelashes. Then one evening, long after his usual bedtime, when the flat is quiet and warm, and the only light is from the flickering of his computer monitor, the Money suddenly comes to life. It (she) struts sexily through his online bank statements wearing red lipstick and matching red stilettos, winking with a feline eye and beckoning him with a curvaceous finger to follow. It (she) invites him to start imagining all the things he can do. Like why shouldn't he buy a sports car? she urges. A better one than that clapped-out old Mazda he has blown £2,000 of his savings on. Why not a Ferrari? A red one, the colour of passion. He's always wanted one, hasn't he? The Money winks and gives him permission to indulge himself. He can travel the world with the hood down, and when he gets fed up of travelling, the Money says, he can settle down in a marble-floored mansion, somewhere warm, with a spectacular view of the sea, not just the wet and windy Peak District. Poetry will surely come pulsing to his pen as he strolls out on to the veranda at sunset.

'Brazil? Rangiputa? Con Dao Islands? Take your pick,' whispers the Money in a husky voice with an exotic accent. 'And you can afford to buy the fine wines now, not the eight quid

99

plonk that Rosie gets in Tesco. And whisky – aged malt. Like that nice tipple Brenda brought out on your first night together – but never again after that. What else do you desire, Mr Pantis? I know, I know. No need to be shy with me. It is every man's dream, to be surrounded with beautiful women. Secretaries, cooks, housekeepers, interior designers, personal assistants, models, life coaches, fitness coaches, all clad in body-hugging Lycra. Whatever. They'll be there to do your bidding, not vice versa, Mr Pantis,' says the Money.

As well as all those beautiful women to keep him company, the kids, Sid and Cassie, will of course visit. They are good kids, and he wants to share his good luck with them. And Rosie too, maybe. But she'll have to learn to shut up. He hasn't yet told Brenda about his good fortune. She will be full of ideas about how to spend it, but they won't always be the same as his ideas. No, he will treat her to occasional surprises, but keep her away from the source of them. 'Mr Pantis, you can be in total control of your wealth,' murmurs the Money.

George and the Money keep up this intoxicating dialogue in the hushed evenings. It is like being bewitched. It is like being in love. It is more seductive than any woman he has yet met. It has taken over his mind entirely, so there is no room for poetry or big ideas about taking back control politically – anyway, all that seems to have become disappointingly bogged down in tedious complexity, whereas money and love are much more straightforward and interesting. He stops worrying about what to do about Rosie and Brenda. He doesn't contact the kids: not a deliberate decision, not something he is proud of – it's just how it is.

When he first rented the flat, he thought that the solitude would help him focus on writing poetry. But it has just made him desperate for company – any sort of company, apart from

Mrs Timms. And that's when he has started to spend a lot of time on the internet, in different chat rooms and forums. He has managed to make friends online with quite a few like-minded people, especially ones of Greek descent. But he has also discovered that there are some serious nutters out there, crazy with greed, crazy with grievance, crazy with bloodlust, lurking with deadly intent at this new global frontier.

Shortly after this, he starts to get phone calls and emails – lots of them. People offering him amazing offers and unbeatable deals, telling him they urgently want to transfer money into his account to help them benefit from a will – and if they do, he'll get to keep half of it. And lotteries he's never heard of wanting to make a payout into his account. And investments in Carbon Credits, beachside apartments in Brazil, buy-to-rent flats in Oldham, Rolex watches, penis enlargement, Russian women desperate for sex, movie investments, and companies in Panama where he can park the money and keep it clear of the taxman so his loved ones will benefit. Loved ones. Huh! If only they knew.

There is a strange email from his Totley letting agency, say-ing they have recently set up a new bank account, and George is to redirect his deposit and monthly payments into that. But when he phones, the agent is surprised and says that all the bank details are the same as before, so he ignores it. He phones Sid, and Sid applauds him for being so sensible as to phone and check.

Then there is an email from his ex-wife Eugenie, saying she has been robbed while away at a conference in Uzbekistan and her credit cards have been stolen. If he can forward some money to her in The Golden Lily Hotel, Tashkent, she will repay him when she gets back and she will be eternally grateful.

He is touched when he gets that letter to think that she still thinks of him, even though he hasn't heard from her in a dozen years. Then he remembers she still hasn't repaid him the £200 he lent her in 1972 to put a deposit down on a new flat when they split up. So he decides to ignore it.

The one that rattles him most is a phone call from his bank, saying there's been some suspicious activity on his account. A woman with a chirpy birdlike voice says they have already set up another account in his name, and all he has to do to be safe is to transfer his money into it. She tells him to call his own bank at once – just to be certain – and sure enough, when he phones his branch, he straightaway gets put through to a young woman who introduces herself as Miss Yewling. She confirms the suspicious activity and advises him to move the money at once. She talks him through the stages of the transfer. It all seems pretty straightforward. But just at the moment that he is about to click on 'transfer', the doorbell rings – a loud, insistent ring.

He panics. 'Hang on,' he says to Miss Yewling. 'Someone at the door.'

It is his neighbour Mrs Timms, with some more of her home-made flapjacks. He grabs them from her rather rudely and hurries back to the phone. It must have taken all of three minutes, but by the time he gets back to the phone she's rung off. Feeling a bit miffed, he rings the bank again, and – here's the curious thing – they have no employee called Miss Yewling, no record of the previous phone call, nor of a new bank account that has been set up in his name. This perplexes him for a while, but he soon forgets about it. By now he realizes he is in love with the Money.

GEORGE: *Spear fishing*

One morning in early October, just as George is lacing up his hiking boots ready to take Heidi out for a ramble on Totley Moor, the doorbell rings. He doesn't get many visitors out here in Totley, so he hurries to answer it, thinking it might be one of the kids on a surprise visit. Or Brenda, missing him, as she claims she does when they speak on the phone. Or Rosie, come to make amends (less likely, but you never know). Heidi follows close behind him with her lead in her mouth. As he pulls back the latch of the door she drops the lead and lets out a low growl.

'What is it, old girl? That's not like you.' He bends to scratch her behind the ears, then straightens up and opens the door.

Two people are standing there. A short, stocky young bloke – in his thirties, George guesses – with a smiling baby face, curly blond hair and a turned-up nose like Bart Simpson, wearing a shiny, pale grey suit which matches his pale grey eyes. And behind him, but taller by an inch or two, a younger woman with bright red lipstick and bright red stilettos, and a wave of heavy, gleaming golden hair that cascades like a sunlit waterfall over her shoulders. The Money has arrived, is his first thought. Later, he can't remember what else she was wearing, apart from red stilettos, or maybe he never noticed.

He is transfixed by her eyes, which are as green as a cat's, and with a slight upward slant at the corners that suggests mystery, magic, raw and elemental sex. If the Money has a human form, this is she. He smiles at her in a friendly way and wiggles his eyebrows, and she meets his gaze but she doesn't smile back.

'Mr Pentiz?' asks the baby-faced man, his cheeks dimpling with jollity. 'I em Mister Sammy Cross from Northern Counties Bank. Fraud Department. This is my assistant, Miss Afrodita.' He gestures towards the young woman, who nods fractionally, still without smiling, and surveys the flat with her up-slanted feline eyes. He has a slight foreign accent when he speaks, which George can't place exactly, but guesses is from somewhere in Eastern Europe. They are taking over everywhere, these days, Poles, Russians, Serbs, Slovaks, Lithuanians, Latvians. Some of the locals resent it. Cross must be a made-up name, an abbreviation of something devilishly unpronounceable.

'Eff you got moment?'

'Not really,' he replies, annoyed by this unexpected intrusion into his morning, but worried that there may indeed be a problem with his bank account after his last brush with the bank. 'I'm just going out. I want to go up on to the moors before the storm gets up.'

'This will take only one minute. We eff discovered your bank card es been cloned. We need to reset security on your account.' He seems unfazed by George's rudeness, almost as though he was expecting it.

'Well, next time, please ring first to make an appointment.' Briskly he picks up the dog's lead. 'Come on, Heidi. Let's go!'

Heidi sticks her nose into Mr Cross's crotch, then into the girl's crotch, and wags her tail. The girl giggles. White, even teeth flash for a moment behind the scarlet lips, and her nose wrinkles cutely.

'May we call tomorrow morning, sir, at ten o'clock?' Sammy Cross calls after his retreating back.

'I suppose so,' he calls over his shoulder as he strides up the lane towards the moor under lowering clouds. He makes a show of nonchalance, but he is spooked.

He gets back from Blacka Hill just as the first big heavy drops of rain start to fall. At once he phones Sid, asking him whether he can come along the next day to give him some back-up, but Sid says he will be teaching end-to-end classes all morning and tells him to call back after work. Brenda has an early dyeing appointment. He doesn't even phone Rosie, or Cassie, who will only get into a flap and start giving him unwanted advice.

'Listen, Dad. Be careful,' says Sid. 'Just remember, by now you'll be a target for spear fishing.'

'Spear fishing? Isn't that something for aboriginal tribesmen, something that takes place in Australia, not in Totley?'

'You've heard of phishing with a "ph"? Where fraudsters send out random emails, trying to get you to give away your password, or click on a link which will upload a piece of malware on to your computer? Well, spear phishing is when they target a particular individual, instead of sending out emails at random, like they did the first time they hooked you. By now the chatter will be all over the Dark Web that you have all this money in the bank that isn't yours. They'll be desperate to get their hands on it.'

He doesn't like the sound of that. He grouches, 'What makes you say it's not mine? Of course it's mine. It's in my account, isn't it? Anyway, what should I do?'

'Just bullshit them, Dad.' Sid sounds impatient, as if he is in a hurry to end the call. 'Say whatever comes into your head.

The main thing is not, under any circumstances, to give away your new password.'

He recites his new password in his head: 'I am George Pantis and I am seventy-nine years old.' IAGPAIA79YO. It is still there. He used it last night to ogle the Money.

GEORGE: *Jesus loves a sinner*

Next day, at a quarter to ten, he is all spruced up and fired up, looking, he hopes, distinguished and debonair with his somewhat sparse hair neatly brushed to one side, which he has allowed to grow back after Brenda's fierce razor-led ministrations. He is wearing a candy-striped shirt and white chinos with striped socks and tan loafers. He wants to make an impression of casual cool. He puts Heidi in the kitchen, closes the door and sits down to wait. His heart is beating a bit harder than normal – which he naturally puts down to the stress. Then the doorbell rings. Ping! He jumps up, spilling his coffee; a splash goes on the white chinos. Oh hell! He dabs at the stain with a tea towel, then he opens the door.

There are two people standing there: a young man in a neat grey suit and a tie, who looks for all the world like a bank employee, and a young woman, very pretty, with clusters of light brown, glossy curls around her rosy cheeks, blue eyes that sparkle earnestly behind dark thick lashes, wearing a cream floral dress and a pale blue linen jacket.

'Come in, come in!' he says, ushering them into the kitchen. 'Have you found evidence of illegal activity?'

The young man clasps his hands together, rolls his eyes up to the ceiling, and says, 'We are all mired in sin, but we can be saved through the mercy of the Lord.'

'Yes, I know,' George replies, 'but what about my account? Has it been compromised?'

The young woman reaches into her bag, and takes out a

black-bound book and a tambourine. 'We are all compromised. We all have black marks on our heavenly account, but in here you will find the road map to get back on the straight and narrow.'

The man cries, 'You know sin? Let the Lord into your life!'

'He's welcome,' says George. 'But what about –'

'Repent! Repent!' the young woman shrills. She clasps George's left hand. 'Sing His praises, oh ye men of sin!' she says.

The young man takes George's right hand and they all hold hands around the little kitchen table. The young man counts, 'One, two, three . . .' and they both burst into song, the woman in a high sweet soprano, the man in a mellow baritone. With her other hand freed from the young man's grip, she plies the tambourine.

> Jesus loves a sinner! Jesus loves a sinner!
> Jesus loves a sinner every day!
> Whatever you've done wrong,
> Reach up to him in song,
> Jesus loves a sinner all the way!

As they sing, George squeezes the young woman's hand. She really is incredibly pretty and she has a heavenly voice. She throws him an arch, sideways glance and carries on singing. He joins in the chorus with a trembling voice. In spite of himself, he feels his eyes brimming with tears. Yes, he has been a sinner, but that is all in the past now. From now on, he will do the right thing. With the help of this young woman and her tambourine.

'Are *you* a sinner?' she asks at the end of the song.

'Yes, yes. I have sinned in thought and deed!'

Their eyes lock together. He thinks he detects a small quiver in her left eye, which may or may not have been a wink. The grey-suited man is gazing raptly at the ceiling.

'It's never too late to throw yourself at the feet of the Lord, and beg for forgiveness,' she murmurs.

'Really? Do you want me to show you how I have sinned?'

There is the same tremor in her left eye, except this time it looks more like a nervous tic. 'That won't be necessary.'

Suddenly the doorbell rings. Reluctantly, George rises to open it, and there is the curly-haired fraud investigator, wearing the same grey suit and white shirt as yesterday. But he is unaccompanied.

'You're . . . a sinner!' cries George.

'Yes, I am sorry I am little bit late, I am sorry if it inconveniences you, Mr Pantis,' he says. He pronounces it 'Pentiz' and he doesn't snigger. 'This will not take long.'

The smart young man stands up, unglues his eyes from the ceiling and grasps the pretty young woman firmly by the hand, pulling her towards the door. 'I can see you're busy. We'll come back another time.'

'But one is never too busy for the Lord's work,' adds the pretty woman, with a smile.

They let themselves out silently.

George waves at their departing backs, and turns to face the fraud investigator. 'You're on your own,' he says. 'Where's your assistant?'

'Miss Afrodita has meeting,' says the man.

He invites him into the sitting room and indicates an armchair opposite the coffee table, which he bought online only last week. It is a room he doesn't use very much, he prefers the congenial disorder of the kitchen. The furniture in here is all new and smells of packaging and fire-retardant, to which the sickly whiff of synthetic Eastern European aftershave is soon added, creating a cacophony of chemical odours.

The man sits down in the low armchair with his knees apart, leaning forward on his elbows, looking up at George with a cheerful smile.

'What's this all about?' George asks.

The fraud investigator, Sammy, takes out a business card from the pocket of his suit jacket and places it on the table, then he takes a bulky machine which looks a bit like the card machines that waiters use in restaurants and places it on the coffee table beside his card. George stares at it with an uneasy feeling.

'The bank needs to reset account, Mr Pentiz. There has been suspicious activity. You have to choose new password. First of all, please could you just re-enter existing password.' He pushes the machine across the table to George.

'I think I'd rather go into the bank and do this.'

'There is absolutely no need, Mr Pentiz.' Mr Cross laughs, a high-pitched neigh like an excited pony, and waves his hands dismissively. 'This will save journey into town centre, Mr Pentiz. That's why I heff come out to your home. It is much more convenient. It is a service we offer to our more . . . er . . . our more older clients.'

'Oh, really?'

Older? Him? They really know how to make a man feel great. Then again, if he drags this encounter out, maybe Sensible Sid will come to his rescue. 'Oh, I see. That's very kind of you,' he says through gritted teeth. 'Can I get you a coffee, Mr Cross? Or would you prefer tea? Milk? Sugar?'

'Thank you. Coffee. Black. Three spoon of sugars.'

George disappears into the kitchen, releasing Heidi to keep an eye on his visitor. While the kettle is boiling, he phones Sid.

'Listen, Dad. I can't talk now. The GCSE class starts in a minute. I'll call you tomorrow.'

George describes the man's number machine to Sid.

'Don't do it, Dad. Or just type in some random numbers,' says Sid.

George comes back into the sitting room carrying two weak, over-sweetened cups of instant coffee, which he sets down on the table to let them cool. Then he picks up the machine and hits a series of keys: 1, 2, 3, 4, 5, 6. Then 'enter'.

'Take your time, Mr Pentiz. Repeat one more time for me.'

Again he punches in the numbers.

'Now new password. Six digits. Also two time repeat. Mm. Thanks for tea. Or is it coffee? Very nice.' Sammy Cross dips his lips into the cup. George slowly punches in 6, 5, 4, 3, 2, 1 once and then twice. He notices that Cross has taken out his phone and seems to be pointing it downwards towards his fingers moving on the keypad. Is he videoing? Shouldn't the machine be connected directly with the bank, by telephone or something?

'Nice. Thank you very much for your cooperation, Mr Pentiz. I go now before rain is starting.' His cheeks dimple. He puts away his phone, finishes his coffee with a slurp, and then stands up.

George shows him to the door and waits for him to disappear from sight, then he goes and sits down at his computer again.

This poem he is trying to write – this saga about the reawakening of a nation from a centuries-long subservience – it isn't coming as easily as he hoped. There is something he needs to say – something that is missing in modern life, that he half recalls from the pre-war past. Something decent and honourable, or maybe something raw and elemental. 'Jesus loves a sinner.' Maybe that is it. Through the window, he watches a rain cloud sweep low over the moor, its edges black and ragged, like an invading army. Like . . . at that moment it releases its rain, and the landscape becomes blurred and grey. Words flow from his fingertips, but he has forgotten how to tell whether they are raw and elemental or merely banal. Or perhaps he has never known the difference.

For lunch he makes himself a deliciously satisfying bachelor meal of beans on toast, and reflects on the encounters of the morning. Life throws curve balls at us, and we have to try and catch them as best we can, he thinks.

An hour or so later, when he glances out through the window to check the weather, he sees a tall female figure crossing the cobbled forecourt. He blinks and looks again. He polishes his glasses. Is she the Money or is she the young woman who is going to save his soul with her tambourine? As she draws closer he sees she is dressed not in a pale blue jacket but in a white raincoat, and her hair is not brown and curly, it is a blonde wave whipped into foamy disorder by the moisture-laden wind. She is picking her way carefully up the steep cobbled path on impossibly high scarlet stiletto heels that keep slithering down in between the treacherous wet cobbles. She raises her head and smiles when she sees him at the window.

He rushes down the corridor to open the door. 'Hello, Miss Afrodita!' he utters breathlessly. His heart is beating. 'What brings you here?'

'Good day, Mr Pantis.' (She too pronounces it Pentiz.) 'I am sorry I was not able to attend earlier with Mr Cross. I think we need to get to know each other more better, do you not agree?' she says slowly. Her voice sounds vaguely familiar. Her English is pretty good, apart from the absence of articles, and the stresses, which sometimes fall on the wrong syllables.

'Sure,' he says, trying not to sound puppyishly over-eager. 'Of course we do.'

There is something charmingly feminine about the way she looks and talks, like the pretty tambourine wielder, that reminds him of the sweet post-war girls of his adolescence, a far cry from the strident booted feminists of today. Eugenie, his first wife, thin, blonde and hazel-eyed, carefully constructed her femininity as something enigmatic and preciously fragile, to be protected and worshipped and then defiled. The very first time he met her, he was hooked. It was just the way boys were brought up to think about girls in those days. Eugenie's fragility, he soon found, was brittle, like ice over a cold, shallow stream. It took all Rosie's passion to warm him up after that.

'Please can we go inside?' Miss Afrodita says.

She follows him into the kitchen and seats herself at his kitchen table, where the unwashed cups from his coffee with Cross and his early morning cup of tea and breakfast cereal bowl are still cluttering the counter. He sweeps them out of sight into the sink. She crosses her legs, letting a scarlet shoe dangle on one of her toes. She lets her green up-slanted eyes wander around the room, before coming to rest on George's face. Her perfume, flowery and spicy, fills the small space. Heidi walks around her, sniffing and wagging her tail approvingly.

'What is dog's name?' she asks. Her voice is sweet and birdlike, with a slight hesitation, as if she is trying to work out as she speaks where to place the accents.

'Heidi,' he says. The tail-wagging steps up a pace.

'That is cute name. What is your star sign, Mr Pentiz?'

'Libra.'

'So you must be very balancing person.'

He laughs and makes a dismissive gesture with his hands. 'I like to think so. And I'm only seventy-nine.'

'Seventy-nine? Uhuh! What is exact day of your birthday?'

'The twelfth of October. Columbus Day, as the Yanks call it.'

She smiles back politely. 'What is mean "Yanks"?'

'You know, Americans.' There is so much he will have to teach her. And she seems eager to learn, a win-win combination.

'October is very pleasant month.'

His birthday will be soon, he suddenly realizes. Must give Sid a ring and take him out for a drink. Rosie, as usual, will probably give him a pair of socks. Brenda? She too has wormed his star sign and birthday out of him and is probably planning a surprise. So long as she isn't planning another spa break; he almost died of boredom last time.

He hasn't yet had a chance to tell Brenda about his good fortune. He wonders whether she knows, because he fears she will be quick to come forward with ways of spending his money on spa breaks and other such nonsense, and will sulk if he does not indulge her. Rosie already knows, of course, but has suggested nothing so far apart from investment advice. But he realizes, because Sid has warned him, that he must be careful not to spread the good news around too widely, just in case it falls into the wrong hands; smiley, smarmy Sammy Cross, for example, he does not trust one bit. But there is something childlike and guileless about Afrodita's behaviour, her naive questions, that makes him want to confide in her.

Her wide-set feline eyes follow him round the room, as he fills up the kettle and puts tea bags into two cups. Then they fall on a pair of framed photos of Sid and Cassie in their graduation outfits on the wall.

'Is this your children?'

'Mhm,' he nods, pouring boiling water on to the tea bags.

'What is their name?'

'Poseidon and Cassiopeia. But we just call them Sid and Cassie.'

'Pretty name.' Nothing in her demeanour suggests that she finds the names unusual. 'When is their birthday?' This fixation with birthdays is getting strange, even for someone who believes in astrology. Then again, it is more appealing than being fixated with sin.

'I can't remember exactly,' he says. 'Rosie, that's my dear wife, takes care of all that.'

'Rosie? Cute name. When she get her birthday?'

'It's in August. Milk in your tea?'

'No. No. I like black. But with sugar if you have. August when?'

'The twenty-second. Same as Dorothy Parker.'

She smiles back politely.

'Dorothy Parker – who is she?'

'The supreme American wit and aphorist. You never heard of her?'

'The Supremes? Yes, I have heard of them. They were long-ago pop group. Your wife was singer with Supremes?'

'Not exactly.' She really doesn't seem to know very much at all. He likes that.

'What about mother? When she was born? Were you close with her?'

'I was. She died two years ago.'

'What mother's name?'

'Sarah.'

'Sarah . . . ? Also very beautiful. What her maiden name?'

'Benton. Why do you want to know?'

All these questions are beginning to unnerve him slightly, and they are particularly strange coming from her who hardly knows him. Will she soon ask him if he is a sinner? If he remembers anything from his bachelor days, it is that women like to talk about themselves.

'Look, what about you, Miss Afrodita? I thought we were supposed to be getting to know each other. You haven't told me anything about yourself.'

'Oh, I'm sorry!' She giggles again behind her hand. 'I very big idiot. I forget I also have to make such natural conversationing. What you want ask?'

Of course what he really wants to ask, what he can hardly restrain himself from asking, is whether she is single, and, er, up for a more intimate relationship. But that would be premature. Instead he asks, 'So where are you from?'

'I am from Sheffield.'

'No. Before that. I mean where are you ultimately from? I'm sorry if you find that offensive.'

Rosie used to say that it is wrong to interrogate people about their ethnicity, because they might get offended. That is high on her list of loopy ideas.

'Why I am offensive?'

'No, no, I was just wondering. Some people might find the question offensive.'

'You find my questions offensive?'

'Not at all, Miss Afrodita. Your questions are charming.' Charming but odd, he wants to add.

'I am glad you think so. And you, Mr Pentiz, where you are from?' she quizzed.

'Sheffield. Born and bred. Best city in England. Two great

football teams. The Blades are the tops.' He puts his hand on his heart and bursts into song.

> Like a greasy chip butty,
> Like Sheffield United,
> Come fill me again.

A look of puzzlement crosses her beautiful face. That is okay, he reckons – not all women warm instantly to football. One day he'll tell her about the first match he went to with his dad. It was an away match at Nottingham, and they returned to Sheffield triumphant, singing on the packed train. Sometimes, for a change, they went over to Hillsborough to watch the Owls. They had different qualities. Like Rosie and Brenda. You can't expect to get everything from just one team, or just one woman, can you?

Brenda, for all her faults, has a genuine passion for the Blades. They used to watch them together on TV, and he'd be jumping up and punching the air every time they scored. Rosie would have called it infantile behaviour.

'They're called the Blades,' he continues.

Miss Afrodita's face registers no emotion.

'Get it? After our local industry, Sheffield knives, swords and scissors.'

Miss Afrodita looks nonplussed. 'They play with scissors?'

'Ha ha. Sometimes they do try to cut the other guys up.' Seeing the puzzled frown on her brow, he adds, 'Just joking.'

'It does good for person's health, enjoy humour, Mr Pentiz.' She nods her head humourlessly. 'Which street you growed up on?' she adds, somewhat mechanically, as if working her way through a list.

'Twentywell Lane. Not far from here.'

'Twenty well? Cute name. And your first school?'

'Bradway Primary. Near where I lived. Look, what is all this about?'

'Friendly conversation, Mr Pentiz. Do you not find me friendly?' She speaks in the same cool, matter-of-fact voice as the Money. Emotionless, yet oddly seductive. 'I think we finish now.'

She takes a long sip of black sugary tea, leaving a lipstick stain like a fallen petal on the rim of the cup, then she stands up.

'Thank you so much, Mr Pentiz. I must quickly go back to office now. Please forgive me. Forgive me even for things you do not yet know about.' Her thick lashes sweep down over her green eyes for a moment and rest there quivering.

'Yes,' he says, mesmerized, but uneasy. What does she mean, things you do not yet know about?

She whips out her phone to call for a taxi. Her fingers are busy on the keys for a long time, he notices – in fact, she is still typing into her phone by the time the Uber arrives.

George strolls down to the Cricketers Inn to think things over with a pie and a quiet pint. It isn't until he tries to phone Sid later that evening that he discovers his phone is missing.

ROSIE: *Feminist sisterhood*

After she gets home from her weekly yoga class, Rosie prepares her supper of only slightly congealed and perfunctorily reheated penne arrabbiata that she discovers in the back of the fridge, washed down by an inch of week-old red wine she finds in the bottom of a bottle in the recycling bin.

It worries her that George has not been answering his phone, and never rings back in response to her messages. So she decides to drop by George's new flat in Totley, thinking maybe he is there all the time, just lying low – avoidance being, she has observed, a favourite tactic of his.

She has only been to his flat a couple of times before, once to have a mosey around and to pick up a pair of curtains that needed hemming, and once to drop the curtains off again when they were done. Although she reckons that curtain-hemming is now probably, strictly speaking, the Bitch's job, she did it for strategic reasons, in order to keep on good terms with him. And she has kept a spare key in the glove compartment of her car. George doesn't know this.

She guesses he has started renting this flat because things aren't working out too well with the Bitch, but he doesn't yet feel ready to come home. He must have found it a bit too close for comfort, she thinks, staying in Brenda's house, the other half of the large stone-built semi, next door to her in Crookesmoor, with the side-by-side front doors, where she could see their comings and goings on the shared footpath. Sometimes he bumped into her or Sunil on the doorstep.

George's new flat is on the ground floor of a converted mill in Totley. Although there are forty flats in the development, it is as quiet as a grave. A forlorn red sports car with a sadly flat rear tyre is resting in a corner of the parking area. She goes over to have a closer look at it. It is not a Ferrari, or even a Porsche. Surely it is his old Mazda, painted red! Badly painted, too – the white gleams through the red on one of the doors. Ha ha!

There is no one at home in his flat, when she rings the bell. Where is he? He must be back from the Canaries by now. She can see the curtains she hemmed hanging in a downstairs window. She fits the key in the lock and steps inside hurriedly. She doesn't want him to come back and find her snooping around. But the flat is eerily quiet, with the great mass of Blacka Hill lowering outside the side window. There is a musty smell of damp dishcloth and sweaty shoes, and the flat is strangely disordered, as if he has gone out somewhere in a hurry. Is he still living here, or has he gone away? It seems as though Brenda hasn't been here recently either – the flat lacks a woman's presence. Maybe they've had a row. On the monitor of his computer is a yellow Post-it note with some letters and numbers: IaGPaIa79yo. Some sort of code – but what does it mean? She takes the Post-it note, folds it and puts it in the pocket of her jeans.

She feels a slow twist of unease in the pit of her stomach, wondering where he is, followed by smouldering rage at the sheer irresponsibility of his behaviour. Why is he putting his family through this worry? At least when he was staying with Brenda, there was some continuity and they could keep in touch. This is nothing but a display of sheer infantile narcissism. At his age, he should have got over that by now! She lets herself out of the flat and gets back in her car, slamming the door, putting her foot down hard on the accelerator as she drives home.

When she pulls up in front of her house, she notices that in the next-door window, a new UKIP poster has gone up, showing Nigel Farage holding out his hands as if in benediction, saying THANK YOU to all who voted for Brexit. And behind the poster, she catches a glimpse of Brenda pulling her curtains across her window to keep out the dark. For a moment, a very fleeting moment, she feels sorry for her: an impulse of feminist sisterhood. Maybe if they could talk they would have plenty to say to each other. They both care about George, don't they? Not that she will trust her hair to Brenda ever again. Bitch.

BRENDA: *Papaya and pomegranate*

Brenda draws the curtains across her small front bedroom window, providing a brightly patterned backdrop to the new UKIP poster she has just put up. Through the window she observes Rosie, the Mad Cow next door, who has just come home from somewhere. It is late. Where has she been? Though she and Rosie don't talk much, she still feels bad about her part in the break-up of the Mad Cow's marriage. She even gave her a free sample of hair conditioner as a way of making peace, after Rosie went berserk and smashed the salon up. It was a nice gesture, and Rosie did not really deserve it, but it didn't cost her anything, and when you live next door to someone, you have to get along with them, don't you? Rosie's type of hair needs a rich conditioner to bring out the bounce in the curls. Last week, she also gave a free sample of Stylia papaya and pomegranate shampoo to Mrs Ali, on the other side, who has rather dry hair that she oils with some stinky oil, and who thanked her profusely.

Women are all different: men are all the same underneath, she thinks, despite their superficial differences. Take George, for example, who at first seemed so spiritual with all his poetry and lovely old-fashioned manners. Underneath it all he is just a two-faced conman, like Sniffer, using her for sex but with no intention of ever leaving his wife, especially now that she has gone and got herself pregnant. As well as being two-faced, he is a bit of an idiot, like the others, always imagining that women are after him. He must think she won't find out about Rosie's pregnancy, or perhaps he doesn't care.

Her mind drifts back to a strange phone conversation she overheard one day, a week or so before George moved out to Totley – he was telling Sid he'd won a load of money on some foreign lottery. Maybe she should have interrupted and told him it sounded like a scam, but she didn't want him to know she was listening. Anyway, he told her soon after that he was going to move into a place of his own, so she didn't follow it up.

He got this gloomy flat right out in Totley, no doubt in order to carry on with other women unobserved, so as a result they now see each other less often. She is sad, of course, because she has grown to love him a little, as you do. But they are very different as people. She knows it can't last, especially now Rosie is pregnant. It piques her that he has even stopped ringing her, but assumes he has met someone else by now. Looking at her neighbour fumbling with her key, she wonders how her pregnancy is progressing.

Recently, she met Sid's Jacquie in the supermarket, and it turns out that she is pregnant too. How strange.

GEORGE: *Red stilettos*

Today is the 11th of October. The last day of George's seventy-ninth year. The day dawns bright and sunny, with autumn colours already touching the leaves of the trees and wisps of mist curling up from the valley. He drinks his tea and eats his Shredded Wheat just as though it is any other day. As he is bending down to clip on Heidi's lead for her walk, he finds his phone. There it is, lying on the doormat in the hall, peeping out from under a pile of letters. How did it get there? Strange, it must have fallen out of his pocket last night when he let Heidi out for a run-around in the yard. He picks up the letters. Three are birthday cards: one from Rosie, with a picture of a mountain; one from Brenda, with a picture of champagne fizzing out of a bottle; and one from Sid, with a picture of a sports car and an 80 number plate. Eighty tomorrow. Cassie, bless her, hasn't remembered. The rest is junk mail with no specified recipient: offers for high-yield investments, low-interest mortgages, car loans, health and accident insurances, domestic appliance insurance, the Liberal Democrats, fitted blinds, local women desperate for sex, country hotels. He sighs and bins them all. Why do they keep targeting him? Sometimes it seems as though they are tuned in to his dreams.

The only letter, apart from the cards, actually addressed to him is a water utility bill. £388! For water! Everywhere you look there is water – it is all around him – in the fine grey drizzle that sometimes descends in the air like a greying net curtain, one disadvantage of living so high up, it drifts in on the wind when he opens the door, obscuring the distant moors. Streams trickle down hillsides and bunch into rivulets that race on down into Totley Brook and meander along the bottom of the valley, colliding splashily with the busy River Sheaf at Abbeydale. Okay, so now he is a millionaire, but they didn't know that when they sent out the bill, did they? Why is water now suddenly so bloody expensive? He picks up the phone and dials Sid for a grumble.

'The water companies spent big on infrastructure when they were privatized, Dad,' says Sid patiently, 'and now they want a good return on their investment. Yorkshire Water is actually based in the Cayman Islands. It's called globalization. Anyhow, happy birthday for tomorrow, Dad. How did you get on with the fraud investigator yesterday?'

'Oh, him? Nothing much happened. Why don't they send someone round to investigate these rip-off water companies, that's what I want to know? Surely there's enough water around here without bringing it all the way from the Cayman Islands? No wonder it's so bloody expensive. What's wrong with good English water? I suppose it's all part of an EU plot.'

'Don't be daft, Dad. You know what I mean.'

Is he becoming daft, now he is about to turn eighty? Well, it isn't over yet. He reckons he has at least twenty more years to live the dream – possibly more, a fit bloke like him, if he gets that prostate seen to. He isn't ready to give up just yet.

Heidi, who has returned to her basket while she waits for him to lace up his boots and put on his jacket, now picks up her lead again and stands quietly behind him with the lead in her mouth.

'Good girl. Come on.' He checks that the phone has stayed in his pocket when he clipped on her lead and has not fallen out again.

As he looks out over the rooftops of Totley, emerging from the mist, he catches sight of an unfamiliar vehicle, a large shiny white 4x4, tilting and swaying as it makes its way uphill over the bumpy cobbles towards the mill apartments. It doesn't turn down towards the residents' car park but pulls up by the turning circle in front of the building, underneath the spreading plane tree, and disgorges its driver. She is a bulky blonde woman wearing a belted grey raincoat. She looks vaguely familiar, as though he's seen her before somewhere, but where? She sees him standing on the doorstep watching her as she approaches, and reaches out a thick meaty hand to him. The door-lock lights flash orange.

'Mr Panties?'

There is a subtle difference in pronunciation between Pantis and Panties, which he has become very attuned to over the years. The woman can't help a slight snigger as she says the underwear version of the name. They never can. He nods but keeps his hand on Heidi's collar. She is behaving strangely; whimpering and straining at the lead.

'I am Mrs Smith from Northern Counties Bank, Mr Panties. Have you got moment? There's been some suspicious activity on your account. We need to run security checks,' she says.

Something weird is going on. He says nothing.

Over the woman's shoulder he observes a flurry of activity. A taxi has raced into the courtyard at speed, followed quite closely by a sleek Toyota Prius with the Uber logo on its side. Out of the taxi jumps Sammy Cross. Out of the Uber jumps Miss Afrodita. The taxi driver also jumps out and starts remonstrating with the Uber driver in a thick foreign accent. Mr Uber winds down his window and shouts back in a thick London accent, 'None of your bloody business!' and gives him the finger.

'It will not take moment.' Mrs Smith hands George a business card, her pointy whitened teeth bared in an artificial smile that seems familiar. Hasn't he seen her before somewhere?

Sammy Cross pays off the cab driver and steps briskly across the yard, with his hand outstretched in greeting, towards where Mrs Smith and George are standing. His hair seems blonder and fluffier, as though it has picked up moisture from the air, shining like a halo in the watery sunlight. Miss Afrodita follows as fast as her red high heels will allow.

'Sammy, please, listen to me!' she is pleading. 'Please, give me time! One more day!'

'Go back into office!' Sammy Cross shouts at her. 'You think you can make idiot out of me? I will teach you lessons you will not forget!' His boyish round-cheeked face is contorted with fury. There is a disconcerting contrast between his playful appearance and the pent-up rage in his voice and face. Sammy Cross hurries forward towards him, ignoring Afrodita. She tries to run after him, but a stiletto heel gets stuck between two cobblestones, and she falls on her knees with a wail of pain. Gallantly, George leaps forward to pull her up, letting go of Heidi's lead.

Heidi at once dashes across to Mrs Smith's big white car, and jumps up to the rear passenger window, where, to George's amazement, another canine face appears, an ugly sly-eyed short-haired face, its big pink tongue hanging out between vicious teeth, panting and foaming like a faulty geyser. Heidi's claws are scrabbling on the shiny white paintwork, and her tongue is hanging out too. Mrs Smith runs back to her car and yanks angrily at Heidi's collar, trying to pull her away.

'Can't you control your dog, Mr Panties?' she yells. 'She may be on heat, and she is wrecking my paintwork!' The white paintwork is scratched right down to the metal in places.

He has never before seen Heidi behave in such an animal way. Miss Afrodita is weeping in his arms, and new ladders in her tights are running up and down her legs; a livid red graze has spread across her knees and red blood is bubbling through her black tights. She steps out of her shoes, leaving them standing side by side on the cobbles.

He turns towards Sammy Cross. 'I say, Mr Cross, Sammy, wasn't that a bit ungentlemanly?'

Sammy Cross shrieks with laughter, his cheeks dimpling. 'There is no gentleman here. Only you, silly old man. This bitch sold your bank number to me. Then she tell me number is change. What you expect?'

George conceals his bafflement. 'I expect a man to behave like a gentleman. Shouldn't you apologize?'

Mr Cross shakes his head and a little smile twists one corner of his lip. This man seems like an absolute jerk, thinks George. If he was younger, he would thump him for sure, to teach him a lesson. The man shrugs and laughs. Over the man's shoulder George watches Mrs Smith cross the cobbles towards them, hanging on to Heidi's collar. Then she lets go of Heidi and squares up threateningly to Sammy Cross, her big arms bulging against the grey fabric of her raincoat.

'You parasite. You say you bought his bank number? Leave him alone! It is not your money in that account! It belong to me!' Mrs Smith steps forward and sticks her chin out with a scowl.

'And who you are, nosy parking lady?' asks Sammy Cross. Behind the boyish clowning is a suggestion of menace.

'I am from Northern Counties Bank, Fraud Department.' Mrs Smith whips another card out of her pocket and holds it out.

Sammy Cross whips a similar card out of his wallet. 'I have seen you before.'

'Snap!' George says, wondering who these two so-called fraud investigators are, who both claim to be from his bank. Which is the real one?

Heidi is still whimpering. Miss Afrodita is addressing the other two in a muffled wail, her hand across her mouth so he only catches a part of what she says.

'I am very sorry I done incorrect thing. I am sorry, Mrs Petra. I am sorry, Sammy. It gone wrong for me this time. Please give me one more day. I can still get . . . his *nommer*.'

His nommer? Does she mean his account number or his new password? She is standing barefoot on the rough cobbles, trembling like a young aspen. Despite his misgivings, George steps forward and puts his arm around her to steady her. The other two exchange sly looks and bring their heads together.

Sammy Cross laughs his shrill laugh. 'If she can get it, we can share half and half; maybe half better than nothing,' he hears him whisper to Mrs Smith, or something like that.

Mrs Smith hisses at Sammy Cross, 'It is more complicated than that, you thief. Money already in that account is mine from massage business. Old fool has got it by mistake, but it is not his money. That girl sold me account details, but he changed password.'

Did he hear that right? What exactly is going on with this account?

'Now I cannot get it out,' she continues to hiss. 'But we can do business together. If you can get password from her.'

'I will get it. Even if I heff to hurt her a little. Or hurt him a little. Money in that account is mine from business affairs. Afrodita has also sold it to me weeks before she sold it you,' Sammy Cross hisses back, then he frowns. 'You are lady with bad dog who has been biting me?'

'Max is bad dog, when it is necessary. But today he is gentle

129

like lamb. He like sniffing. Sometimes he like biting.' She laughs cheerfully. 'We can talk, Sammy. Then maybe we can do business. Do you want lift back to Sheffield?'

George is still smarting from her description of him as an old fool. He may not have caught exactly what they said next but he saw them whispering with their heads together. As Mrs Smith opens the car door for Sammy Cross, to give him a lift, the ugly dog leaps out and races around the forecourt until he comes to rest by the scarlet stilettos, one of which is still firmly wedged between the cobbles. He sniffs and tugs. Heidi runs after him, barking and jumping, trying to grab the shoe. It is a great game. The taxi drivers seem to be having a tussle too. George backs towards his door, pulling Miss Afrodita with him, away from the angry drivers and the excited dogs, but the dogs ignore them and carry on with their game.

The Uber and its driver have disappeared from the entrance to the yard, and the cab driver is lying groaning on the ground beside his cab, its engine still running. As George watches, he staggers to his feet, saying, 'Bloody immigrants! They think they can come up from London and steal our jobs! We have to do NVQ Level Two to get an Uber licence in Sheffield!'

'Max! Come here, boy!' shouts Mrs Smith.

The dog pays no attention to her, and leaps up on to Heidi with his wet pink erection. Heidi seems pleased.

Miss Afrodita covers her mouth with her hand and giggles. 'It is very embarrassing,' she says, 'may we go inside?'

He takes her by the hand, leads her into the flat, and closes the door.

GEORGE: *Birthday, Columbus sets sail*

It is George's birthday. He is eighty today and he has broken free from his past life. He has made it past the finishing line! He has the loveliest birthday gift a man could desire: he's sitting beside Afrodita in the first-class compartment of the East Midlands train as they thunder southwards towards London St Pancras. Without her scarlet high heels, in a pair of clumpy flat black shoes that he bought for her in a local shop when he dropped Heidi off with Cassie, Afrodita does not look quite so spectacular: her hair is less sleek but still glossy, her mascara smudged, making her inscrutable feline eyes seem wider, more kitten-like, more vulnerable above her high-curved cheekbones. For the first time, he notices a faint shadow of dark hair on her upper lip. But he finds her lovelier than ever, as she is now: shy, confused, defenceless (apart from him, of course, he has appointed himself her defender), snuggled into his oversized green fleece that she has borrowed from him and squeezed on over her tight white suit.

She is staring into her cup of tea. At last she says in a low whisper, 'I did not want to deceive you, George. You are a good man, but . . .'

But what? he wonders. He still can't quite believe in this unexpected relationship with this beautiful woman. It seems like a fantasy – on a different plane to his relationships with Rosie and Brenda. More like the long-gone passions of his youth, when he was intoxicated with the physicality of women, and did not have to deal with their messy contrariness. He wants this relationship intensely, not just a quick physical consummation but something tender and enduring. His whole body pulses with excitement, and his left side, which is casually in contact with her right side through the green fleece, keeps throwing out stabs of fire. They have not yet made love, but they surely will. It is only a matter of time. In the meantime, as he understands it, he is escorting her back to her mother's home in a remote village in Albania and away from the villainous clutches of Sammy Cross and Mrs Smith, who mean her some unspecified harm because of some financial mix-up – so much he has established, and it is enough for now. He dares not ask what will happen when they get there until he is sure she is willing, because he does not want to frighten her away by revealing the urgency of his desire for her.

'. . . but you are too much innocent. I know already my mother will like you. We are going back to home of my mother in Kashtanje, Albania. Nobody will catch us. We will be safe there.'

They sit side by side in silence, listening but pretending not to listen to the young woman who shares their table, a large-bosomed redhead with mauve fingernails who is talking loudly into her mobile phone – to George it sounds like boyfriend trouble – while the landscape flashes past, the crooked spire of Chesterfield, the wide sweep of the River Derwent at Belper, the flat featureless fields and bored-looking cattle of the East Midlands. Sometimes a flurry of rain obscures the view.

'Dear George, your country is very beautiful,' says Afrodita, breaking the silence at last. 'My country is beautiful also, but too poor. Before was poor and peaceful, but now we are always in war, I don't know why; radio is telling us there are so many people who wish to harm us. When you see my home where I grown up, you will forgive me.'

'Nothing to forgive,' he murmurs, inwardly a trifle alarmed. 'I love you as you are, Afrodita. You can tell me everything now.'

She sighs and takes him at his word, seeming to shrink further inside the old green fleece, so that now only her fingers are poking out of the sleeves. Then she reaches across and lets her fingers rest lightly on his thigh.

'So listen to my story, my dear George, and forgive me if you can.'

'I'm listening.' He wiggles his eyebrows.

'I am born in Zur, in south of Kosovo. It is small place, but it is very calm and beautiful, hills all around. My parents been farmers. They work hard in field every day, for hours they are bending backs under hot sun. Still they remain poor. For me it was happy time because I did not know there could be another life. We always get enough to eat, sheep's meat, vegetables, fruits, chickens and eggs. Plenty eggs.' A small smile flits across her lips.

'I have two brothers and one sister. I been most clever daughter in our village, and so I receive scholarship for study. When I had eighteen years, I went to university in Tirana, which is Albania capital city. I am study business economics. Our teacher in Tirana is communist of old school, and he tell us many examples of how some people got very rich in business in very quick time but not by honest method. Then started my desire to become rich. My teacher said to us, "All wealth is created by labour. Riches come to those who steal labour of others. In beginning of every great fortune is one great crime. Soon crime is forgotten, but riches remain." '

She looks up to check that George is still listening, and her wide green eyes narrow and blink. 'I see it is true. However hard I work, I will never be rich just from work. I must steal another's work, or I must steal from those who have already stolen it from others.'

George can feel his heart thudding as she speaks, so loud, it seems, that he wonders whether she can hear it too. He realizes that she knows about the money in his account, and she wants to get her hands on it. He should have guessed, he tells himself with a sigh, but you always hope, don't you?

The lady with the tea trolley stops beside them and, seeing the redhead opposite dabbing at her eyes with a tissue, tops up her cup of tea.

'Here you go, duck. Chocolate biscuit? That'll make you feel better. How about you, sir? Madam? A piece of shortbread?'

She notices Afrodita's tear-heavy eyes, and pours out her brown liquid balm, and George and Afrodita curl their fingers around the hot cups as she trundles away to the end of the carriage and through the sliding doors to the next coach.

'While I was in Tirana I met Sammy Kroçi,' Afrodita continues. 'That is his real name, but it is too difficult for English, so in England he carries name Sammy Cross. He was at this time air pilot, with Aeroflot Airline. He was from Podgorica and he was learning aeronautic engineering in my university. He was very beautiful, with round blue eye and little upturned nose, and yellow hair curling upon shoulder, I never before seen such beautiful man. He was always very happy, smiling and laughing all time. We used to meet for coffee in café in university, in evening we gone walking beside beautiful Lana River. It is very romantic place in moonlight. Soon we discover we have much in common. We both admire persons who got riches and desire to get rich. It was his wish we get married and we plan to do business investment together in tourism. We fall in love and we make plan to marry.' She squeezes his hand. 'I was very young.

I did not understand at that time what type of man is he. He is not good man.'

'Go on,' he says.

'In old times my country was beautiful and peaceful, but now is everlasting war. Neighbour kills neighbour. Good men become bad. While I was away in university my parents had to run away from their home in Kosovo into Albania because of too much fighting. There my father dead, and my mother move away to stay with her family in place where she come from, place name is Kashtanje, name for beautiful forests of chestnut tree that growing close by there. My mother's parents got very old and they also die. Then started a new war. My brothers gone away for soldier and my sister moved to job in Pristina, so my mother alone in Kashtanje and she cry for me to go home.' Her voice has dropped to a near whisper.

George bends his head and listens.

'Kashtanje is very isolated rocky place sticking out in middle of sea, on one side beautiful golden beach, on other side bay with harbour, behind great forests of chestnut trees. Sometimes men come by boat to trade chicken, goat meat, sheep meat, all animals we feed with chestnuts, very tasty. My mother make business there with chicken, fat chicken, very healthy with good taste. When she gone to Kashtanje she know all secret partisan bunkers left over from Hoxha days, but now Kosovo Liberation Army has secret base there with clinic.'

'Clinic?'

'For treatment of woundeds. But there is now other operation.'

'Operation?' He doesn't like the sound of that, but her sweet sing-song voice reassures him.

'All that was very long ago, George. Now Kosovo is peaceful. One day I got visitor, when I was alonely in Kashtanje.

It was Sammy. He borrow motorboat from Russian business-man he know at Tirana, and he come to Kashtanje to harbour. He ask me to marry him. I say I cannot leaving my mother. When he gone away to join army I am very sad.

'I have been dreaming to escape my poor existence at Kashtanje and to return to Tirana. In business studies I have been learning that to make tourist business in this country is great opportunity, but to make high-class tourism you need invest money. And we got no money, only chicken.

'Daily life in Kashtanje is boring. No one to talk with except mother. Every day same. Hot sun. Wind from sea. Every day eating only eggs, chickens and chestnuts. Even bread is made from chestnut flour. No one ever come to this place, only some trading boats to bring flour, cooking oil and gasoline, buy chestnut, egg and chicken from us. And sometime navy ships pass by and sometime on far horizon we see Greek cruise ship at night, far away in south, full of bright lights.

'There was then war, we heard on radio, and many fighting, but not in Kashtanje. I got no interest in this politics. I was only desiring to wear beautiful clothes and to eat beefburger. I was regret I did not accept to marry Sammy. And I was start to remember again what my teacher said. I thought, if it is necessary to commit one crime, I will do it. Soon crime is for-gotten, but riches remain.'

The redhead sitting opposite them on the train has put down her mobile phone and stares as if listening to Afrodita, frowning a little, twisting a strand of hair around her finger. She is staring at the automatic door in front of which the tea-trolley lady has just stopped.

Afrodita continues in her low stilted voice, apparently relieved to be unburdening herself, and he holds her hand and pretends to listen sympathetically – though, in truth, he is growing increasingly alarmed. Her talk about crime and Kroçi, aka Cross, has unsettled him; it seems the two have known each other for a long time, and there is obviously more to their relationship than being colleagues at the Northern Counties Bank.

'Afrodita, I can help you. You don't need to commit a crime.' He whispers it softly, so softly perhaps she doesn't hear, or perhaps she has committed the crime already.

She continues her story. 'In business study in university we have studied internet for online commerce and tourism opportunity, but I discover from other student that there is also Dark Web, where all things are bought and sold that must be kept hidden –'

'But what I don't understand, Afrodita, is how come you ended up in Sheffield?' George interrupts.

'I finish my degree in Tirana top in my year, and I have opportunity to study abroad. I come in Sheffield for complete master's degree in international business, and Sammy said he will come also, he got air pilot job at Doncaster International Airport. I am so happy.'

The redhead's phone rings. She answers it and exclaims, 'What?' She presses the phone so tightly to her ear that maybe she does not hear what Afrodita says. She is staring intently at the trolley lady's disappearing back. George turns to follow her gaze.

There is a sudden commotion, and a shrill burst of whinnying laughter that rings through the quiet carriage. The trolley lady's serene progress towards the exit has been halted by a man in a light grey suit, with curly blond hair and a turned-up nose, who is pushing to get past her in the opposite direction. It is Kroçi, holding a small revolver. George ducks down under the table as soon as he sees the revolver, pulling Afrodita with him.

The tea-trolley lady rams the heavy trolley into Kroçi with quite some force, buckling his knees and pushing him out through the door, which automatically closes behind him and swallows him up. Then opens again. Then closes again. His arm, with the gun, is now trapped in the door. The tea lady holds down the 'close' button, grabs the hot-water jug and douses Kroçi's arm with boiling water. He lets out a blood-curdling cry and drops the revolver.

'That'll serve 'im right,' the tea lady declares. She picks the revolver up and drops it into the other stainless-steel jug, which contains milk.

Then a tall figure in a peaked cap – it must be the guard – appears behind the glass door in the inter-carriage space. It's difficult to see everything that's happening there, but he seems to grab and heave Kroçi from behind.

After a few minutes the train squeals to a halt at a station. Passengers alight and disembark. On the rainy platform, George sees Kroçi pick himself up, shake himself down, and stare around him in bewilderment. A tall figure in uniform, talking on a mobile phone, approaches him.

The doors close. The train moves off and picks up speed.

The tea lady exclaims, 'My goodness! We're in Leicester already! And I haven't done Coach A yet!'

Afrodita emerges from under the table and whispers, 'I think he following us.'

BRENDA: *The key*

On George's birthday, Brenda tries once or twice to ring him, but without success. He's left that annoying answering machine message on – about circumstances beyond his control. Huh! Men. He's probably off gallivanting with someone else. Or maybe he and the Mad Cow have gone somewhere together. Still, she sent him a card to show she hasn't forgotten him.

At six o'clock she gets home from the salon, to see Sid standing there, a worried look on his face.

'Brenda, sorry to trouble you,' he says, 'but can you lend me the key to Dad's flat? It's his birthday and he's not answering his phone, and I just want to check whether he seems to still be living there, and if there's anything that might give us a clue where he's gone.'

Brenda is tired after a day on her feet, and she thinks that Sid is just being polite; he probably believes she knows where George has disappeared to and where he is hiding. But she does not. After George moved out to Totley, although they didn't actually split up in so many words, they haven't seen much of each other.

So she is surprised when Sid asks her for a key to the flat, thinking surely Rosie also has a key? But maybe, she reckons, Sid doesn't want his mother to know he is going over there looking for George. Brenda fumbles in the little drawer in her hall table where she keeps the spare keys, and hands it over. She doesn't think it will do any good, but it may make Sid feel better.

'Bring it back, pet, when you've done. And tell me if you find anything. I want to know who he's with.'

'Will do,' says Sid, pocketing the key.

After Sid has gone, she heats up a luxury chicken korma with pilau rice from her freezer, and settles down in front of the telly to watch her favourite programme, *Crimewatch*. It's amazing how wicked and devious some people can be. And a surprising number of them are not British. Like this girl that has been reported missing from a bank in Sheffield – tampering with people's accounts. It just shows you can't trust anybody these days, not even banks. Very nice-looking girl – they showed her picture. Looks like butter wouldn't melt in her mouth. Hang on a minute – isn't that George's bank? Could it have something to do with his disappearance? What's he been up to – and more to the point, who with? She doesn't want to land him in it, but she wants to know where he has disappeared to. Something serious is going on. She gets out her phone and keys in the *Crimewatch* number.

GEORGE: *The landing of Columbus*

From St Pancras station George and Afrodita take a taxi to Heathrow. Normally, he would take the underground, but he still wants to impress Afrodita.

'One hundred and six bloody quid?'

'That's it, mate.'

'Next time I'll get an Uber.'

The cab driver shrugs.

They seem to have shaken off Kroçi but then George catches a glimpse of him standing in a queue at the Duty Free.

At the check-in desk, Afrodita produces an Italian passport with a flourish, and whispers to him, 'In my country, everyone has Italian passport.'

He was already beginning to have doubts about Afrodita, even before her revelations on the train. Now he realizes she must have criminal contacts to have obtained the passport illegally. He begins to wonder, what else has she been doing illegally?

'Is everything going to plan, Afrodita?' he asks as they clear Passport Control.

'Of course, my dear George. When we arrive in Roma we get train to Brindisi. In summer there is direct flight but not now. From small harbour south of Brindisi we must get fishing boat to take us to Kashtanje where my mother is living. There is no road, only way is by sea.'

Knowing that she probably wants his money more than she wants his body has not cooled his ardour, but it has made him wary. He will settle for a quick physical consummation, now he realizes there is little possibility of a long-term, tender and passionate affair. Can he get to sleep with her, and still keep up an enduring, tender and passionate affair with the Money? He slips an arm around her in a protective way, to hold her tight. Her body yields against his. He feels her warmth and compliance.

'You okay, my dear George?'

'Of course. Spiffing. Never been better.' He lies with conviction.

The flight lasts two and a half uneventful hours, and he watches a film, drinks two glasses of wine and a small glass of whisky, eats tasteless chicken, and strokes Afrodita's hair when she rests her head against his shoulder. And he falls asleep.

In his dream, Rosie and Brenda and Afrodita merge into one enigmatic multi-qualitied female figure, who may now also resemble his mother. She leads him along an endlessly long carpeted corridor which vibrates with a deep soothing rumble like a mechanical birth canal. He wakes up as the plane begins its descent. He is not sure what he has got himself into, but there is no going back now.

In Rome, they take a metro train to the central station, then another long train journey, when he manages to doze off again, to a little harbour where a fishing boat is waiting for them. It is all as she said. It is a long crossing on the small boat, throughout which Afrodita flirts with the fisherman, with little giggles and sideways glances and light-hearted remarks in an unknown language, until the man is docile and passive like a lump of putty in her hands.

George watches the performance with fascination. He is beginning to wonder who she really is.

At last, a long wooded stretch of land arises out of the sea above a steep cliff and a broad crescent of sand, and Afrodita gives a small shriek of excitement. He can't tell whether it's the mainland or an island they have come to. There is a scattering of white-painted cottages climbing up the hill, which, as they approach, appear to be vacant, with blank, blind windows. They have arrived at her mother's village on the Kashtanje headland, Afrodita says, but it seems to be quite deserted; there is nobody there apart from Afrodita's mother, an inscrutable grey-haired old lady with a deeply wrinkled face who comes on to the beach to greet them and who speaks not a word of English, apart from hello. She embraces her daughter and covers her with kisses, then shakes George's hand and repeats her one word of English several times.

Afrodita is behaving quite oddly, one minute flirting with him, as she did with the fisherman, then lapsing into long silences or talking mainly to her mother, in a language he cannot understand. From their sideways glances and smiles he guesses they are talking partly about him. Well, that is only to be expected. But what are they saying? George wonders. The old woman croons and murmurs words of affection to her daughter, and strokes her hair. Afrodita makes affectionate gestures to George, little kisses and hand-squeezes and so on, but she has started up her questioning about names and birthdays again. Behind the sweet musicality, her voice now has a hard, urgent edge as she throws the questions at him and fields his answers.

And there is still the problem of Kroçi. George puzzles over his sudden appearance on the train, and again at Heathrow. Has Afrodita laid a trail for her former lover, or did he simply follow them? George recalls with a shiver the man in a light grey suit, standing as still as a figurehead in the prow of a fishing boat trailing in their wake. True, Afrodita cunningly gave him the slip when they arrived, by disembarking on a low, unpopulated island; then she and George held hands and waded across a partially submerged causeway to Kashtanje, leaving the man floundering behind as the tide came in. He had to turn back. But he is bound to return. George knows he will be somewhere on the headland, waiting for them.

George is beginning to regret splitting up with Rosie and even Brenda. But he's still inwardly fuming that they seem to regard him as an old fool, or some kind of runaway pet to be bossed around and brought back with his tail between his legs. That is not at all what he has in mind. Oh no. He is still, after all, George Pantis, a mature handsome man, highly desirable to women.

BRENDA: Suck it up

Two days after George's birthday, Brenda gets home from her salon at six o'clock to find Sid standing there on the doorstep, dripping with rain, holding out her key to George's flat, which he borrowed a couple of days ago.

'You'd better come in out of the rain,' she says. Sid's blue cagoule is dripping on to the doormat. 'Did you find anything?'

Before he can answer, she spots another hurrying figure, clutching her coat around her, appearing out of the blur of rain. Rosie is dashing up the path towards her front door, holding her hand above her head in a desperate attempt to keep her hair dry, just as Brenda opens the door to Sid.

'Sid?' says Rosie in a questioning voice, seeing the blue cagoule.

'Hi, Mum!'

'Sid, what are you doing here?'

'Er . . . I was just calling round to see you, Mum, but you weren't in . . . and the truth is, I'm just a bit desperate for a pee, so as you weren't in . . .' He looks shifty.

'Hello, Sidney,' Brenda says, opening the door and calling out to him. 'Come on in, duck.' (Yes, she knows he is really called Poseidon, but she can't bring herself to say it – it's so pretentious, isn't it? Fancy lumbering your kid with a name like that.)

'No, he bloody won't!' Rosie grabs his arm. 'It's bad enough you stealing my husband. I'm not going to let you steal my son.'

This confirms Brenda's opinion that her neighbour really is a Mad Cow.

'Come on in, pet.' Brenda grabs his other arm and gives a sharp tug, pulling both him and Rosie, who is hanging on tight like a limpet, tumbling in over her threshold.

'I've just put the kettle on. And I've got a Victoria sponge. You like cake, don't you, Sid? I expect it's too patriotic for you, Rosie Frilly Panties.'

'What's that supposed to mean? You've got some funny ideas, Brenda.'

'Or maybe you're on some Gwyneth bloody Paltrow purity diet, telling you it's unclean to eat cake,' retorts Brenda.

'Calm down, Brenda,' Rosie says in a school-teachery voice, as if she is trying to control a room full of lower-class rowdies. 'No need to shout. I'd love some cake.'

This is too much for Brenda.

'Don't tell me to calm down! You lot are always telling us what to do, what not to do, what's good for us, what we should eat, how we should think, what we can and can't say, who we can and can't have in our own bloody country. You think we're ignorant,' she puts on an exaggerated 'fake posh' accent, pursing her lips and mimicking Rosie, 'and it's all for our own good. You think we don't know what we voted for, we're all thick, or evil racialists. Well, let me tell you something, Rosie Panties, we won, you lost, and you'd better suck it up. That's democracy.'

She can feel herself shaking and starting to sweat. Her voice has risen to a shriek. She has been bottling this up for weeks, or maybe years, since she was at school herself.

'Suck it up. What a horrible expression, Brenda. What does it mean?' her neighbour asks in that same cool middle-class voice.

Brenda is too flustered to think of a reply. What she's always wanted to say to Rosie is how sick she is of being patronized by the middle-class know-alls like her. She didn't intend to get emotional, but she can't help it. She slams down the sponge cake on the table, next to the *Daily Mail* that she hasn't had a chance to read, she's been that busy on her feet all day. She gets three of her best gold-rimmed china plates, and hands Sid a knife. He cuts the cake carefully, trying to make all the slices equal in size, bless him. He is a teacher, too, but he doesn't go out of his way to make her feel thick. Then she fetches three matching gold-rimmed cups and saucers.

'Don't tell me to calm down! I'll never calm down until we get what we voted for! And if they try to diddle us, there'll be riots in the streets!' She reaches for the tin of tea bags. 'Yorkshire tea good enough for you, Frilly Panties, or do you want something more superior? Dried dog turd infused with oriental herbs? Morning-gathered toenail clippings?'

'Yorkshire tea would be great, Brenda. Milk but no sugar.'

Rosie has gone all quiet. Brenda feels a bit guilty, but she can't control herself. She pours the water over the tea bags and while it is drawing, she has another go.

'Now you're in my house, you listen to me for a change. I'll tell you what's good for me and my country. Because we've got to take back control from your bloody elite that have ruled over us for years – your posh-boy David Cameron, your rich-boy George Osborne, your slime-ball Tony Blair, who caused the problem in the first place by letting all the immigrants in, your crazy Jeremy Corbyn, your smarmy Gary Lineker, your millionaire J. K. Rowling . . .'

She can feel her heart beating as she recites the names of those privileged people she can't stand. She can tell she has really succeeded in winding her neighbour up when she sees a superior smirk settling on Rosie's mouth, like hair dye that only takes on its true colour when you add developer.

'You're potty, Brenda!' Rosie smirks; Brenda is warming to her role as 'developer'.

'. . . and the Governor of the Bank of England, and the lying *Guardian* newspaper, the know-all universities and the biased BBC, and the corrupt MPs that are just out for themselves . . . all them upper classes that think they're better than us just because they've got money stuffed away in tax islands, and they've been to private schools and posh universities and they think that gives them the God-given right to rule over us!'

'How sad. You've got an inferiority complex because of your lack of education. But maybe you really *are* inferior,' Rosie hisses across the table.

She's got Rosie well rattled. Good. Brenda may not have been to university, but she knows she isn't daft. She pours out three cups of tea and shoves the milk jug towards her neighbour.

'There you go again, Frilly educated Panties. You really do believe you're superior, don't you? But you're not so superior you could hang on to your husband, eh? That's why you had to pretend to be pregnant, to try and get him back. Well, that's a game two can play.'

Rosie goes red from the neck upwards. She sneers, 'Most men will go after sex, which is the lowest common denominator. Sorry, that's a mathematical term. I suppose it's too complex for you. But life is complex, you know, Brenda. Politics is complex. Sometimes one needs experts. What do you mean I am pretending to be pregnant, anyway?'

'Mum. Brenda . . .' Sid tries to intervene.

But Brenda cuts across him. 'Well, I'm an expert when it

comes to men, Rosie Panties, and I could see George was upset because of your cold, heartless behaviour. All that women's lib crap you go on about. Women's rights. Human rights. European Court of Rights. It's all crap. Like fake pregnancy. When it comes down to it, nobody has any rights. He told me all about your sex life. Lack of.'

Well, that does it. Rosie lets out a short strangled-sounding shriek. 'Bitch!' Then she picks up her cup of tea and lobs it across the table at her.

Brenda dodges to the side. Some tea splashes on her new white cable-knit jumper from Reiss, which she hopes will come out in the wash, but fortunately most of it misses her, and the cup smashes into the granite worktop behind, sending thousands of little bits of china flying everywhere. Pity. It is part of a pretty Royal Albert china set from Atkinsons.

'Missed again. You people are so clever, but it's all mouth. You're useless when it comes to anything practical.' Now her blood is up and she is mad with anger. She picks up the teapot, full of scalding tea, and swings back her arm to take aim. 'Now let's see if I can hit the target!'

Rosie ducks beneath the table. Who knows how it would have ended, but Sensible Sid raises a hand.

'Stop, Brenda! Stop, Mum! Please stop fighting! Look at what I found in Dad's flat!'

He reaches in his pocket and pulls out a dagger in a scarlet leather sheath, and slaps it down in the middle of the table. The two women stop in their tracks. Brenda's arm is still raised, with the heavy china teapot wobbling slightly in the air. Rosie reaches out and grabs another cup of tea from the two left on the table, and takes a deep gulp. They both study the object Sid has brought. When Brenda looks more closely, she sees it isn't a dagger at all; it looks more like a broken-off stiletto heel from a scarlet shoe. Rosie pokes at it gingerly, as though it may bite her finger.

Brenda picks it up and turns it over. 'Louboutin,' she says, with confidence. 'You can tell because they always have red soles, and there's a scrap of red leather from the sole still stuck on. I bet you didn't know that, did you, Rosie Panties? They must have cost her well over five hundred quid.'

Rosie rolls her eyes and mutters, 'What sort of a woman spends five hundred quid on shoes like that?'

Obviously the Mad Cow doesn't have much knowledge of fashion, and it shows. On the Chamber of Commerce committee there are some women with two or three different pairs of Louboutins.

'The sort Georgie is shagging now,' she replies. She meets Rosie's eyes with a glint of triumph. Then she gets up slowly from the table and fetches a dustpan and brush to sweep up the shards of china.

Rosie reaches for a tea towel and mops up the tea spilt on the table and floor. 'Sorry about the mess, Bren,' she says in a quiet voice. 'I don't know what got into me. Do you mind if I use your loo?'

'Go ahead. You know where it is.' Her voice is quiet too. It is like the calm after the storm.

'Of course I do.'

The two semi-detached houses are mirror images of each other, though Brenda has a new white bathroom suite with a bidet, whereas Rosie's thirty-year-old avocado suite has loads of chipped and cracked prawn-coloured tiles around it, and is always full of damp knickers hung out to dry.

While his mother is out of the room, Brenda pulls her chair up close to Sid and addresses him in a low voice.

'Did Jacquie tell you I saw her in the supermarket? She told me she was pregnant. Don't you think that's strange? Jacquie and me and Rosie, all pregnant at the same time. The babies will be like siblings, although they're really – well, I don't know how to describe their relationship.'

'Mum's not pregnant.'

'That's what she told me.'

'You must have got the wrong end of the stick,' says Sid.

'I don't know how she managed it, at her age. Could be fake, I reckon. Did I tell you, I'm pregnant too? IVF of course. All you need these days is a condom full of cum and a freezer. Sorry, Sid, is that too much detail for you?'

Sid has turned pale and puts his hand across his mouth as he mutters, 'Well, congratulations on the pregnancy, Brenda . . .'

'Anyway, I got talking to Jacquie. I'm so excited you're going to be a father too, Sid, I'd better get knitting for all of us. By the way, did you find anything of interest in George's flat?'

'All I found was a pile of junk mail in the hall. I picked it up and stacked it on the hall table.'

'Anything else?'

'There was a business card from a Mr S. Cross, Fraud Department, Northern Counties Bank. He came round to my house once, looking for Dad. And I found three birthday cards on the window sill in the kitchen, from which I deduce that Dad must have disappeared on or shortly after his birthday. There was an opened water bill dated two days ago, which I remember him grumbling about at the time, and a more recent unopened electricity bill, postmarked yesterday. That gave me a time-window for his disappearance.'

She nods. 'Good on you, Sid. No sign of any other women?'

'Only that.' He points at the scarlet heel on the table. 'It was in the rubbish bin in the kitchen. It definitely doesn't look like the sort of thing my mum would wear – or you, Brenda. That's why I picked it up.'

'If you find out who he's gone off with, you'll tell me, won't you, pet?' she says.

'Sure I will, Brenda.' Then he pauses and mumbles, 'But . . . what if he's dead? For all we know, he could have been murdered. And the girl who the shoe fits is . . .'

There is a sound of scuffling, and suddenly the door bursts open. Rosie flies into the room, as though she's been listening outside the door, yelling, 'What girl?'

'The new girl he's gone off with, Rosie Panties.' Brenda knows she is being catty, but sometimes her neighbour seems to be asking for it. 'The one that was on *Crimewatch*. What if she's been murdered by George?'

'That doesn't sound like Dad,' mumbles Sid.

'So you watch *Crimewatch*, do you, Brenda?' Rosie asks in a mocking voice.

'I just happened to be watching the telly and *Crimewatch* came on, and I recognized the name of George's bank. They said a girl who works in a bank in Sheffield has been reported missing by her employers. Now Sid's gone and found that *thing* in his flat!' She points at the broken-off heel with an exaggerated shudder. 'Looks like our Georgie has a secret life.'

'Hmm. Maybe,' says Rosie. 'Or maybe he *wants to* have a secret life, and this flat is the first step in that direction. For a man like George, the woman you haven't yet slept with is always more attractive than the one you go to bed with every night. Maybe he would like to have a secret life – it's much more exciting than you or me, Bren.'

'Sounds like he's just lost the plot. He's getting on a bit, your hubby.'

'Yes, but he thinks he can have a last fling. Or a few last

flings. He always liked women, Brenda, and maybe that's why he's moved out to his own flat in Totley, where he can carry on unobserved.'

Typical Rosie. Brenda can't help liking her, even if she is a Mad Cow. She has to have the last word on everything, whether it is George's adventuring or the Common Market. She has to have the last word, even when she is wrong.

'Believe me, Rosie, I told him not to move out to that bloody flat in Totley, miles away from anywhere, but he was in a funny mood. I don't know what got into him. Maybe he'd already met *her*.'

Or maybe it has something to do with that phone call she overheard, about winning a lottery, she thinks, but she doesn't voice her thought to Rosie, who probably doesn't know about the money. She pokes the broken-off heel gingerly, like it is a biting snake, still alive. 'We were getting along ever so well, too.' She catches Rosie's eye and adds quickly, 'I don't want to upset you, pet, but I just couldn't stop myself falling in love with George, especially once I fell pregnant. He's a good man.'

'I know he's a good man. I don't need you to tell me,' Rosie growls, ignoring the throwaway line about Brenda's pregnancy, as if she assumes it must be fake. 'But he has his faults.'

The two women move their chairs closer to each other, conversing in low voices. Brenda is enjoying the exquisite pleasure of toying with Rosie, winding her up tight like a mechanical puppet and watching her responses.

'He's kind of spiritual,' she continues. 'Thinks about the big things in life. Not like my bloody ex, Sniffer, who only thinks about money and dogs.'

All the memories of her time with Sniffer come rolling back: the rows, the violence, the passionate sexual making up after. As she talks she watches Rosie, who is squirming under the scrutiny. Sometimes she thinks her neighbour has led such a privileged life she doesn't know what the real world is like. Well, she will let her know now. 'Sniffer took control of all my savings when we lived together, read my diary and my phone messages, went mad if he saw me talking to another man. Then he turned and went off with that criminal Kosovan brothel-keeper who pretends to run a pet-grooming parlour.' The pain still hurts. Tears mist her eyes.

'So you decided to get even by nicking another woman's husband?' Rosie's voice is hard and curious.

'At first it didn't mean nothing, pet. I was just having a bit of fun. Just playing around. I felt free, once Sniffer had gone, but I was lonely. By the time George came along, I'd been on my own that long, I was longing to feel a man's body next to mine.' Rosie's eyes have turned into hard narrow slits as she watches her. 'But then I really started to love George. His voice. His eyes. The feel of his arms around me. He was so different to Sniffer. I started to yearn for the life I might have had if I'd met him sooner. I loved the way he used to . . .' She can't help it. She starts to cry theatrically, dabbing her eyes carefully with the tissue, so as not to smudge her mascara.

'The way he used to what?' Rosie asks in a nasty voice. 'Do give me the sordid details, won't you?'

'Massage my feet after I'd had a hard day. That's not sordid. Ah, it was nice!' She chokes back a sob.

'He did *what*?' Rosie's eyebrows shoot up.

Brenda smirks. She has hit the bullseye there!

'And I loved the way he used to look into my eyes and say poems straight out of his head.'

'Oh, that!' Rosie snorts. 'You can have enough of poetry, you know. What else?'

Sid's head is flicking from side to side like he's at a tennis match.

'I loved the way he talked about his kids. I always longed for kids of my own. Sniffer and I never had any kids,' she snuffles back a tear. 'George thinks the world of you, Sid. And Cassie.'

'Sid's going to find him, and bring him home,' Rosie says, in a proud voice. Typical Rosie. 'Aren't you, Sid?'

'Maybe,' says Sid nervously.

'I know. I lent him the key,' says Brenda.

'I didn't know you still had a key to the flat, Brenda. Why didn't you give it back?'

Brenda shrugs. 'I'd forgotten all about it until Sid asked for it. Anyway, I thought George might want me to pop round if he was feeling lonely one evening. You know what men are like.'

In her heart, Brenda suspects George's disappearance is something to do with this money he thinks he's won. But maybe he hasn't told Rosie, and Brenda is not about to break it to her – she'll only try and get her hands on it, possessive, scheming self-righteous cow that she is. How he wants to spend it is up to him. Some of it may even come her way, or at least they can have a nice holiday or two.

'No, I guess I don't!' Rosie replies with a snap. 'But I'm a fast learner.'

'Not fast enough. Anyway, enough of the blame game for today, Rosie,' she says in a placatory tone. 'This is serious. What do you think we should do now, pet?'

'I reckon we've got to put aside our differences to save him.' Rosie slurps her tea. 'From *that* woman.' She pokes the heel with her finger. 'Maybe from himself. Poor George.'

'Poor George. You would say that.' Brenda takes an angry bite of cake. 'You're bound to think that, but he's no victim, your Georgie. He knows what he's doing.' Rosie still doesn't get it, thinks Brenda. Maybe she's being deliberately thick, or maybe she's just led a very sheltered life. 'Though he's been a bastard to both of us, and got us both pregnant and dumped us.'

'What do you mean, got us both pregnant? I'm not pregnant, Brenda! Are you?'

Brenda bows and shakes her head. 'No, I just said it, because I thought you were, Frilly Panties. I thought you were faking it to try and get George back.'

So she was wrong about Rosie's pregnancy. Very wrong, thank goodness! But right about George's general unreliability.

'But although he *has* been a bastard, he could be in some sort of danger now. I reckon he's gone and jumped in head over heels, out of his depth, with this new woman. You can never tell with women who wear red stilettos. It's up to us to rescue him, don't you think?'

Rosie nods thoughtfully, as if it's just beginning to dawn on her that George is up to something. 'We have to save him from himself, because he's a bit of an idiot. And from a woman like that, because he's a bit of a tomcat. I expect you've discovered that already, Brenda. He won't stay faithful to you for long.'

'Alright, have it your own way, Rosie Panties,' she sniffs tearfully. She is more inclined to be charitable now that she realizes the pregnancy story was just a trick of her imagination. Tears of relief stream from her eyes. 'Just try to think of it the other way around, for a minute. According to the police, the girl's gone missing from the bank where she was working. Her employer reported her missing. But nobody reported that George was missing. He just did a runner. See what I mean?' She taps the side of her nose and winks through her tears.

Rosie snorts like a horse. 'You mean that makes George a killer? Don't make me laugh, Bren. I know he's an idiot in many ways, but he's never shown any signs –'

'Not to us that know him, Rosie. Anyway, apparently the girl was already under suspicion when she went missing from her workplace. The police showed me a full-length picture of the woman and asked me if I recognized her.'

'Was she wearing red stilettos, with one heel missing?' asks Rosie, giggling.

'I couldn't see her feet, pet,' says Brenda. She can't help having a soft spot for her neighbour, even if she is a Mad Cow.

'What has poor George got himself into now? He may be in danger; or maybe he's already dead.' Rosie's voice has gone quiet and thoughtful, as if she's talking aloud to herself.

The idea is too horrible to bear thinking about, so Brenda doesn't think about it.

'I lent Sid the spare key to George's flat. That's how he found *that* thing!' She points at the heel.

'I searched his computer,' Sid chimes in. 'I saw he'd been booking flights with British Airways.'

'What flights?' Rosie asks in an excited voice. 'We've got to get the day and flight number.'

'I drew a blank there. Nothing of interest. One of you two should go up there and have a look around, in case I missed something.' Sid stands up and pushes his chair away. 'I'd best be going back home. Will you two be alright now? No more fighting?'

'No more fighting!' they say in chorus.

Then Brenda adds, 'Sure we'll be alright. Don't worry about us, Sid. Us bark is worse than us bite.' A warm feeling comes over her, like a doggy blanket, smelly but comforting. She looks at Rosie, at the way her head is bowed and her skinny, fidgety hands are clasped together. What has she done with her wedding ring? Suddenly she feels a bit sorry for her, as well as for herself. George has deceived both of them.

'We're going to put aside us differences and join forces. We'll work as a team from now on,' she says. 'Won't we, Rosie Frillies, my mad old love? Your hair looks nice now. It suits you short.'

Sid lets himself out the front door.

ROSIE: A CCTV image

Half an hour later, Rosie has returned home, and just got her nightie on for bed when the doorbell rings. Thinking it must be Sid or Brenda, having forgotten something, she pulls on her dressing gown and goes downstairs. But when she opens the front door, it isn't Sid or Brenda. Two cops are standing there on the doorstep, a woman and a man. After introducing themselves as DCI Gibbs (the woman) and DS Colson (the man), they flash their ID badges at her and ask whether she can spare a moment.

'Of course,' she says, her nose quivering with curiosity.

'Mrs Pantis?' they ask. 'We'd like to have a word with your husband.'

'He's not here.'

'Do you know where he is?'

'No. As it happens, I've been trying to track him down myself. You'd better come in.'

They follow her into the hall, and then into the kitchen, and sit down at the table. She offers them tea, but they decline.

'We're looking for him because when we put the story on *Crimewatch* about a young woman who has disappeared from a Sheffield bank, a viewer rang up to say she thought your husband has an account at that bank and now he's disappeared too. We want to identify a man who was seen with the woman in question and eliminate him from our enquiry.'

'What enquiry?' A shiver runs through her. Brenda mentioned *Crimewatch*! Who still watches that? Only the sad elderly crime-obsessed readers of the *Daily Mail*. What could it possibly have to do with her and George? 'Could I see the image?'

They have come prepared. They produce a grey, grainy photo, a blow-up of a CCTV image, which they spread on the table. It is George alright, she can tell at once from the stubborn set of the mouth and eyebrows, and the way the wisps of hair stick out over his ears where it has grown back from Brenda's hair zealotry.

'Is that your husband, Mrs Pantis?'

'Yes,' she whispers. Her heart is beating so hard she is struggling to get the words out. 'Yes, that's him. But where is he? And who's he with?'

They exchange swift glances. The woman cop says, 'We can't say at present. But we can confirm that it's a criminal investigation, Mrs Pantis. We'd be grateful for any help you can give us.'

The thing that puzzles Rosie obsessively is that although the image is cut off vertically in the middle, he is clearly holding hands with someone. But who? It isn't Brenda's hand – her hands are middle-aged, brown-spotted, plump and wrinkly, discoloured from dye, glittering with bracelets and rings. She likes a bit of bling. The hand in the photo is slim, young and ringless. Besides, Brenda is here, next door, and George is . . . where is he?

ROSIE: Sheer narcissism

After the visit from the cops Rosie really starts to worry. That night she doesn't sleep well. A series of vivid nightmares followed by hot sweats keep her awake, and the next night the nightmares return, so she is tired as she gets herself up and dressed for work on Monday morning. She notices two missed calls on her phone, but decides to open them later. She is counting down the days to half term; she has a difficult year group she is still getting to know.

She is just getting into her car when her phone rings again. She glances down at the caller's name, sees it is Cassie, and decides not to answer.

A few minutes later it rings again. This time it is Sid on his mobile. He tells her that Cassie had a visit from the cops on Friday night, while they were drinking tea with Brenda, and she's worked herself up into a state. She couldn't get through to Rosie, so she rang him last night and left a message with some hysterical tale that George has been murdered by a mysterious woman he's been seen holding hands with in front of a Bitcoin machine in London.

'Poor Dad,' says Sid. 'He's obviously got himself into some kind of mess with this lottery money. Maybe he's bought Bitcoin with it. No wonder he wants to disappear. Someone who has just come into that amount of money from an unknown source is bound to be vulnerable to spear phishing. But murdered? It couldn't be true, could it, Mum?'

Rosie sighs. 'I wouldn't put it past him. Sheer narcissism, if you ask me, just to get us all running around after him. I expect he'll sort himself out. Either that, or Cassie's got the wrong end of the stick.'

'You don't seem to care, Mum,' Sid accuses. 'Dad told me that a Russian girl who works at the bank, and said she was at school with Cassie, tried to get him to reset his password.'

'I don't think Cassie was ever at school with any Russian girl.'

She puts the phone down and drives to work a little faster than usual, cutting up other drivers aggressively.

During her lunch break Sid rings to say he's just been down to the Northern Counties Bank. The manageress confirmed that she knew his father but told him that under data protection legislation she could give him no information about his father's account, nor about the bank's employees. If he had any worries he should go to the police, she informed him sniffily. They did not keep records of employees' ethnicity. Then she added in a quick surreptitious whisper, glancing around to make sure no one was listening, that there was a young woman who worked there who spoke Russian but who was really from Yugoslavia. Or Albania. Or Kosovo. She had apparently gone missing without telling anyone where she was going, and a check had shown up some irregularities in her work. The police are looking for her. If he found any news of her, would he please inform the bank?

'Thanks for doing that, Sid,' Rosie says. 'Don't tell anybody, will you? We don't want the whole world and his dog to know about George's money, do we?' What she means is, 'I don't want Brenda to find out.' She knows that Sid is still pally with Brenda. 'Just in case there is anything dodgy,' she adds.

When George said he had won seven million quid on some fishy foreign lottery, her first reaction was to snort sceptically – either he was confused, or it was wishful thinking. Her second reaction was fury – did that mean the Bitch would get half of it?

No, Rosie determines, that will never, ever happen.

BRENDA: *Vital clue*

Next day, after work, Brenda drives over to George's flat, taking the key Sid has returned to her, thinking that Sid (being just a bloke) may have missed some vital clue. When she opens the front door, inside all is silent and musty. These modern flats are so badly ventilated, she thinks, without a good coal fire to draw the fresh air in.

There is a pile of mail stacked neatly on the hall table (Sid must have left it there), but the bed is unmade and there is dirty laundry scattered on the floor – T-shirts, socks, pants, tissues – and the kitchen sink is full of unwashed crockery. Instinctively, she starts to tidy up. She can't stand mess. A teacup with a red lipstick-print on the rim is in the sink. Hm. Could be Rosie, but she doesn't usually wear lipstick, or it could be someone else. The bins have not been emptied and are beginning to stink. The place is full of fruit flies hovering around the unemptied compost container. George's phone, passport and wallet are not there, but his toothbrush and shaving kit are in the bathroom. She feels out of her depth, playing the detective as she tries to work out whether this means it was a hurried departure or a planned one. Like Sherlock Holmes, she's looking for the vital clue to where George has gone, a clue that is so bloody obvious it's hiding there in full sight.

On the window sill in the kitchen are three birthday cards: there is the one from herself, with a picture of a bottle of spuming champagne – not very subtle, but George, bless him, isn't very subtle. One is from Sid, with a picture of a car with an 80 number plate; and Rosie's card is not too subtle either, with a picture of the Matterhorn – a big dick if ever there was one. 'You are my strong and stable rock' says the caption.

She works out that George must have disappeared sometime between his birthday on the 12th of October, because his birthday cards have been opened, and the 'use by' dates of the 14th of October for the milk, sausages and two cheesy pasta dinners she finds in the fridge. Why is he eating all this rubbish? Obviously nobody is cooking for him.

There is an opened water bill – what a rip-off! – from a few days ago, and an unopened electricity bill, which she opens, postmarked the 13th. So he must have gone away in those couple of days.

What's this? On the desk beside the computer is an envelope with a six-letter word in capitals scribbled on it: NINYAS. She puzzles over it for a minute, then copies it on a bit of paper and stuffs it in her handbag. NINYAS: looks like a booking code of some sort. She'll have time to decode it later.

There is one more unusual thing that turns up in her search, hidden under the bed: a single scarlet shoe minus its heel. It seems to be the companion to the heel that Sid showed her and Rosie, even down to the scrap of red sole that was torn off.

There's nothing else. She sweeps her gaze around the flat and wonders again what made George choose such a dismal out-of-the-way place. Perhaps he wanted to put some miles between himself and her next-door neighbour, the Mad Cow Remoaner. Who could blame him?

She is just about to let herself out when she hears the sound of a dog barking in the yard. She glances out of the window. There's a big muscular Staffie running around in circles outside. It's Sniffer's dog. She would recognize that dog anywhere. It's big enough to be a pit bull cross, but Sniffer says it isn't a pit bull because they are banned under the Dangerous Dogs Act. It was mooching around Rosie's door the other day, before she got home.

What is it doing out here? she wonders. Is Sniffer with it? Is it on the loose? A minute later she sees Pattie Smith stomping up the forecourt on her big stout legs, with a dog leash in her hand. A chill mist descends on her heart to see her old rival in these unexpected surroundings. Apparently, nowadays she sometimes calls herself by her real name, Petra Simic, but in those days she was just plain old Pattie Smith. She's the slag her Sniffer went off with. Anyway, she stomps right up to George's apartment and raps on the door.

Brenda opens it, folds her arms across her chest, and looks her in the eye. 'Yes?'

'Is George here?' the slag says.

'He's gone away,' Brenda says.

'He must have gone off with that Kosovan bimbo and her Serbian boyfriend,' the slag says. 'They've run off with my money.'

'I don't know anything about that.'

'I know where they've gone. I can help you to find him before they kill him. Can I come in?'

SID: A portal into another world

A week later, Sid, Rosie and Brenda have set off to find George and bring him home. Pattie Smith, she of the small blue van that Sid pranged on the Ring Road, has suddenly and mysteriously teamed up with Brenda, and is now their guide.

Rosie has arranged for a colleague to cover her teaching for the next week. Sid has a reading week coming up, and Rosie has reassured him that Jacquie will be okay till he gets back. Brenda has locked up her salons, with a notice 'Closed until further notice' hung in the window.

'I know where they are gone, and where they going,' Pattie says in a dramatic guttural whisper. 'They will fly to Rome, then get train to Brindisi, then catch fishing boat to secret place on Albanian coast. Sam Kroçi told me it.'

Thanks to the booking code that Brenda found in George's flat they know George and another passenger, a woman with an Italian name, went to Rome, and booked themselves on to a flight on the 12th of October, which was George's eightieth birthday. The other four have booked a flight to Rome as soon as they can.

Rosie says, 'Watch out, Brenda. It's Europe. It's full of foreigners.'

Brenda growls back wearily, as if from habit, 'I don't know what you're getting at, but whatever it is, it's pathetic, Rosie Panties. We won. You lost. Just get over it, can't you?'

'No, I bloody well can't! It's my duty as a citizen of this country to put a stop to this nonsense,' retorts Rosie, also wearily.

Sid, with a weary sigh, wishes they would stop fighting and concentrate on the task in hand – rescuing his father, which he supposes is what this quarrel is really about. Everybody has Brexit fatigue, but Rosie and Brenda are still at it, screeching 'facts' at each other as they board the plane to Rome.

They have left it too late to get seats together, and maybe that's just as well, thinks Sid. He is next to a young couple who hold hands throughout the flight and, watching their interlocking fingers, his mind flips to Jacquie, wishing he was holding hands with her. Rosie is sandwiched between two handsome Italian blokes, while Brenda looks on enviously from her window seat next to a nervous elderly couple. Pattie is up ahead in an aisle seat and keeps glancing round to make sure she has not lost anybody. Pattie must be Italian, thinks Sid, because she is travelling on an Italian passport. Strange. He would never have guessed she was Italian – she does not look or dress like an Italian, nor does she have an Italian accent.

From the airport at Rome they catch a taxi to Roma Termini station. Under Pattie's instruction, the taxi races through the traffic-clogged streets of Rome, past the glittering shops and teeming restaurants overflowing on to the pavements, round a spectacular ruin.

Roma Termini train station is vast and chaotic. Everyone seems to be shouting at each other, or into their phones, and rushing in random directions, bumping into bewildered-looking Americans. There is an all-pervasive smell of hot brake fluid and coffee. No one knows anything.

Brenda barges up to the information desk and asks, loudly and slowly, 'Where is the train to Brindle Sea?'

'Brindisi,' says Rosie.

'That's what I said.'

'No, you didn't. You said "Brindle Sea".'

Brenda shrugs. 'Same difference, innit?'

Rosie replies, putting on her hoity-toity Key Stage 4 teacher voice that is familiar to Sid, 'No, it's not at all the same, Brenda.'

'It's what Pattie said.'

Rosie eyes Pattie venomously. 'That impostor who's trying to defraud my husband?' she hisses at Brenda. 'Who is she anyway?'

'She's a criminal – a *foreign* criminal. She should be sent back to where she comes from, but she keeps changing her mind about where that is. Anyway, like most of them she seems to be above the law. One rule for us, one rule for them. She runs a brothel up Attercliffe, on the main road between Rotherham and Sheffield, as well as others in London. So-called massage parlours. Imports girls from her own country, telling them they're going to be au pairs in rich English families. When they get here they find they're stuck in a whorehouse in a run-down area on the outskirts of Sheffield. Not that it makes any difference – they can't go out, anyway.'

'How awful. How come you know her?'

'Went off with my Sniffer. Now he works for her. In fact, the girls work for both of them. He just keeps them under control with his dogs. They're raking it in, the two of them. Like pigs in shit.'

Rosie is quiet. Sid can see her brain whirring, trying to work out what's the correct response to this slurry of wrongdoing.

Brenda reaches out and takes her hand. 'Don't worry, I'll look after you, pet. Let's us two stick together.'

Rosie nods mutely.

The overnight train for Brindisi leaves shortly after 10 p.m., in ten minutes' time. They career through the station and barge through the departure barrier just as the guard starts to blow his whistle. He pauses to let them scramble aboard. Sid grabs the handle of the last door of the last carriage, and hauls himself up and in through the door, then he reaches down and pulls up Rosie, Brenda and Pattie and all their baggage on to the high step. They collapse in a heap on top of each other inside the train.

The guard toots his whistle, the train starts with a jolt and picks up speed. Sid mutters to the others, 'We're on our way. But to where?'

They ease themselves into a foursome, seated around a table. Pattie sits next to Sid. Rosie and Brenda leave their bags on the facing seats. Brenda says, 'We're just going to find the loo, poppet,' and they disappear.

The train has sped up, and is swaying from side to side as the doors at the back of the carriage slide open, and Brenda and Rosie stagger in.

'Much cleaner than British trains,' says Brenda.

'That's the EU for you,' says Rosie. 'They have regulations.'

'You don't need regulations for toilets,' retorts Brenda. 'Just a sufficient supply of toilet paper.'

She plonks herself down opposite Sid, with Rosie next to her, opposite Pattie.

'George has got himself in a right pickle, hasn't he?' She addresses Pattie chattily.

Pattie replies, 'What is mean "in pickle"?'

'It means pickle. Like pickled cucumber,' Brenda says.

'He got in cucumber?'

Rosie shrugs. 'It's an English saying,' she says, and adds, 'we've come to help George get away from these criminals and bring him home. Whatever he's done, I forgive him. In the end, it's all water under the bridge.'

'What is mean "water under bridge"?' Pattie queries. 'It

170

mean at end she will kill him, and throw body in water under bridge?'

'No, pet,' says Brenda. 'Rosie loves him. She's his wife. Or ex-wife. Just like I'm Sniffer's ex-wife. You don't just stop loving someone when he goes off with someone else, you know.'

Pattie glances up at her malevolently. 'This ex-wife, she know everything? Maybe you think she even know password?'

'What password?' says Brenda.

'Password to bank account, what we must get from him before Afrodita will get it. If she will get password from him, she will take all money for herself. She is bad woman.'

'What money?' asks Brenda.

'My money from massage business that I have put in this account,' Pattie replies. 'He has been changing password. Now I cannot get it out.'

Sid pricks up his ears. Did he hear that right? It seems as though Pattie is after George's password too, but her English is unclear and she is talking in a low voice. Oh dear, what a mess, he thinks. Poor Dad!

Darkness accompanies them as they leave behind the suburbs of Rome, and the train moves north through a neat landscape of cultivated fields and vineyards. But after a while they leave this behind, and as the train turns its course and heads east, the terrain becomes more mountainous and wild. They travel through pretty, shuttered-up towns with creeper-covered walls and pass through little stations without stopping, past yawning guards patrolling the platform with their drowsy dogs, and some busier places with their bustling railway stations even in the dead of night, where passengers alight and disembark. Behind the stations there are many grand porticoed buildings and a sprinkling of lights. From time to time they are plunged into total darkness as the train enters a tunnel. Sid starts nodding off. It's been a long day. Rosie and Brenda are sitting side by side in grumpy companionable silence, their chins and eyelids drooping. The train thunders on through the night.

After a while, the rhythm of the train sends Sid to sleep, so he can't remember much about the journey. Once he opens his eyes to see, after a minute of darkness, that the other three have rearranged themselves. Rosie is now sitting beside him, while Brenda is sitting next to Pattie, resting her head on her shoulder. In the seats beside theirs, a noisy three-generation Italian family who embarked at the previous stop are sharing bread and salami; the kids are polite and docile, but the adults are all yelling at each other and at them. As the light begins to rise with the approach of dawn they see, out towards the east, the silver gleam of the Adriatic Sea.

About five hours after their departure, a voice barking over the loudspeaker announces that they have arrived in Brindisi. There is a sudden screech of brakes and a sharp jolt.

'Here we are! Wake up, everybody!' chirps Pattie raucously, like an assertive magpie.

The jolt has unbalanced one of Brenda's bags, stowed overhead, and it flies open. A shower of bottles and jars rain down on Rosie's head. She turns on Brenda, declaring that this is the last straw. Brenda flaps around, trying to fit everything back into her bag. Sid tries to help. Rosie passively obstructs. Pattie watches impatiently, tapping her fingers on the back of the seat.

Outside the station is a small row of taxis, the drivers dozing at the wheel. Pattie commandeers the last taxi. Then she gets out her mobile phone and starts talking very rapidly in a language that Sid cannot understand; he listens carefully, but it

172

doesn't sound to him like the Italian he remembers from holidays.

Theirs isn't the speediest driver, but once they have left the town centre, with its scattering of hotels and restaurants, and navigated the suburban straggle of poor roadside houses, shuttered-up shops and petrol stations, he picks up speed a bit. Then Sid becomes aware that they are being followed. A pair of bright, low headlights is sitting on their tail, always the same distance behind, whatever twists and turns they take. Soon they have left behind the scruffy port and are following a winding coastal road through dark hamlets and broad-eaved villas set back off the road and surrounded by neat gardens and shadowy cypress trees; from time to time the vista opens up and they see the Adriatic on their left, heavy and lazy, gleaming like polished lead. After about half an hour, their taxi veers off to the left down a rutted sandy track through dunes, signposted 'Marina di Brindola'. The headlights follow. The driver glances nervously into his mirror. Sid's heart is beating hard. Their taxi pulls up abruptly on a level stretch of sand, stopping beside a small wooden jetty where a fishing boat is moored, bobbing up and down on the lazy water. A man steps out from the cabin, over the coiled ropes and nets, and watches them.

'Venti-tre,' demands their taxi driver when they have all piled out of the cab. Pattie has the money ready in euros. When did she get it out? While she's paying him, the car that has been following them pulls up alongside, and three guys get out – they are wearing black leather jackets, baseball-style caps and wire-rimmed aviator-style shades, even though it is still quite dark outside. To Sid, they look chunky and tough, though one of them is just a boy. Like central-casting bad guys, they carry guns, at least the two bigger ones do, and their low-slung combat trousers seem to be bulging with pockets stuffed with concealed weaponry, but they are not speaking Italian – he can't tell what their language is. No matter, thinks Sid, they sure do look like villains.

Pattie addresses them in the same unknown language, and points at Sid and Rosie and Brenda. The bad guys race down to the jetty and start stomping up and down and yelling at the fisherman, who is fiddling with his outboard motor. He shakes his head. The first bad guy barks at the fisherman in Italian, then he and the boy jump on board the vessel, while the third villain comes back up the dunes towards Sid, Brenda and Rosie, waving his gun. The taxi has left by now, so they have little choice but to obey when he gestures for them to get aboard the fishing boat. Pattie leads the way. The boat has a strange, putrid fishy smell and appears to be leaking slightly through several small holes in the sides that look like bullet holes. With eight of them on board, it sits dangerously low in the water, especially once all Brenda's polka-dot baggage is stowed in the bow, but the sea is calm, gleaming sombrely in the dawn light.

The fisherman in charge of the boat Pattie has commandeered for them is a short, stocky man with greasy black grey-streaked hair and bad teeth. He has deep wrinkles, due to age or to spending too much time in the sun. He looks sleepy, as though he wants to get home to a sweet espresso, rather than set out to sea again.

As soon as everyone is on board, the first gangster points at himself with a stubby tobacco-stained finger and introduces himself loudly as boss-man Samir, and then points at the other two. 'This my middle brother, Neptun. This my bebby brother Tonibler. In Kosovo many children are called Tonibler. Today he accompany us to learn how to do business. *Vail Vail*' he cries at the terrified fisherman.

The man at once fires up the motor, and off they go, bouncing at speed across the wide flat sea. The land, with its sprinkle of lights and buildings, recedes at an alarming rate. There are one or two other boats out on the Adriatic, even though it is still very early, and they are hungry as well as tired.

The fisherman doesn't seem to be entirely in control of the boat. Pattie has disappeared into the tiny cabin and Rosie and Brenda look terrified; they grip on to the side-rail when the boat rears up in the water and lands with a slap on the waves, showering salty spray over everyone. The black-jacket guys chortle. This is their idea of fun, and the terror of the women seems to excite them more and more, so they urge the fisherman to go faster. There are no life jackets on board. While they are still within sight of land, Samir lights a cigarette, then gets his cell phone out and starts to check his messages, chuckling to himself and shaking his head, like a maniac. The younger one, the one called Neptun, makes a long, serious phone call that Sid doesn't follow. The boy, Tonibler, is also using his phone, texting like crazy with his thumbs. Soon they are out of sight of land and the phone calls end abruptly. The endless sea slips by beneath the bows.

Despite the cool breeze and the salt spray, Rosie and Brenda have dozed off again, leaning against each other, their jaws relaxed, their mouths open, snoring lightly. Sid feels his head nodding in sympathy to the rhythm of their snoring. He tries to keep himself awake by making up a song in his head.

> I once met a guy called Samir
> Who said you have nothing to fear
> And reached for a bottle of beer.

As if on cue, the bad guy Samir pulls out some bottles of beer from a case under the seat and hands them around. Rosie and Brenda wake up with a jerk, shake their heads, and doze off again. The fisherman shakes his head too, although it is probably his beer they are drinking. Pattie, Sid, Samir, Neptun and Tonibler take one each. The beer is very fizzy and still slightly warm from the heat of the previous day. Sid sips slowly, swishing it around his mouth. The other four down the contents with a few glugs, and throw the bottles overboard into the sea.

Then something strange happens. As they sit low on the horizon, the boat's motor chugging away, sending out clouds of bluish smoke, a shimmering mist rises out of the sea like a veil and envelops them in its translucent folds, so everything seems wavering and unreal. Afterwards, Sid will often try to recall the feeling of dissolving self that came over him, the melting away of the everyday boundaries between reality and unreality. It is as if they have passed through a portal into another world. But he can't remember how it happened.

What he remembers next is that suddenly he opens his eyes with a start. He is still holding the bottle of beer in his hand, though it is almost empty now. The sun has risen. The sky is pale blue, with colourful streaks of pink, like a magic show at the circus. The sea fret has disappeared as mysteriously as it arose, and the sea all around them is bright and sparkling, as though sprinkled with sapphires and rubies. A brisk wind has covered the sea with dancing silver waves.

Rosie and Brenda yawn, stretch and rub their eyes.

'Where are we?' murmurs Brenda.

'Italy,' says Rosie. 'In Europe.'

'Oh God,' says Brenda. 'I'm desperate for a pee.'

Rosie opens her mouth to say something else but closes it again.

In about half an hour the sky clouds over and clumpy grey clouds amass with menace on the horizon. The sparkling dawn has disappeared as swiftly as it appeared. A cool wind has started to blow. The sea is getting choppy. After a couple of hours, just as Sid's stomach is beginning to growl with hunger, a flattish island emerges from the waves in front of them; they see scrubby trees and bare low hillocks. But the boat does not stop here; it speeds on, the fisherman staring ahead and guiding it skilfully between partly submerged rocks, biting his lower lip with concentration.

After they have left the island behind, they see the bulky shape of a dark land-mass up ahead, and they pass another fishing boat coming towards them, sitting high in the water. The fisherman switches off the motor, and the boats glide towards each other. The fishermen greet each other like long-lost friends or brothers. Sid can't tell what they are talking about but he guesses from their gestures that it is about them. The man on the other boat turns round and points, and Sid sees beyond the outstretched arm a headland with a jumble of shallow cliffs forming a natural harbour, sheltering a wide white beach. There are no apparent signs of human life, apart from some grey buildings like domed bunkers, set far back from the beach among a grove of trees. As they draw closer into the shore, he sees brown lumps like tree stumps on the sand that appear to be moving; these turn out to be brown fluffy chickens, pecking about among the seaweed. They scatter at the noise of the approaching motor.

When they reach the shallow water, the fisherman cuts the motor, removes his flip-flops and jumps over the side of the boat, grabs the painter, and hauls the boat towards the beach. Then he reaches out a hand, indicating that they too must jump into the sea, which is about thigh deep at this point and very clear, so Sid can see a small shoal of fish darting around near the prow.

Samir and Neptun go first. Without removing any clothing they make quite a splash. Then they beckon to the others. Tonibler puts his hand over his mouth, makes a Native Indian war cry, and leaps.

Samir holds out a hand to the women. 'Vieni, vieni,' he says.

Pattie jumps to catch his hand, also without removing anything. Brenda carefully removes her kitten heels, stows them in her capacious shoulder bag, which she grips under one arm, and then leaps bottom first, holding her polka-dot travel bag above her head with the other hand, making an even bigger splash as her bum hits the water.

'Come on, Rosie Panties. Don't be scared! Just shut your eyes and jump!' Brenda turns round and holds out one hand to Rosie.

Rosie takes off her trainers, tying the laces together and slinging them around her neck, then she reaches for Brenda's outstretched hand and jumps, soaking her jeans and the bottom of her T-shirt.

Sid goes next. Splash! The water is deeper and colder than he thought, soaking him right up to the waist.

Once they have all disembarked, the fisherman clambers back on board, switches on the motor, reverses the boat a few metres, and chugs away. Too late, Rosie realizes that her suitcase is still on board. She swings round and shouts and waves wildly at the boat as it disappears out of sight behind the rocks. Samir fires a few perfunctory shots at it, which don't even penetrate the wood. When Rosie turns back, she finds herself staring into the barrel of his revolver.

'No worry,' says Samir. 'Now you must do what I say, certo. Put up hands in air and walk slow-slow in front of me.

We will go first to special clinic, but you have nothing to fear.'

'Nothing to fear,' Pattie nods and murmurs in assent. 'I know this people.'

A shudder runs through Sid. He remembers what he has read on the internet. Rosie turns her head and catches Brenda's eye, who nods imperceptibly and puts up one hand. The other hand is still gripping her travel bag.

Lifting their knees out of the water, and curling their toes into the sand, they wade towards the shore.

GEORGE: A green Marks and Spencer carrier bag

This is how George next sees Rosie; she is splashing towards him like Amphitrite out of the sea, raising her feet to lift her knees clear of the water, her arms held high, a look of utter panic on her face. Behind her are Brenda and Sid, also splashing. Behind both of them are two gangster types and a boy, waving them forward with handguns, and the sinister blonde woman he knows as Mrs Smith. Out at sea, a fishing boat, similar to the one he and Afrodita came in, is chugging away out of sight. Watching from the shade of a derelict wall about thirty metres back from the beach, George slips out of sight around the corner before the new arrivals can spot him. He races back towards the thatched cottage where Afrodita is sitting in the shade of a chestnut tree beside her mother, holding a dead chicken between her knees, plucking it skilfully and collecting the discarded feathers into a green Marks and Spencer carrier bag, letting the blood from its cut throat drip on to the sand. More chickens, oblivious to the death of their flock-mate, are clucking around them, pecking at the dry ground.

'Quick! The others are here!' George cries. 'Sid, Rosie, Brenda. And that woman called Pattie Smith.'

With squeals of alarm, Afrodita and her mother run indoors, leaving the dead chicken and the bag of feathers. He runs after them, and a dozen or so chickens cluck inside in his wake, before he bars the door. They (the humans, not the chickens) make their way up a ladder to an upper storey under low eaves, where strings of onions and peppers are hung to dry, and peep out through a hole in the thatch.

'Some gangster types seem to have taken them hostage,' George says.

'These are not gangsters,' says Afrodita, 'they are Kosovan Liberation Army. They was classified terrorists, but now they US allies, so you have nothing to fear.'

'I see,' says George.

From his vantage point under the eaves he watches Rosie down below; she pauses and looks around her, as if wondering which way to go. She looks terrified, and George wishes he could call out to her with some words of reassurance but he doesn't want to attract the attention of the bad guys. Despite Afrodita's reassurance, they still look quite like gangsters to him. Brenda, also bare-footed, is standing close to Rosie, hanging on to her travel bag and glancing around nervously at the gunmen. Sid is there too. He looks numb with fear and moves robotically.

'Do not be afraid, dear George. They will be alright. There is nothing to fear at Kashtanje. Sammy Kroçi will not find us here,' whispers Afrodita at his side. 'Everything is changed since Sammy was here last time. We were not in this house. I did not think he would try to follow us to this place.'

George doesn't say anything because his mind is possessed by uncharacteristic self-questioning thoughts, and is going around and around in circles of doubt. Did Afrodita lay the trail for her former lover? Whatever possessed him to think that Afrodita would have the slightest feeling for him? He is not sure of her age, but she looks about the same age as Cassie. Rosie, he knows, frets that Cassie has fallen for an older man, but is Cassie's beau *so* much older? What interest could a young beautiful woman like Afrodita have in an elderly retired schoolteacher? Is she really drawn by his wit, his gentlemanliness, his well-honed seduction techniques, his superior intellect? All these charms worked, once upon a time, on 25-year-old Rosie, but that was many years ago. And then he starts to ask himself what possessed him to give his account number to an unknown woman on the phone in the first place? What madness led him to be so smitten by Afrodita's beauty that he has followed her to a distant corner of the Adriatic, when two lovely mature Yorkshire women, interesting and complex like a vintage wine, are already eager to indulge him? Of course they are not as beautiful as Afrodita, he muses, but they are quite alright, and a lot less dangerous. He is beginning to wish he'd stayed in Totley.

'George,' Afrodita whispers, 'my dear one, if only you will give me your password we will be okay. We will lose some money but we will be free.'

'But . . .' He notices there are traces of blood on her fingers: it must be from the dead chicken. 'But it's my money. I won it in the Kosovan State Lottery.'

'Are you so sure?'

'Who else's could it be?'

'Maybe it belong to Mafia. Maybe it belong to Mrs Petra.'

'The lady with the mobile pet parlour? You must be kidding.'

'Pet parlour business is not real, it is just front for massage business.' She taps the side of her nose and winks. 'She is also Albanian lady. I have known her a long time.'

'Oh yes? How do you know her?'

'She is my bank customer in Sheffield, she tell me she want open short-term bank account in Northern Counties. I think maybe it is to wash money so she no pay tax. I not ask what for. I ask what percentage I get.'

'You gave her my bank account details?'

George is still convinced that the lottery itself and the prize he 'won' must have been genuine. After all, the Money was there, safely settled in his bank account, when he left England. He is certain that if he gives Afrodita his password that's the last he'll see of it, or of her.

'I did not give, I sell.'

George nods in puzzlement, and this is enough to encourage her to continue her strange confession.

'After I come in England for study master's degree I get twenty hours a week job in Northern Counties Bank. I need work to send home some money for my mother, and my tutor give me reference. But I have not forgotten my idea to make one big crime. Now I start to look around for my lucky, and Mrs Petra is my lucky.'

'So you set out to rob her of her ill-gotten gains?'

'Ill-gotten gain? I not understand this word.'

'It means she got the money in a criminal way.'

'I do not see so big difference between criminal and not criminal. There exists many ways to wash criminal money and make it clean. England is big centre for washing money.'

'This is what you did?'

'Of course. In England I study hard and I take part-time job in bank. Night-time I search Dark Web for business opportunity to make more money. In Kosovo our mafia have good contacts with Italian Mafia. In these days sex business is better than drugs business, because penalty is less and profit is more. Mrs Petra is UK partner of sex business.'

'So that's where my account comes in?'

'These mafias need clean account for washing dirty money. Account is only use for very short time, transfer dirty money in, then after one day transfer all money out and close it up. Northern Counties Bank has many old dormant saving accounts of customers who take out all money when interest rate gone down. I sell detail of account to smuggling gangs, they pay me with Bitcoin, and they look after my mother. Usually account owner does not find out. I build up my business this way.'

'That's who you sold my account details to?'

'Forgive me, my dear George.' She smiles apologetically. 'It was too easy to guess your password, my dear George. Millions of people are using "PASSWORD" password. You are too careless.'

'Not any more, I'm not.'

'When I met Mrs Petra first time,' Afrodita continues, 'she was already bank customer and I recognize her name Simic is from my country, but now she change to Pattie Smith. We start to talk. She said she need to open bank account quick for short time, one day only, to pass money through one bank account into another account so owner cannot be trace.'

'So you offered her my bank account?'

'I can see you not using it.' She giggles sweetly, and lowers her eyes. 'She give me ten per cent. Mafia only give me two per cent. She say she got money in massage business. I think she just want to escape tax. But I already sold your bank account with password to KLA mafia who make kidney business in my country. Kroçi is working with KLA to extract kidney for black market. Sometimes they extract kidney from girl before they sell her to massage business. They also wanted to put money in account for very short time.'

'But who did you sell my account to?'

'To both, my dear George. That is my problem. First I sell to KLA mafia for kidney business. I think they have finished their business and I can also sell account again to Mrs Petra. But when I sell her details of this account I did not check that mafia money was took out. That is my big mistake. Now mafia want it back.'

'Oh dear. I see your problem. One bank account, which happens to be mine, and two lots of criminals who are after what is in there. You naughty girl! And now I have changed the password, so all the money is mine.'

She continues with a smile. 'Now I got big problem. Password has been changed by you, dear George. I can no longer give them their money back. I need to get that new password or they will kill me and they will torture you. Better you give me password without torture. What you think, eh?'

'Mhm.'

So that's what she's after, thinks George. Well, he had started to suspect it was not his body she wanted, but nevertheless it is disappointing to find it confirmed so bluntly.

'Please, George, my dear one.' There is a tone of supplication, of obeisance, in her voice that he finds quite arousing and gets his imagination going into overdrive with all kinds of improbable scenarios. In the broken light that filters through the threadbare thatch, the curve of her cheek towards her chin is enchanting, and her sweet voice tinkles like a bell. Unshed tears lend lustre to green eyes that smoulder in the half-light. Perhaps he was foolish to think there could be any mutual desire between them, but his libido has raced ahead of his common sense, as has sometimes happened in the past, though never before on this scale. Men are vain and foolish creatures, he tells himself with an indulgent smile. He has sadly concluded that without money he will no longer be of any interest to her; but so far he still has the money. No one can get it out without his password. Can they?

'We will be together,' her voice continues to tinkle in his ear. 'We will take out half and we will use it to build big modern hotel on Kashtanje to make tourism business, and we both get very rich in short time. Already there is runway here built by KLA. Sammy and Petra Simic can share what money is left after we take out half. They will fight each other, but they will not do bad thing to us.'

'One big crime, the basis of every fortune. Is that it?'

She nods silently.

'Let me think about it,' George replies.

But he has already made up his mind. His poet soul shrinks at the thought of the sheer hassle that will be involved in building and running a hotel with Afrodita. His idea of hotel management has been formed by that old John Cleese programme *Fawlty Towers*, which he used to watch with Rosie, laughing their heads off as everything that could possibly go wrong did go wrong. Now it will be for real, and Afrodita and he will be the unfortunate hoteliers.

Besides, he tells himself loftily, he is not a criminal, and to put a big tourist hotel on Kashtanje also seems a crime against nature that will destroy the wild beauty of this secret place, the equivalent of building a high-rise block of flats on Totley Moor. So many lovely, formerly wild places have been destroyed by the relentless money-making march of tourism. He does not want to be a part of it. He does not voice his reluctance straightaway, he will play for time. Now he just grunts and wiggles his eyebrows in a way that women seem to like. Afrodita giggles and clutches his hand.

He glances at the patch of sky that he can see through the thatch. It has turned as dull and dark as slate, as if someone has suddenly roofed them in, and there is a faint moaning as the brisk breeze grows steadily into a wind that finds its way into the crannies of their hiding place. It feels as though a storm is on its way. Afrodita's mother has gone to round up the chickens, leaving them alone together.

They huddle together in their eyrie under the thatch as the

light turns inky and the wind rises. From time to time they can hear distant voices in another part of the headland. He can make out Rosie's familiar shriek, and a squawking of chickens, then a single gunshot rings out and the echo reverberates for a while around the rocks. Then silence. Then a new sound breaks the silence: the phut-phut-phut of an outboard motor, getting louder as it approaches.

As the wind swirls and gusts from a new direction, they catch the sound of Kroçi's high-pitched laugh, carried in by the wind. Afrodita shivers and George puts his arm around her shoulder.

'Sammy Kroçi believes I already got password from you. He believes I wish to keep money for myself. He will kill me if I do not tell him.'

Can this be true?

'I will protect you, Afrodita,' George says without conviction.

The words are carried away by a gust of wind.

SID: Project Fear

Sid, Brenda and Rosie stumble out of the sea, avoiding the eddies of seaweed which catch at their legs until they are on dry sand. They walk behind Pattie and ahead of Samir, Tonibler and Neptun, who wave them forward with handguns across the wide sandy beach until they reach a belt of shingle. There was a scattering of chickens here when they first came ashore, but most of them seem to have taken fright at the noise of the boat and have headed clucking into the undergrowth around the margin of the bay. Neptun takes a pot-shot at one of the stragglers. Tonibler claps with delight. Sid tries to recall what Samir said about the clinic. This does not seem to be at all the kind of place that would host a clinic. On his left, Rosie and Brenda are still squabbling, this time about who is to blame for delaying Brexit. As if that has any relevance to the situation now, thinks Sid.

He knows he must remain alert, but he feels an overwhelming sense of weariness, partly from exhaustion because he has been travelling non-stop for thirty-six hours, and partly from the angry, noisy wind, the paralysing fear and the feeling of disorientation. He wishes he was at home with Jacquie and the baby and wonders if he will ever see them again. Rosie, who must be feeling tired too, has burst into tears and now releases a torrent of invective against George, whose narcissism and naivety she blames for her plight.

'Oh, chuffin' 'ell, Rosie!' says Brenda. 'This is the wrong time to go snowflake on me.'

'I'm not a snowflake. I'm just tired. And hungry.'

'Here, eat these and shut up!' Brenda shoves a small bag of salted peanuts, filched from the plane, into Rosie's hand. 'Ssh! Listen!'

Rosie munches silently, and takes a sip of the bottled water, which she spits out again. Together they listen. Beyond the sound of the wind rattling the dry leaves, beyond the stormy roar of breaking waves on the rocky coast of the Adriatic, is the phut-phut-phut of a motor. A moment later they hear voices, shrill women's screams, and a burst of gunfire.

'Come on! Don't be scared!' Brenda grabs Rosie by the wrist.

'I'm not scared!' retorts Rosie crossly, but she *is* scared, Sid knows.

'Sometimes you've just got to be brave and say no to the voices of Project Fear! Have confidence!' Brenda laughs.

'Confidence in what?' Rosie mutters sourly. 'I just want to assess the situation, that's all. Don't jump until you can see you're clear of the cowpats, as my mother used to say.'

Out at sea, a tempest is brewing up, crashing the waves on the rocks and lashing the wind-bent trees. A mass of black clouds have blocked out the light from the sky. Rosie lets Brenda pull her along.

Now Sid notices a large yacht, painted in camouflage grey, rocking in the shallower waters beside a sandbank. It must have snuck in behind them. Maybe that was the motor he heard. On second sight, it looks less like a large yacht and more like a small speedboat. Three men in battle fatigues are on the deck, talking and gesticulating animatedly; Pattie cups her hands around her mouth and shouts something at them. One at a time, they jump from the stern into the choppy sea; then three young women, whose hands are tied together with a rope threaded between them, are brought up on to the deck, and another soldier pushes them overboard, while the men in the sea catch the end of the rope and tug them along, so they stumble and splash and scream in the swirling, eddying water, which is sometimes up to their waists, sometimes up to their chins, pulling them off balance. What a pitiful trio, thinks Sid, and wonders what their fate will be. Struggling and staggering, at last they make it on to the beach, where they sit down for a moment, close to tears, their wet clothes clinging to them, before their captors jerk the rope to pull them up and away.

Sid, Rosie and Brenda, along with Tonibler, cower back into the shade of a pair of pine trees and watch open-mouthed as the procession passes only a few metres away, while Samir and Neptun step forward, call out to the women and wolf-whistle, until Pattie puts a finger to her lips and shushes them. The three men drag the women up the beach towards the complex of concrete buildings that sprout like sinister mushrooms among the tall dark trees. This also appears to be where Sid and his fellow-travellers are headed. After a few minutes, the men go back to their boat without the women and disappear below deck.

But now here comes another strange figure; Kroçi, the fake fraud investigator whom Sid once met when he was looking for George, comes scuttling sideways along the sand like an evil crab with a knife in his hand, looking wet and bedraggled.

'Afrodita! Where are you?' Kroçi cups a hand around his mouth and yells into the approaching storm. Only the wind and waves respond.

'What's he on about?' Brenda whispers loudly.

'No idea, Bren,' says Rosie, 'though Afrodita does sound like a pretty name for a girl. Maybe the one George was holding hands with in the police photo? The idiot.'

Uh-oh, thinks Sid. What has poor Dad got himself into now? A love triangle with gangsters? Not a good idea. There is no sign of George, but he thinks he must be here somewhere. Sid wants to break away from Pattie and the gunmen and go in search of his father, but he doesn't feel he can leave his mother and Brenda on their own with this charming lot. Besides, heroism is not really his thing.

Kroçi is walking around on the beach now, his head bowed as if he is looking for something on the sand. After a while he catches sight of the grey boat moored in the bay, and he makes his way carefully down towards the sea to get a better look. When his pointy city-dweller toes are almost at the water's edge, he stops and waves, but just then the motor of the boat springs to life and it phut-phuts away to moor closer to the headland, Kroçi following along on the dry sand and over the headland for a better view.

Samir and Neptun raise their weapons as Kroçi wanders out of sight on to the headland, stumbling on the rough ground when he reaches the rocks; then they return to their main task of marshalling their three captives along the shore to find a path through the wood towards the mushroom buildings half-hidden in a thicket of trees. Though they still have their guns trained on the three captives, they are distracted, chatting to each other and to young Tonibler, with bursts of raucous laughter, as though they are recounting anecdotes. From their hand gestures Sid guesses the anecdotes are about women. A few large warm drops of rain have started to fall, and he can smell a storm approaching.

Hunger, thirst and fatigue are destabilizing him. He is not used to so much travelling, but he tries to maintain a clear head, which is quite difficult as everything is bathed in a mist of unreality, akin to the sea fret that overtook them on the

Adriatic. Day seems to have turned into night. It is now about midday, but the sky is deeply overcast, black with storm clouds, and a sinister warm wind rips in circles around the bay. Just as they reach the biggest of the mushroom-like buildings, a jagged flash of lightning illuminates the sky, and a crack of thunder crashes, almost simultaneously, above their heads. The heavy clouds release their downpour.

They make a dash for the door.

SID: *Thank you for your donation*

Inside, the largest concrete mushroom-type building does indeed look and smell like a primitive clinic – a strong smell of disinfectant covers a scent that is sweetish and slightly putrid. The shallow-domed walls and ceiling are painted white, the grey concrete showing through where the paint is too thin. A faulty neon strip light buzzes on the ceiling and there is a row of orange plastic chairs along one wall, where Samir gestures to them to sit. With much scraping of chair legs, all seven of them sit down. Brenda stows her polka-dot travel bag under an empty chair.

The three young women they saw earlier on the beach are already here, dripping wet, their clothes clinging to them, slumped in three plastic chairs, apparently drugged or fast asleep. Now he can get a better look at them, Sid sees they are dark haired, pretty and very young – maybe in their late teens. What are they doing here? They do not look at all in good shape. Sid's heartbeat quickens with pity at their plight. This situation does not bode well for the girls, nor for the rest of them. Neptun goes up to get a closer look, and brushes the hair back from the face of the girl nearest to them. Samir shouts something at him, and they both giggle like schoolboys.

Leading off this central space that serves as a waiting room are several closed doors, giving the waiting room a closed-off, claustrophobic feel. Sid scans them, looking for a potential escape route. Through a small closed window in the far wall they all watch the progress of the storm, the flurries of rain, the great trees tossing their branches, the wind howling and moaning and sometimes dropping to a menacing whisper before a new violent outburst. It seems to Sid as though all of nature is in torment.

Behind one of the closed doors Sid hears a sound of groaning and coughing, then a soft woman's voice repeating something apparently soothing, and a clatter of instruments. He listens, his pulse beating with terror. Suddenly there is a louder clang of metal on metal, as though an instrument has been dropped into a metal container, and then the door opens wide. Inside is a primitive operating theatre, with a raised bloodstained bed on which a groaning, writhing figure is lying, face down, under a powerful overhead light. Into the waiting room steps a small wizened man in green surgical scrubs and a blood-stained apron, wearing wire-rimmed glasses, behind which bulge watery blue eyes. One eyelid droops.

'Welcome! Welcome to Kashtanje clinical centre! My name is Dr Zaj, clinical director! Soon you will all have opportunity to make donation to help glorious Kosovo Liberation Army!' He holds out his arms in greeting to them. Sid notices that he has a slight tremor in his hands. 'Welcome to the patrona, Mrs Simic, who helps us to complete this important work!' He bows towards Pattie. 'You are very welcome, lady.'

Neptun says with a grin, 'Afterwards you will sleep soundly. You will have only small scar on back for souvenir when you leave here, but you will feel and remember nothing. We thank you in advance for your donation.'

Dr Zaj retreats into the operating room, closing the door behind him.

'What donation?' asks Rosie in a shocked whisper.

'Kidney,' whispers Tonibler.

Sid feels an urge to vomit, but swallows it down. His fists are clenched tight, his nails cutting pink crescents of fear into his palms. He looks around at the doors again, trying to suss out an escape route.

Then the operating room door flies open again, and a trolley-stretcher draped in a bloodstained sheet is trundled out by a short man in a light blue uniform. On it lies a big man with a mass of frizzy ginger curls, wearing only underpants and what looks like an old school tie around his neck, but no shirt. He is so pale that he appears to be totally drained of blood beneath his freckled skin. He is still groaning horribly.

Dr Zaj tuts and shushes him. 'No need for such drama, my friend! All will be well! Try to sleep. Pain is only temporary. We little bit short of anaesthetic,' he explains to those in the waiting room. '*Nyet problema!* Anaesthetic is not necessary – it causes dependency in patients. They recover more quickly without. But first you must take some refreshment. Erblina!' He snaps his fingers and returns to the operating room.

An overweight woman in a nurse's uniform with a fancy beribboned headdress, crisp and white with many folds like the sails of a galleon, floats up with a stainless-steel tray carrying a flat, sticky white cake cut into slices. Three slices are already missing, and there are three glasses of a cloudy tea-coloured liquid. She hands them around to Sid, Brenda and Rosie with a little bow. Sid notices that there is a bloodstained thumb print on the side of his glass.

'Drink!'

Eagerly Sid takes the cake and the glass of liquid. He is famished and thirsty after the journey, but something tells him not to consume them. He sniffs.

'Drink!' whispers Neptun. 'Is better for you.'

He takes a bite of the cake, but does not swallow. His throat is scratchy and dry, and he feels a great urge to sip the liquid, but manages to spit it out silently, so it dribbles down his chin. Brenda takes a sip of her glass of brownish tea. Sid lunges forward to stop her and accidentally knocks his mother's cup to the ground.

The nurse Erblina says, 'No matter. I will get more.'

She disappears into a side room, a separate but linked dome-mushroom which seems to be kitted out as a kitchen. The short blue-uniformed man brings an empty trolley, on to which the first of the three comatose women is lifted; then she is wheeled away to the operating room. Through the open door, Sid catches a glimpse of her being undressed unceremoniously and lifted clumsily on to the operating bed beneath the dazzling light by Dr Zaj and the little blue-uniformed man. Dr Zaj, with his back turned to them, goes to wash his hands in a steel basin in the corner. Then the other man closes the door with a click.

As Sid listens to the crying behind the closed door, his ears pick up another sound that seems to come from outside, gusted in on snatches of wind. It is a man's voice, calling, 'Afrodita, where are you?' He listens intently, but he cannot tell whether or not it is his father's voice.

A sudden gust of wind rattles the building and flings open the door to the operating room, where to his horror the girl is lying naked on the bed, face down, shaking and whimpering. The nurse steps forward with a syringe and re-covers her with the bloodstained sheet that has slipped on to the floor. Dr Zaj is still washing his hands in the basin, rubbing them together and twisting them around and around under the running water.

'Oh my God! We'd better help them get out!' cries Brenda in

a horrified whisper. Her head, which was drooping before –
from the sip of liquid pre-med in the tea – jerks up. 'Come on,
Sid! Come on, Rosie!'

'Careful, Bren. They're probably foreign,' Rosie replies with
a smirk of malice. 'You might catch diseases off them.'

'Stop trying to be clever, Rosie Panties. This is serious.'

Rosie flicks her hair back and pokes out her tongue, then
laughs triumphantly as though she has scored a hit.

'Sssh!' Samir admonishes, and levels his weapon at them.

GEORGE: Steady and slow-burning

From their hiding place beneath the ragged onion-smelling thatch, George hears the shrill call of Kroçi, and he observes somewhat clinically Afrodita's heightened responsiveness, a fresh flush in her cheeks, a bright alertness in her eyes. He realizes, even if she does not realize it herself, that she is still partly in love with the fake fraud investigator, more than with him, George. But she will try to fake amorous intent at least until she has wormed his password out of him. Well, he can still outsmart her. He has the trump card, the password. Or does he? His brain has been whipped by the wind into a swirling golden fuzz, like Afrodita's hair.

As the afternoon wears on, he notices that the mother has been gone for quite a while. She went out to lock up the chickens from the approaching storm, leaving the two of them alone on the upper floor of a rickety wooden dwelling that seems to be held together by a giant tree that loops through the flimsy structure with its mighty branches. Now's my chance, he thinks. How lovely she is, with that pensive look in her eyes, her prominent cheekbones, her hair wind-tousled like spun gold. He reaches out his hand and touches it. But Afrodita does not respond. She smooths her hair. She is still preoccupied with Kroçi.

'Afrodita, where are you?' Kroçi calls. The words are carried in on a sudden gust of wind, faint but unmistakeable.

'He call to me, dear George,' whispers Afrodita, shrinking back into the shadows at the sound of Kroçi's voice.

'Sshh!' he whispers back. 'He won't find us here.'

Sid, Brenda and Rosie, he has observed, are not with Kroçi but with some other guys – maybe they were never with him at all, or maybe they got away, though he doubts they can escape from the headland in this storm. There is no overland route, Afrodita told him. The only way to arrive and leave here is by sea or by air. They must still be somewhere on Kashtanje.

A woman's voice down below startles him. He looks down through the thatch, expecting to see Rosie or Brenda, but instead he sees the grey-raincoated self-styled fraud investigator Mrs Smith, who visited him in his flat in Totley with her sex-mad dog.

'Who is this woman, Afrodita?' he asks.

Afrodita peers down through the fringe of the thatch.

'That is Petra Simic, Mrs Pattie Smith in English,' she whispers. 'She is also wanting password from your account. Her money is in there.' She turns towards him and takes his hand. 'Please, George, tell me password. You can trust me. You know I love you.'

The trouble is, George realizes, he does not trust her, not one bit, especially after her confession, but he is too much of a gentleman to say it aloud. Moreover, he's quite sure she does not love him, and he acknowledges that although he desires her and longs to hold her in his arms, and kiss that soft curving cheek, that strawberry mouth, it may not amount to love. Does he love her? Is love not something steady and slow-burning, like the feeling for Rosie that has grown quietly in him over thirty-five years, quite distinct from this sudden eruption of aching passion? Where does this desire with its passionate urgency spring from? It has led him into some tricky situations, but never before one as tricky as this.

When he doesn't reply, lost as he is in thought, she pleads again.

'Please, I will give you whatever you like, my dear George.' She lays a hand on his knee, and lets it stray upwards, finger by finger, towards his crotch. He feels a rush of pleasure accompanied by a rush of shame. This is kind of creepy. Creepy but tempting.

Then all of a sudden, coming from the opposite direction, he hears a new sound – a woman's long, anguished scream. Rosie? Brenda? His heart thumps and seems to stop. Now, from his thatched hiding place, he sees Kroçi coming into view in the clearing in front of the cottage, but he is not alone; he is with someone, a slight, grey-haired woman dressed in black with a red headscarf. He is holding her, dragging her along by one arm as she cries out and struggles to free herself. It is Afrodita's mother. Kroçi has a knife and is holding it to her throat, barking words in a strange language. She falls silent for a moment, then lets flow a torrent of words in which he thinks he hears Afrodita's name.

Beside him, Afrodita stiffens. 'He got my mother. He will kill her. I must go to him.'

'Don't go, Afrodita. Stay with me. Do not fear for your mother.'

'He hate my mother. It is because of her I not marry with him.' Tears spring into Afrodita's eyes. Her lower lip is twitching. 'Please, George. Just give me your password, then I will return. I know Sammy; he believe I got your password already, but I am keeping it for myself, because I want keep all money for myself. If I tell him password, he will not harm us.'

George's heart races with a panic-driven pulse. Now Kroçi has Afrodita's mother as a hostage, the whole situation is getting desperate. A new obsessive thought has begun to trouble him. Did Afrodita tell Kroçi they were coming here and invite him to follow them? Has she set it all up, or is her mother really in danger? He struggles to remember his password. What was the unforgettable sentence Sid said to him?

'I am George Pantis and I am seventy-nine years old.'

'That is too long for password.'

'No, just the first letter of each word. That's the new password.'

'Say password again.'

'I am George Pantis and I am seventy-nine years old.'

'But you tell me you have a new birthday, you are age eighty.'

But did he change it again in the run-up to his birthday? He honestly can't remember.

'Okay, eighty then.'

'Are you sure? I must be right or he will kill me.'

Did he in fact change his password after he spoke to Sid? Or did he only intend to? And did he use upper case or lower case? Or just upper case for the initials of his name? Doesn't it have too many digits for a password? So which digit is superfluous? How can he have forgotten? He used the password every evening at home when he visited the Money in his account. And should the computer or George himself forget, it is written down on a Post-it note stuck to his monitor at home. A lot has happened since then. The harder he tries to force himself to recollect, the more confused he becomes. If he puts it out of his mind and stops trying to force it, the memory will surely float back, as memories do. Otherwise, he'll just have to wait until he gets home and finds that Post-it note.

'You might have to try them both.'

'Okay, my dear George. I thank you.'

Afrodita kisses him lingeringly on the lips. Her lips taste of secrecy and forest chestnuts. His heart zips into overdrive. He reaches out a hand to touch her thigh as she makes her way down the rickety wooden ladder.

SID: Something lumpy inside

The big hairy man on the stretcher groans, stirs, and then his groan unwinds into a long, quivering sob of pain.

'Aargh! Am I still alive? I knew I should never have come here to work with these barbarians,' he moans. He has a slight Scottish accent.

Sid gets up and lays a hand on his arm. The big hairy man winces and groans again. His eyes are still closed and his teeth are clenched. The waistband of his underpants is soaked with blood. 'Don't touch me. I'm a dead man!'

'No, you're not. You'll live,' says Sid, trying to recall Jacquie's brisk voice when she rebukes his bouts of hypochondria.

Will he ever see Jacquie again? The thought of Jacquie waiting for him at home only underlines the hopelessness of his present situation.

'Who are you? What are you doing here?' Sid asks him.

'Angus Aberdeen. Aargh! United Nations Special Envoy! We try to do a humanitarian intervention on their behalf, we bring them law, democracy, civilization, and they steal our body parts, bloody criminal bastards!'

'Shut up mouth!' snarls Pattie.

A faint bell rings in the deep cave of Sid's mind – where has he heard that ludicrous name before?

Behind the closed doors, the young woman on the operating table screams for help, and starts howling a word that sounds a bit like 'Mummy' over and over; then at last she goes silent. Sid's hair is standing on end. There is something raw and primitive about the cry, which takes Sid time-travelling straight back to an incident in his childhood, when he fell off his bike and cut his head and blubbered wildly while Rosie cradled him in her soft arms and murmured words of comfort until he was silent.

'Ah! They must have put the needle in at last,' Angus gasps at the girl's sudden silence. 'But they've not got much morphine left, so they're trying to spin it out. You only get a fractional dose. The drug smugglers haven't arrived yet, because of the storm. They bring the morphine when they come, and they take away the harvested kidneys in a refrigerated container on their speedboat. Big global market for stolen kidneys. Transplant tourism. They're in competition with China and Brazil. Petra takes care of the girls, she exports them to England, minus a kidney.' He groans again. 'You'll be lucky if there's enough morphine left for you when it comes to your turn.'

'I don't intend to go under the knife,' Sid replies in a whisper through clenched teeth. 'I'm just pretending to be drowsy.'

'Neither did I,' moans Angus. 'Better take the pre-meds. It may be all you'll get.'

Rosie and Brenda are shivering and holding hands, wide-eyed with terror. Brenda reaches towards the comatose girls on the chairs and slaps their cheeks with her palms to try and wake them up, but Samir fires a warning shot at the far wall, and she sits down abruptly. Almost at the same moment, an almighty thunderclap and a flash of lightning crack overhead like an explosion of fireworks, causing the lights to flicker wildly. The neon strip light in the waiting room flickers once or twice, then dies for good. In the operating room, the mighty overhead light is dead. Soon the room is plunged into near-darkness, as though Samir has shot out the light with a single bullet.

Dr Zaj rushes into the waiting room. In his right hand is a scalpel. In his left hand is a stainless-steel dish brimming with blood and something lumpy inside.

'What is happen? Electricity kaput!' he cries, wiping the blade on his apron. 'I cannot operate now! Kidney refrigeration kaput!'

The fat nurse also stomps in, wiping her hands on her apron. Another flash of lightning reveals, through the open door, the young girl lying, face down, naked on the operating table, her arms dangling helplessly beside her, a green jewel glittering on a ring on her middle finger that they forgot to remove; Sid gasps. Until now the whole adventure has seemed bathed in a mist of unreality, but the girl's plight brings home to him sharply that he must do something. But what?

Sid is not normally the heroic type, but he realizes that it is up to him to rescue her, and himself. This is his chance, his now-or-never moment, the moment when he will discover what sort of guy he is. Reluctantly, the knowledge dawns on him that if he is ever to get out of this place and see Jacquie again, he is going to have to make it happen himself. His heart is beating hard, his mouth is dry, his palms are moist. He is paralysed with indecision.

Then a song from Ee-You and the Ramonas floats into his head. It seems like a memory from another life, the life he was once on course for with Jacquie and the baby, and it galvanizes him into action.

> Oh brother listen to my song!
> When you see that something's wrong,
> You don't have to try
> To be silent and strong!
> Na! Na! Na! Na!

Then comes a great gut-stirring guitar riff that he used to try to imitate. There are different versions he knows, with a slight variation in the lyrics, by Angela and the Muttis, and the Blue-Eyed Barnier Boy.

He hasn't got his guitar, of course, but he can vocalize. Crouching low, with a resounding yell, 'Yaaah!' he gives Angus's trolley a mighty shove so it careers crazily across the room and bashes into the knees of the seated gunmen. Angus tries to sit up, then decides to lie down flat. Sid hears their shouts and the clatter of a gun falling to the ground. A round of shots from the other gun sprays randomly around the room, but the bullets bounce harmlessly off the chairs and trolley. Only Dr Zaj is hit in the leg, and he staggers once, then falls to the ground, dropping the stainless-steel dish which hits the ground with a bell-like clang. A dark bloody lump of something pulpy slithers across the floor. Sid stares in horror, wondering – is this what human kidneys look like?

Another flash of lightning reveals a bold female figure in mock-crocodile kitten heels, shoving the boy Tonibler away with some force and throwing herself down on top of the gun that's on the ground. She snatches it up, levelling it at Samir, and yelling, 'Stick 'em up! Samir, you heard what I said! Up! Drop your gun!'

To Sid's amazement, he does throw it on the floor. Pattie and Tonibler make a dive for it, but Rosie is nearer and gets there first. She picks it up, gripping it in both hands to examine it, pointing the barrel at herself, at Sid, at Brenda, at Pattie. She has no idea that a loaded gun may go off if handled incorrectly.

Sid grabs it from her. 'Give that here, Mum!'

He points it at Pattie, Neptun and Samir, just like they do in the movies. The precise, compact weight of the gun in his hands gives him a heady feeling of confidence and boldness. All at once he feels like a different tough-guy version of himself, in a different movie. Not Sensible Sid any more, but Brave and Decisive Sid. Neptun, gunless, grins and raises his palms; his bristly lips part, showing big strong teeth. A gold medallion of the Virgin Mary hangs around his neck.

Tonibler begins in a chatty tone, 'One day, I will come in England to work wit girls. I will get plenty rich. Zis girls already got plenty English passport. Shtolen from tourists. I speaking good English, yes?'

Brenda tuts and shakes her head. Rosie starts to say something, but thinks better of it. She kneels down and slaps the two dozy young women who are still in the waiting room, until they regain consciousness.

'Wake up! Wake up! We must get away from here quick!'

The fat nurse Erblina waddles over to help Dr Zaj, who is sitting on the floor, trying to staunch the blood that spurts from his leg with a wodge of gauze bandages. Dr Zaj howls, 'Ai, ai, ai!' and yells something in which Sid catches just the word 'morphine'.

The nurse Erblina snaps, 'No! Morphine all finish!'

There is another double flash of lightning, thunder crashes close by, and everything seems to happen all at once. Suddenly the door of the waiting room bursts open and three guys toting revolvers, wearing black leather jackets and bad haircuts, bounce in, legs akimbo. Their heads are soaked with rain, and rain drips off their jackets. They're wearing shades, and it's a wonder they can see anything through the dark lenses, but they fire off a few shots randomly just to show they mean business. One of them hits Dr Zaj in the other leg. He yells curses and writhes on the ground again. They don't seem to notice that Brenda and Sid are armed and the other gangsters have been disarmed, because it's so dark in the waiting room. Sid is too confused to draw attention to himself by challenging them. He guesses from the fact that they all talk to each other in bad English that they are from all over the world, that this is a global operation and English is the only common language they have. They nod companionably to Samir, Neptun and Tonibler, who starts to shout some kind of warning but is cut off by another thunderclap. Then the first one declares, 'Geroin is arrive. Come quick, Erblina!'

'Oh, thanks be to God!' The fat nurse Erblina jumps up and runs to the door with surprising nimbleness, shouting, 'Come, Miki!'

The blue-uniformed male nurse emerges from the operating room. They follow the gangsters, leaving Dr Zaj writhing on the floor.

On the way out, the first gunman asks Erblina, 'You got girls?'

'Three,' answers Erblina.

'Good, our team in London is waiting,' he says. 'You give them geroin now, they not causing no problem after.'

'Come on, love! Wake up! We gotta go!' says Rosie, pulling on the arm of one of the sleepy girls, waiting their turn to be operated on, after the nurses and gunmen have gone out into the rain. 'Take your chance to get away while you can. C'mon, Bren. C'mon, Sid. Help me!'

'You go for it, Rosie! Sid and I'd better stay here, to guard these dangerous criminals.' Brenda throws Sid a meaningful look.

He realizes that she has decided it's up to them to stay behind and keep Samir, Neptun, Tonibler, Pattie and Dr Zaj covered until Rosie and the two girls can get away. Then they have to rescue Angus and the naked, unconscious girl on the operating table, before Dr Zaj can recover sufficiently to take out her kidney.

With a yell and a heroic flourish of a clenched fist, Rosie pulls the sleepy, sedated girls on the plastic chairs towards the door, and out into the storm and lashing rain.

A few minutes later, coming from outside, they hear the sound of men's voices raised in altercation and one, two, three gunshots. The door crashes open. In staggers George, clutching a wounded hand, surrounded by a bevy of frenzied chickens.

GEORGE: *The Big Bad Wolf*

George waits for Afrodita after she climbs down the ladder in answer to Kroçi's call, but she and her mother seem to have disappeared with him and show no sign of returning. George has no idea where they have gone. Should he go and look for them? But, he thinks, Kroçi is young and armed with a knife and he, George, is neither young nor armed. Besides, what will he do when he finds them? Maybe when the storm has passed, then I'll go and look for them, George resolves.

Having decided to do nothing just yet, he relaxes a little. He wishes he could fall asleep like that, in his rain-soaked clothes, but his baseball cap has gone, his back is sore, his neck is horribly cricked, his stomach is growling with hunger – but at least he is alive. He stretches his arms above his head, breathes in deeply and listens. There is no sound, apart from the surging of the waves. The shrieks, the gunshot all seem like faraway bad dreams.

Soon he will find Rosie and take her back to Sheffield, and everything will be alright again. He will look up his password on the Post-it note on his computer screen, withdraw some money, buy a better sports car, and set off on a world tour with her. Yes, okay, he'll buy something nice for Brenda, too. He will give Afrodita and her mother some money to replace any chickens that have blown away and build a new cottage out of bricks, with proper plumbing. Okay, maybe even a modest hotel. Nothing too fancy.

His head is full of such benign fancies as the storm continues to rage, making the chestnut trees dance in a frenzy, bending the tallest pine trees almost horizontal and once or twice pulling their roots out of the soil, which is just a shallow peaty layer overlaying the stony ground. The whole structure of his precarious shelter shudders with its force. Only the roots and branches of the mighty chestnut tree hold it together.

Suddenly a violent gust snatches up the flimsy thatched roof and tosses it about until it is all broken up, the reeds whipped up into a fountain of straw, then it is tossed up in the air again and scattered across the ground. After the wind come wet gushes of fat raindrops that soak his clothes. Jagged giant legs of lightning stride across the sky.

Feeling both scared and exhilarated by the storm, he descends the rickety ladder and goes in search of something to eat. No one is around in the cottage. Pots and pans are scattered around, but he can't tell whether it's from the storm or from human action – after all, he has observed over the years that Rosie's kitchen often looks as though a storm has hit it. The reeds from the thatched roof are strewn about on the floor and on the ground outside, but apart from that the cottage is intact.

'Afrodita? Where are you?' he calls, but there is no reply.

In an overturned enamel pot, he finds some cold cooked chestnuts, which he wolfs down. They settle into his belly comfortingly, like porridge. He washes them down with a swig of brackish water from a plastic bottle. There are plenty of eggs, but he has no way of cooking them, and he is not desperate enough to eat them raw. He scrapes out the remains of the chestnuts and scatters them on to the ground for the chickens, who peck them up gratefully, and follow him, still pecking, as he nips behind the nearest tree for a pee. There he finds his baseball cap and pulls it down hard over his brow.

'Watch out, little brown hens!' he shouts out loud to the

chickens. 'The Big Bad Wolf is on the prowl.' They cluck companionably and shake their feathers. Then he sets off towards the beach, with his chicken entourage, in search of some human life – Sid, Rosie, Brenda, Mrs Smith, Afrodita, her mother and Kroçi. They must all be here somewhere; but where are they hiding? The small wild headland with its plantation of chestnut trees and its silvery beach is not large enough to conceal such a lot of people.

A couple of hundred metres away across the bay, in the shade of a group of trees, is the wall he was hiding behind when he first saw Rosie splashing ashore, and beyond that a cluster of grey dome-roofed buildings that have darkened in the rain and have a sinister air, like toadstools that have sprouted up overnight, or alien spacecraft. Afrodita pointed them out to him when they first arrived, and said they were now a clinic with their own landing strip. Followed by his clucking entourage, he makes his way in that direction.

When he is just about there, he encounters a fat woman in a strange ribbon headdress coming down the opposite way, with a wizened little man in a blue tunic, and three mafia types in shades and black jackets.

'Hi!' He raises his hand in greeting. 'I'm George.'

'Hi, George!' says one of the black-jacket guys, and points his gun and shoots him in the hand. Ow! It's not a deep hit, more of a skin graze on his little finger, like a kind of warning greeting, but it still stings like hell.

'Was that necessary?' he yells. It seems like just bad manners but, to be on the safe side, he throws himself on the floor.

The gangster takes some pot-shots at George's chicken followers. Then he puts his gun back in its holster, and the gangsters and nurses continue their stroll down towards the beach.

George writhes on the ground, clutching his ears, and wishes he was at home in cosy, predictable Sheffield, where he could pop in and ask Dr Khan to take a look at his finger. Not that one is often shot, in the hand or elsewhere, in Sheffield. He misses his family, he misses the comfortable and only-slightly-smelly home he used to share with his wife Rosie. He wishes he could hold Cassie in his arms – not the stiff, bossy Cassie of today but the sad-eyed ginger-haired twelve-year-old Cassie. He misses Sid – Sensible Sid – who would surely soon think of a way out of this dire situation. Will he ever see any of them again?

What a relief it is to open the first door of the complex of grey buildings and find Sid sitting there.

SID: Women can be mean

'Hi, Dad!'

The last thing Sid expected was for his father to burst in surrounded by chickens. If anything, Sid was expecting his mother to come back with the two girls she was trying to rescue. He fears they may not get far if they encounter Erblina, Miki and the gangsters. The other girl, as well as Angus, are still in the 'clinic'. They look like they are in deep shit. Well actually, Dr Zaj doesn't look too good either, but Sid reckons it serves him right. Pattie looks nervous but unharmed. Samir, Neptun and Tonibler look as cool as a glass of iced beer.

'Come and join us.'

'Hello, Sid. What a wonderful surprise to find *you* here! What's going on in here, Sid?'

'Oh, a bit of this and that. Kidney removal, mainly. And a bit of sex trade. And drug trafficking, weather permitting. Don't worry, Dad, nothing we can't handle,' Sid, the new heroic Sid, chuckles drily. Then he notices the bloodstain on his father's hand. 'Are you hurt, Dad?'

'It's superficial. Just a bit of a graze on my little finger. Is Rosie here?'

'She escaped a few minutes ago. But Brenda's still here.'

The girl in the operating room has started to groan and shiver. Brenda has gone in to comfort her, leaving Sid alone to guard Samir, Neptun, Tonibler, Pattie and Dr Zaj.

'You okay, pet?' Brenda asks the girl, who lets out a string of stuttering words in a foreign language.

214

'No understandee,' declares Brenda loudly. 'You gotta speakee English.'

The girl falls silent.

Brenda waves her gun-free hand towards George and says, 'Hi, George. Welcome to the madhouse. There's all sorts going on here today. We've got the whole bloody United Nations. Jabber, jabber, jabber. Totally incomprehensible. Make yourself at home, pet.'

'Hi, Brenda,' says George in a faint voice. He walks into the 'operating room' and gives her a peck on the cheek. Sid can tell by the way he's looking at it that he is unnerved by her gun. 'Just because you can't understand it, that doesn't make it incomprehensible, you know.'

He is still a know-all, thinks Sid. In spite of what he has gone through, he hasn't learnt a thing.

Brenda doesn't say anything but her cheeks are flushed and her eyes bright with excitement as she raises her gun. Turning his head to follow the line of her gaze towards the door, Sid sees a group of figures standing there, silhouetted against the light from the open door. They are the three gunmen from the boat, the fat nurse Erblina, and the wizened blue-uniformed male nurse called Miki. Except that the gunmen are not carrying guns; like Erblina and Miki, they are staggering under the weight of huge, heavy holdalls.

'It is too far from beach to carry!' groans one no-gun gunman, plonking down his holdall in the doorway.

'Zis drog much heavy,' groans the other.

'Come. Stop moaning. Bring geroin.' Erblina leads them into the side kitchen and lights the propane gas stove, which explodes into life.

From behind the closed door, Sid hears all kinds of clattering and expletives. The first gunman, the pushy one, opens the door and says, 'Erblina, now show me girls.'

Erblina indicates the drowsy girl still awaiting her surgery on the operating table, who has had no actual morphine yet.

'Here is she. I don't know where is others. Maybe gone toilet.'

'You must give them morphine now,' says the second no-gun gunman. 'Then they quiet not making trouble. We can take jar of kidneys you have prepared.'

Erblina nods, loads the syringe, and advances on the girl in the operating room.

But suddenly Angus yells out, 'Over here first! I've already been cut, and the pain is killing me! I need morphine!' He lurches from his stretcher-trolley.

Erblina sticks the hypodermic into a vein in his arm and Angus breathes a huge sigh of relief. He rolls on his back, and the syringe falls with a clatter on to the floor. Miki picks it up and prepares it again, this time for the girl.

The no-gun gunmen shout, 'Stop!' and raise their gunless hands menacingly, but Brenda struts out of the operating room and waves Samir's gun at them, barking commands, 'Go! Sit!' She directs them to sit beside Pattie, Neptun, Samir and Tonibler on the orange plastic seats in the waiting room. The two lots of baddies nod sheepishly in acknowledgement of each other, and mutter what seem to be unfriendly remarks about Brenda. They are evidently not used to being bossed about by women.

'Nyet problema. I will get more morphine for girl.' Miki goes into the kitchen, and a few minutes later Erblina comes out with another syringe, advancing towards the girl who is waiting on the operating table to have her kidney cut out. But Dr Zaj is out of action.

'Here, please, Erblina! Me too!' he groans from the waiting-room floor, clutching his wounded leg.

Erblina turns on him. 'Shut up, you no-good parazeete. I seen you feeling little titties of young girls on operating bed.'

Tonibler puts his hand over his mouth and giggles.

'Heff pity, Erblina!' The doctor holds out an arm that is surprisingly muscular.

'God will heff pity!' She sticks a needle into his vein.

Too late, he realizes that there is nothing but air in it. She gives him a kick.

'You shut up and die,' she says. Then she turns to Sid and says, as if by way of explanation, 'This Dr Zaj is my no-good husband.'

The doctor screams, gurgles, twitches for several minutes, then goes still. Erblina kicks him into life again, and sits down to watch his suffering. Her eyes meet and hold his defeated gaze with a smile of satisfaction. Women can be mean. Not Jacquie, of course.

After about an hour has passed, the rain falls vertically instead of horizontally, in large round drops. The storm has started to abate, and the branches of the trees wave with less agitation. The girl on the operating table and Angus on the trolley have started to come round.

'Mu . . . mu . . . mu . . . !' moans the girl.

'After you come in London you will get plenty morphine,' Erblina tells the girl.

The no-gun gunmen and Pattie nod with enthusiasm.

'I come wit?' pipes up Tonibler eagerly, his rosy young cheeks dimpling with anticipation. 'I help you. I like zis type of work.'

The others throw back their heads and laugh until their tears roll. 'Ha! Ha! Ha! Hahahahaha!'

While they are helpless with laughter, Sid decides it is the time to make a move. Brenda catches his eye, nods discreetly and winks at George. Keeping the bad guys covered with their weapons, Brenda, George and Sid back slowly, slowly towards the door, then Sid eases the door open and holds it while the others slip outside. Brenda has kept her gun, but manages also to retrieve her polka-dot travel bag from under the chair. When Brenda, George, five strangely subdued chickens, the drowsy, slouchy girl (who has covered herself in a white coat) and Angus (who has managed to heave himself up on to his feet and stagger) have all let themselves out through the door, Sid follows.

Once they are all outside, and the door swings shut behind them, he stops still for a moment to assess the situation. How far away is the beach? he wonders. It can't be too long before the others try to get back to their boat, he reckons. To discourage them from thoughts of following, he fires off a round of shots at the base of the closed door. At the sound of gunfire, the poor traumatized chickens squawk and flap their wings as they skirt around the bodies of their fallen cluck-mates on the ground outside the clinic. The humans stare at the chicken carnage and bow their heads.

They have emerged into an altered landscape. All around is evidence of the devastation caused by the storm. The concrete mushroom buildings themselves are intact – they seem as though they were built to survive a nuclear blast – but broken vegetation is scattered everywhere, tangled with bits of litter and other assorted debris from the sea. Two great trees along the path have been uprooted, and a pole carrying the electricity cable to the clinic is on the ground. They pick their way over and around it.

At last, when Sid, Brenda and George are out of sight of the clinic, Sid turns round and starts to walk forwards, fast as he can, towards the sea, stumbling through the debris and fallen branches. Though he tries to look confident for George's sake, and Brenda's, he is filled with apprehension. How will they escape from Kashtanje? How will they find Rosie and the other two girls?

GEORGE: Union Jack shorts

George, who has never before thought of Sid as the heroic type, is impressed by the way his son has managed to get him and Brenda, and two drugged-up strangers, and even some chickens, away from that sinister toadstool-like building and on to a track towards the sea. Where did he learn such resourcefulness? He looks at his son with a new respect. The wind has dropped now, and the treetops are only swaying lightly. There is no sound, apart from the gentle surge of the surf, and a low sun lightens the sky, with pale clouds sprinkled like rose petals on a Wedgwood blue porcelain plate.

He's given up on Afrodita. His passionate feelings for her, if they ever amounted to love, have vanished like a dream when morning comes, like the afternoon storm that has suddenly evaporated into this benignly still early evening air. He looks back on that all-consuming delirium, that storm of passion, with a kind of puzzlement. Where did all those intense feelings so suddenly spring from? And where did they vanish to? Would he and Afrodita have been great together? He will never know, and neither will she. Does he feel regret? Just a tinge. Then again, George tells himself indulgently, if we never did things that we later regret, we would pass through life like sleepwalkers and experience nothing in the journey. He wishes her no ill, but he sees now that he is not the man she desires. He supposes that she, her mother and Kroçi are here somewhere on Kashtanje. But for now, all he needs is to find Rosie and bring her back to Sheffield, where the Money will surely be waiting for them. He cups his hands around his mouth and calls her name. Sid orders him to shut up, but he takes no notice.

'Rosie, where are you?' he yells.

There is more evidence of the storm's force as they approach the sea. Great mounds of seaweed have been torn out of the water and gathered up in a dark churning mass under the surface, or heaped in mounds on the sand, and a mighty gnarled tree trunk has been tossed up on to the beach, as if by a petulant giant. At the water's edge is a scene so gruesome that it strikes horror in George's heart. The spume is tinted with garish flecks of pink. A body is lying there, face down, half submerged in the water, rolling casually with the surf. Tresses of long golden hair drift on the current. A wave turns the body, revealing a horrible gash widening across the throat through which the blood is leaching out into the salty water. A single flip-flop is bobbing in the waves a few metres away. A shoal of little grey fishes is darting around it. Two brown chickens, also dead, bob up and down on the waves nearby.

'Afrodita?' he cries, and with an anguished scream he runs into the water. Then he stops in his tracks and stares. It is a body for sure, but it is not Afrodita. It is a man – apparently a young dark-skinned man, maybe an African, naked but for a pair of Union Jack shorts. The body is broken up, as though it has been pounded and mangled in the sea for quite some time – one arm is missing, torn off at the shoulder, and one leg is torn off at the knee. What he mistook for long hair is seaweed that rises and falls with the waves. A victim of the storm. Or a victim of circumstances? How long has he been in the water? Where did he come from? How did he get here? A story of crime, politics or passion? Whichever, some stories have truly terrible endings, to be avoided at all costs. He bows his head.

'Dad, calm down; it's terrible, but it's not Afrodita,' says Sensible Sid. 'Don't make so much noise, Dad. We're still in earshot of the clinic. We've got to get away from here.'

George looks around and catches sight of three figures further along the beach, perching on an upturned rubber boat. As he draws close, he recognizes Rosie, her face buried in her hands, rocking with grief and shock. With her are two pretty dark-haired young women, their cheeks also bathed in tears. But he can see at once that neither of them is Afrodita.

'George!' Rosie cries, jumping up and wrapping her arms around him. 'George! You bloody idiot. Thank God you're safe! I've been so worried about you!' She chokes back a sob in her voice. 'I love you.'

'I love you too, Rosie. I don't know what came over me. I'm sorry.'

One of the young women stands up, revealing a lithe slender figure clad in shorts and a tight T-shirt. She grasps George's hands in her firm young hands and looks into his eyes. 'You are husband?'

An Afrodita moment comes over him, but he steels himself, and simply says, 'Mhm.'

'Did you see that body in the water, George?' moans Rosie, wiping a tear from her eye. 'What's the world coming to? How will it all end?'

'Is it someone you know?' he asks flatly, to mask his relief at having found her.

'We're all part of the same human family, George, aren't we? The human race is destroying itself!' She sniffles, clasping her hands in a wringing movement. 'George, what on earth is that thing you've got on your head?'

'Oh, this is just an old baseball cap.'

'Look at him! Such a lovely young man! No older than Sid! He lost one of his shoes!'

She starts to weep again. George bites back his irritation. There she goes again, taking on the agony of the world, he thinks. No wonder she and Brenda clash. Of course Rosie can't help it; it's part of what makes her nice. Part of what drew him to her in the first place was her all-embracing niceness. But it can get wearing.

Brenda has followed him along the beach, and is standing looking at the drowned boy with her lips pursed, a sphinx-like expression on her face, then she glances up at weeping Rosie, but she doesn't say anything, she just takes a clean tissue out of her bag and dabs her eyes, then hands one to Rosie.

'How the hell are we going to get back to Sheffield?' George says in a neutral tone, to defuse the tension.

In the same moment, Sid is there beside them, hugging Rosie in his arms.

'Hey, Mum, don't cry. It'll be alright now.'

She sniffles on shamelessly while Sid consoles her, thinking she's crying with relief because of finding George, and maybe she is. Then Sid heaves the rubber dinghy over, revealing two handguns like nesting birds curled together on the sand. George grabs one, and one of the pretty girls grabs the other, winks and says something he doesn't understand that ends in a grunt of unmistakeable satisfaction.

'I think this boat must be theirs. The bigger boat is moored over there, away from the rocks.' Sid points out to sea at a sleek grey speedboat moored some three hundred metres away. 'Come on. Quick! We haven't got much time! We've got to reach it before they do. I hope we can get this thing going. They're coming after us!'

They drag the rubber dinghy over to the water's edge and

into the surf. Sid holds it steady while the rest of them wade in up to their thighs and scramble on board. Someone carries Brenda's travel bag. The semi-comatose young man from the clinic, smacked into consciousness by the cold water, stretches out a hand and introduces himself to George. 'Angus Aberdeen. United Nations. Special Envoy.' The three pretty girls start to chatter among themselves in an unfamiliar language, and they pass the five flapping chickens from hand to hand, until they are all on board and perch, clucking with content-ment, in the bow – a brown feathery chattery posse. Brenda covers their retreat with her weapon; when it comes to her turn to get on board she tosses the gun into the boat first, then flings herself, face down, on to one inflated side of the rubber dinghy. As they pull her arms, she scrabbles to heave herself on board, one leg at a time, losing one of her mock-crocodile kitten-heel shoes, which floats away on the water to bob up and down peacefully beside the flip-flop of the drowned man.

Angus Aberdeen yanks the cord to get the outboard motor going and the little dinghy chugs away from the shore. Just in time. The six bad guys, Petra and the two nurses break out of the woodland and run down on to the beach. 'Stop! Stop! Stop!' They jump up and down in the eddies of water and yell, but they are too late. The dinghy phut-phuts steadily towards the speedboat.

Over to their right George sees a kayak-type boat coming fast around the headland. Two slight bent-over figures are wielding the paddles furiously, without looking up. As it gets closer he sees the kayak is heaped high with a strange brown cargo which appears to be writhing and moving. As their paths cross, he recognizes Afrodita and her mother, and the kayak, he can see, is loaded and piled high with plump brown chickens, which are trying to perch on the edge of the boat but keep sliding down into its interior, then trying to clamber up again with much flapping of wings.

'Hi, Afrodita!' he waves and yells, but she and her mother do not slacken their paddling to wave back. A moment later George sees why – Kroçi has joined the other bad guys and Petra on the beach. They run into the water in pursuit, but when they are waist-deep they give up. George takes a pot-shot at them with the handgun he found on the beach, but it doesn't go off. Rosie squeezes his hand consolingly. One of the pretty young women aims at the bad guys on the beach, but they are out of range by the time she has worked out how to release the safety catch.

As they approach the waiting speedboat, they see there is an iron ladder leading down into the water. Sid seizes it and hangs on to it while they all climb up. The Scotsman Angus pulls himself up and takes charge at this point. He has an air of command, even though he is wearing nothing but an old school tie and bloodstained underpants, and has a horrible fresh irregular scar on his back.

'All aboard? Let's go!' he shouts.

There is a floor hatch leading down some steps, and in a cabin they find a couple of young guys in shades and quasi-military uniforms playing cards and smoking in a corner. Angus and Sid grab them unceremoniously by their collars, drag them upstairs and push them overboard, while they are still within reach of the shore. The two swim like crazy towards the headland about fifty metres away. Angus also finds a spare quasi-military outfit down there, hidden under a bench. It is a couple of sizes too small and absurdly short in the leg, but once he's squeezed himself into it, his voice sounds more Scottish, thinks George, and there's no shutting him up.

'Guys, this is a known drrug-rrunner vessel, so we have to

be careful,' he says. 'The anti-mafia police will be looking out for us up and down the coast; on the other hand, they may have been paid off to turn a blind eye. So we may get away with it. In my opinion, we should head for the little port of Vohurr, which is just a few miles north, up the coast from Kashtanje, and then catch a regular ferry to Bari in Italy, like tourists. Once we're back in the EU we'll be safe, subject to international law.'

'I don't understand.' Brenda challenges him with a flirtatious wink. 'I thought we were in Europe now.'

'We are now in Albania, which is in Europe geographically but not in the EU, though it has applied for EU accession, but it still has some criteria to fulfil. So you see we are not now in EU territory,' Angus replies with exemplary patience, given the pain he must be in. 'Albania is a lovely country, but these people, these drug lords and their hangers-on, they're what is holding Albania back; they trade drugs into the cities of Europe, and innocent country girls from all over Eastern Europe into the European sex trade. Now they've started diversifying into fresh body parts for the burgeoning private clinic transplant industry. It's a growing business, with demand far outstripping supply. Each fresh kidney fetches nearly half a million dollars. And if they do get caught, the penalties are less severe than for drug trafficking. We sent in a United Nations taskforce to put a stop to it, but they've all disappeared except me. And I'll be lucky if I make it back to England.'

'That's where we're headed,' says Sid in tetchy voice. 'Now shut up and navigate.'

SID: *We don't know yet what's true or false*

Angus is beginning to get on Sid's wick, with his pretentious know-all public-school drawl, laced with a touch of faux Scottish, not to mention the way he has taken over Sid's role as leader of the group. In fact, he reminds Sid a bit of Cassie's beau, Ivor. But it is also quite a relief that he has taken charge. Sid was finding the hero role hard to keep up, especially with his mum and dad watching so proudly.

Angus navigates the speedboat up the coast, always keeping within sight of land. It is a wild, rocky, well-wooded coast, with small silver beaches, and little scatterings of dwellings poised at the water's edge. They get to Vohur as the sun is going down. There the three girls vanish without a trace; they don't even say thank you or goodbye. Sid can't help worrying, and hopes they'll be okay after their ordeal. They have each taken a chicken.

Angus says, 'Dinna worry. They know how to look after themselves, girls like that.'

Girls like what? How the hell does he know? thinks Sid.

They book into a family room in Vohur's only hotel, a quaint brick-and-stone building overlooking the harbour, with peeling aquamarine paint on the ceiling and rose-trellis-patterned wallpaper. They devour a bland, fishy supper washed down with strange, sour rosé wine on the hotel's outdoor terrace where all the single males in town appear to have congregated to smoke, drink and have noisy arguments. Everybody ignores them when they stand up and say goodnight before heading upstairs to bed. Brenda and Rosie share the double bed, but they lie back to back and don't cuddle, though they have obviously grown to like each other; George and Angus get the two singles; Sid squeezes into the cot, with the side down and his feet hanging over the edge; their two remaining chickens roost on George's bedhead.

Early in the morning, they queue to board an ancient open ferry across to Italy, which Brenda pays for with some euros left over from the Canaries holiday. The ferry is crowded with head-scarved women, men pushing motorbikes, and Italian tourists. There are lots of chickens, including their two which they sur-reptitiously manage to leave behind. Someone will eventually adopt them. Brenda, who gathered up everyone's passports into her polka-dot bag after going through Passport Control in Rome, now hands them round as they approach Customs again. They are only slightly damp. Angus doesn't have a passport, but claims to have been robbed and beaten up. He whips up his shirt to show his jagged scar to the officer, who faints at the sight. Another officer averts his eyes and waves him through.

In Bari, which is a little way up the coast from Brindisi, Angus and George visit a tourist clinic. George insists on get-ting a sticking plaster for his wounded finger and they bond over details of their suffering. Their wounds are dressed without the weary medic asking how they were acquired – assuming, being tourists, their injuries must be in some way related to drunkenness. She gives them some painkillers, and discharges them. While Angus is still being cleaned up and bandaged, George and Sid hit the town and buy him a loose colourful shirt, some more underpants and shin-length shorts. He looks absurd, but normal for a tourist, Sid thinks, with a touch of satisfaction. Brenda and Rosie, meanwhile, set off to find some food for their journey back.

As Bari is on the same rail line to Rome as Brindisi, they catch the same train back to Rome. It seems a much longer and prettier ride in daytime, along the coast and across the mountains, when they can sit back, devour the view and their picnic of bread and salami and tomatoes, which Brenda and Rosie bought in Bari. Sid remembers with a shudder their journey into the dark unknown, and feels a twinge of gratitude that they are all alive.

From Rome they get a taxi to the airport and manage to get seats on two separate flights to Gatwick, in the course of which they gain an hour. At Gatwick they meet up again and get a train that goes directly from Gatwick to St Pancras station. Angus decides to tag along with them, saying it is ten years since he left the UK. He doesn't have anywhere else to go because his parents were already dead when he left, and everyone else thinks he is dead, and he doesn't want to create shock waves by appearing, suddenly resurrected.

There, in St Pancras, gloriously decked out in red-brick Gothic under a splendid glass-and-iron dome, they change for the train up to Sheffield. It seems to Sid unbelievably expensive; almost as much as the flight from Rome.

So, have they got away with it? he wonders.

Some things have changed irrevocably. It feels like he is coming back to a different country, even though they have only been gone for just over a weekend. England seems poorer and grubbier than he remembers it. In his mind's eye, London is still a great capital, a bastion of wealth, progress and civilization, a place where he could never afford to live, but his physical eyes see litter blowing about everywhere in the streets and on the tube, free newspapers full of near-naked women blowing in the gutter, discarded drinks cans and fast-food containers, and the people look overweight, poorly dressed and pasty-faced. Can things have changed so much in a few days? He phones Jacquie from the train.

'Oh, Sid! It's great you're back. I was so worried about you. I've missed you.'

She has missed him? Isn't he the lucky one? His eyes mist up, he doesn't know why, and his throat suddenly feels sticky, as though full of honey, as it often does when he struggles for tender words. He has so much to tell her, he starts arranging his recollections in his head while they are still vivid, but already they are slipping away into the past.

'I missed you too. How's the baby?'

'The baby's well and kicking. I had a check-up today. Everything's okay. Due date mid-March. They've still got questions about my right to be in the UK after Brexit, but at least the baby will be a British citizen. But listen, Sid, I've applied for a transfer from Leeds to Sheffield.'

'That would be so great! Do you think it'll happen?'

'We'll talk about it later. I'll meet you at the station. I'll tell Cassie you're back, and see if she can come and meet you too!' The train goes into a tunnel and they lose the connection.

The journey from London to Sheffield takes two hours, during which they all drink tea, munch shortbread and madeira cake, and piece together their story from its many different fragments, but everybody has a different take on it, and it soon acquires a dreamlike aura, as though it is a patchwork, an embroidered story, a magic fable, not something that really happened at all. Sid keeps catching sight of Brenda giving his father little sideways 'look-at-me' glances and fluffing up her hair, but George is reading the *Guardian* and doesn't seem to notice. Rosie notices, but just sniffs and acts superior.

It is not long before Brenda and Rosie are quarrelling again.

They start off talking about the drowned man, and of course that leads right on to immigration and that leads on to Brexit. George tries to make peace by wiggling his eyebrows.

Then Brenda starts talking about the way she disarmed the gunmen.

'Oh, shut up, Brenda! It was Sid that disarmed them,' says Rosie. 'You just make things up that suit you. Like Brexit. Like we're going to manufacture goods and export them to the whole wide world. Like that fake hair conditioner you gave me.'

'That hair conditioner? It wasn't fake. Maybe you put it on wrong. Just like you believe the establishment experts that say everything's going to go wrong for the British economy once we leave Europe. It's called Project Fear. Anyway, what's that got to do with the gunmen?'

'Well, for a start, the gunmen were genuinely scary and the fake hair conditioner genuinely removed my hair. It wasn't just "Project Fear", as you call it. You just make up a version of the story that puts you in a good light.'

'But it's true, isn't it? Sid?'

He goes red – funny, that's not how he remembers it at all, but he wants to keep out of this argument.

He realizes that the differences between Rosie and Brenda are irreconcilable because the differences are not about the 'facts'. It's because they're different people with different upbringings, different experiences, different outlooks on life and different ideas of what's right and wrong. No amount of information, true or false, is going to alter that.

'We don't know yet what's true or false. Only time will tell,' he mumbles. They both nod in agreement and George wiggles his eyebrows.

SID: An object of desire

The train judders to a final halt and passengers start to reach down their luggage from the overhead racks and sidle towards the doors. Sid feels a great sense of unburdening – he is glad to be back in safe and predictable Sheffield again, after the horror and trauma of the last few days. They have been through so much, it feels as if they've been away much longer – an entire lifetime, in fact. They have all changed, and some of the changes are undoubtedly for the better. Sid cannot put his finger on what has changed in him – on the outside he still looks like the same owlish and slightly plump guy, but on the inside he feels more confident and decisive, if also softer and more weepy. How is that possible? Look at the way he weaponized that trolley by bashing into the knees of the gunmen – he did it, didn't he? Not Brenda? And then he led the escape by dinghy from the beach. It's as though being strong has allowed him to be soft at the same time, like toilet paper.

But the main change has been between George and Rosie. They seem to have got back together again, and they are acting all lovey-dovey like he hasn't seen them in years, though the strange thing is that now Rosie seems to have taken over control in the relationship from George. He wonders, how did that happen? They don't seem to talk about Brexit any more, which is still dragging on tediously. It no longer seems very important.

As the train pulls into Sheffield station, a broad radiant beam, like sunshine chasing away clouds, sweeps across his father's face. He reaches out his arms, grips Rosie's shoulders, pulls her forward and kisses her. She stiffens momentarily at the contact with his unshaven scratchiness. But she evidently hasn't forgotten the days of the Che Guevara moustache. Even at eighty, his father is still a very good-looking man.

Jacquie and Cassie are there to meet them at the station as they disembark. He folds his arms around Jacquie tenderly, then takes her sweet earnest face between his hands to kiss her, and he feels an unfamiliar prickling sensation behind his eyes. Strange how his recently discovered 'hero' self is prone to weepiness, he thinks, blotting his eyes on his sleeve. Cassie, who can also be prickly but in a different way, hangs back with a pout on her face as if wondering why no one is paying her much attention, until his parents enfold her in a three-some hug.

Standing just behind Cassie and Jacquie is another bloke he doesn't recognize, a squat, muscular, ugly bloke who introduces himself as Gerrard Snifton. When she sees him, Brenda goes scarlet, fluffs up her hair and makes a little kissy-kissy pout with her lips, like she recently did at George.

'Sniffer! What brings you here?' she squeaks.

Mr Snifton, aka Sniffer, explains that he bumped into Cassie in the Ponderosa Park; she was walking Heidi and he was looking after Pattie's dog. The dogs started chasing each other and playing together, and Cassie and Sniffer recognized each other from when they had lived next door to each other. 'She told me you were coming back. I hope you don't mind me coming to meet you, flower.' He leans forward to give Brenda a peck on the cheek.

Brenda flings her arms around him and kisses him unrestrainedly on the mouth. 'Oh, Sniffer, I've missed you so much!'

'Me too, flower.'

She begins to blub, and unzips her spotted shoulder bag, which matches her spotted travel bag, and hands around a packet of tissues. Only George and Angus hang back, shy and dry-eyed. A week ago, Sid realizes, he would have been among the dry-eyed, but times are changing fast and he has changed too.

He goes over to give Cassie a big hug, and she starts to cry without inhibition. Angus, he notices, can't stop himself from staring, which Sid supposes must be the effect of the long, red-gold hair. He spots his mother looking at Angus, and he can tell at once what she is thinking: she is thinking about fixing up a date for them, as is her wont. She dislikes Ivor almost as much as Sid does, and she hasn't yet realized that Angus can be just as pedantic.

Sid makes perfunctory introductions.

'Hey, Cassie. This is Angus. Angus, this is my little sister, Cassie.'

Angus stares intently at the flaming hair, and at the carved flower-clip that pins it back from her forehead.

'Is that an ivory hairclip you're wearing in your hair?'

'It's only plastic? It's fake ivory?' Cassie bleats.

'Just as bad,' admonishes Angus. 'It encourages poaching by giving out a false message of ivory as a luxury product. An object of desire, if you like,' he adds.

'Desire?' Cassie murmurs. She takes off the offending clip and silently sticks it in her pocket.

Why? This is so out of character for Cassie.

Sniffer has brought his car to the station multi-storey – it is a massive, unashamedly manly black 4x4 with bull bars at the front and a dog grille behind the back seats. They all pile into it with their luggage. Brenda sits up in front with Sniffer and Cassie. As she clambers in, Brenda wiggles her bum and gives

George another of those fleeting sideways 'look-at-me' glances. Maybe she can't help it, maybe it's just an instinctive gesture, thinks Sid. He guesses she won't be trying to split his parents up now she's got Sniffer to keep her occupied.

Rosie throws Brenda a mean look and sits herself ostentatiously upon George's knee in the back. George still has a beatific look on his face, and his expression doesn't change. Jacquie and Sid nestle up close, to allow more space for Angus. Angus stinks, really bad, and has gone a nasty greyish colour. Heidi and Pattie's dog, Max, snuggle up behind the dog grille in the back.

As they cruise through the familiar streets, Sid thinks how lucky he is to have made it back to Sheffield, how great it is to be here, even in autumn, when the trees, what remains of them after the Council's decimation, are turning gold and a thin sleety rain is bringing down the remaining leaves and making the pavements slippery. He looks happily sideways out of the tinted window as the familiar places slip past like images on a screen, murmuring the names of his favourite haunts.

Jacquie tells Angus his wound is probably infected, that's why he stinks, so on the way home they make a detour up to the Hallamshire Hospital to get him checked out. The admissions team tut-tut over his wound in horror and decide to keep him in.

SID: *Organic*

Over the next few days, Angus's bedside becomes a site of pilgrimage and confession.

Sid goes down to the hospital at two o'clock the next day, and greets Angus with a handshake, like men do. Angus is sitting upright in his neatly tucked-in hospital bed, looking perky, and cracking pleasantries in a broad Scottish accent with the bustling nurses who are tucking him in, in spite of the tubes that are dripping fluids into him and out of him.

'I suppose I'll be seeing much more of you, now you've taken a shine to my little sister,' says Sid.

The Scotsman chuckles. 'How did you guess, mate? Is it so obvious?'

'Have you got friends and family you want me to contact for you now you're in hospital?' asks Sid. 'A girlfriend?'

'I've been gone for ten years, and everybody thought I was dead when the KLA captured me. Well, I nearly was. I managed to escape but before I could get back they recaptured me. My girlfriend mourned me and then got on with her life, I suppose. I haven't heard from her. There doesn't seem any point in showing up now. I may as well make a fresh start.' He grabs Sid by the hand. 'Tell me about Cassie.'

Sid winces at the force of the man's grip. He's going to have to get used to the idea of this big hairy mouthy man with his faux Scottish accent as his sister's new boyfriend. Still, he's better than Ivor. Before he has more than a minute to give this scenario much thought, Cassie comes in and gives Angus a kiss on the brow, then plonks a bunch of grapes, still in their brown paper bag, in the plastic bowl on his bedside table. It is the same bowl which the nurses use for soiled swabs and dressings (though it is empty now).

'Organic,' she says.

'Thanks, hen,' says Angus.

There must have been some intimacy between them already. He doesn't realize yet, thinks Sid, that Cassie doesn't usually consider anyone apart from herself. He smiles to himself. The Scotsman has met his match.

ROSIE: Comfort and joy

Rosie takes the bus from home into central Sheffield next day after lunch, intending to do a bit of shopping. How safe, dull and humdrum it all seems.

She is relieved to be back in Sheffield, and relieved that this folly of George's seems to be over at last. He hasn't apologized yet, or admitted he was in the wrong, and she is not going to press him. He's told her he is moving back in, and she has decided to give the house a bit of a make-over for this new phase of their lives together, having experienced the luxurious modernity of the Bitch's bathroom, and sunk her toes into the thick pile of the Bitch's bedroom carpet. (Okay, so Brenda did not actually invite her to visit her bedroom, but she left the door open, didn't she? And Rosie was curious to see where it had all happened.) Anyway, she's made up her mind to have a scout around the shops now, to see what is available. Shopping has never been a big thing for her, apart from food – she enjoys shopping for something to eat for the whole family.

But the shock of coming back from the Adriatic to autumnal Sheffield has made her realize that, even more than a new carpet, she needs a new coat to see her through the coming winter. Usually, this might have been a cue to hit the charity shops, but now that George has won all this money, which Brenda seems not to know about, she thinks to herself, why wait? She has decided to look around in Coles, aka John Lewis.

The window displays of the department stores in town glitter with promises of comfort and joy, and in the store itself there is a purposeful bustle of people getting their shopping done in good time for the scarcity that Brexit will surely bring. Outside in the street, the shops, especially the bargain shops, are busy.

The students are back and the centre of town is filled with bewildered-looking Chinese youngsters wandering around looking for the ingredients of delicious meals that will remind them of home, not all this foreign muck. Rosie smiles benignly at them.

But behind the bright lights and glitter, the town centre seems bleak and shabby. Eddies of dead leaves and litter swirl in on a gusty autumn wind and settle between the market stalls on the Moor. Bodies huddled in sleeping bags are already bundled up and bedded down in the doorways of closed-down shops. As soon as the sun goes down, the cold will draw in, maybe even a frost.

At the top of the Moor she hears a brass quartet playing the mournful strains of Gresford, and the banner of the Corton-wood Colliery Band sags sadly between its two poles behind the musicians. When the song is finished the former once-proud miners rattle a miner's helmet at the passing shoppers for change. Cortonwood was the first pit to close, in 1984, and in their street they held weekly collections for the miners and their families when they went out on strike. Now they collect for the local food bank.

Thinking of this pricks her bubble of pleasure at the new coat she has just bought, and puts her in a pensive mood. Has she been too extravagant, when so many go without? Well, at least the Bitch won't get it. Brenda seems to have surrendered any claim on George's lottery win, if she ever even knew about it. Rosie pulls the new coat tighter around her, hunches her shoulders against the wind and sticks her hands deep into the silky lining of the pockets, then she makes her way to the bus stop to catch the bus home, intending to walk from there to the hospital.

Twenty minutes before the end of visiting time, Rosie waltzes into Angus's side room in her new expensive coat, a startling shade of scarlet, exquisitely soft to the touch, snug around her shoulders. She is holding a bunch of dahlias and some stems of white laurel in her hand. Sid and Cassie are already there.

'Angus! How are you?' She leans over to give him a kiss on the cheek.

'Ouch! Mrs Pantis, don't press so hard!'

She shifts her weight and sits down on one of the two bed-side chairs, smoothing her coat beneath her as she sits. 'Sorry. Is that better? These are from my garden. Actually, the white laurel is from a bush in the Bitch's garden, but she won't miss it. She isn't tuned in to the rhythms of Nature. Is there a vase I can put them in, Angus?'

Cassie jumps up. 'I'll go find one, Mum?' She wanders off, and Angus follows her with his eyes.

'I thought you and Brenda had made up, Mum,' Sid says.

'You don't understand women, Sid,' she replies. 'We have and we haven't. But she's still a Bitch, isn't she? Anyway, George has decided he's moving back home with me. I don't know how to break the news to the Bitch.'

'I don't suppose Brenda will mind, Mum. She seems to be besotted with Sniffer.'

Rosie frowns. 'You think this is just an insignificant female spat, Sid, between two women over a man. But it goes much deeper than that. You don't realize the way the country's changed, the way everyone has become angry and intolerant. Rival tribes are getting ready to slaughter each other. Only

240

Brenda thinks it'll all be over soon and everything will go back to normal.'

'You don't think that?' Angus chimes in.

'No, I do not. Whatever goes right or wrong afterwards, there will always be someone – immigrants and elites or saboteurs – left to take the blame, so it will never be completely over.'

'Don't be so gloomy, Mum,' Sid says. 'Won't we have a laugh about it?'

'There'll be nothing to laugh about. We'll be reduced to eating home-grown cabbages and wormy potatoes, without even a nice glass of red wine to wash them down with. But we won't talk about it, because we're British. Like our marriage breakup, the Brexit fallout will be buried in a deep pit, and we'll just not mention it again. Once George has moved back home, I'll never talk about his dalliance with Brenda.'

SID: Welcome back to the real world

Sid feels a hit of pure unalloyed joy when Rosie announces that George is moving back home, like he used to feel when he was a little boy, when he never doubted his parents' constancy, before they started arguing. He studies his mother's face for clues as she talks, framed by the scarlet collar of her new coat. One of them must have given way on something, but what? Maybe he'll never find out. Everything will be back to normal, leaving him and Jacquie free at last to embark on their own family life, their own adventure, without having to worry about their parents! He sees no signs that George and Rosie will ever resolve their differences about Brexit – and, to be honest, they no longer seem to care very much. They have fallen in love all over again.

He has plenty of other things to worry about – some jobs-worth at the hospital in Leeds is questioning Jacquie's right to be here after Brexit, despite her commitment to the NHS, making her confused and tearful, and Sid keeps wanting to tell her it probably doesn't matter as they'll probably get married. But he hasn't actually asked her yet. He's still taking in the good news about his parents. He wonders, does Cassie know yet? How will she take it? Surely they are both too old and too cool to be affected by the amorous toing and froing of their parents.

Cassie has been gone a while, looking for that vase.

Rosie glances at her watch and smooths her coat. 'George will be here any minute. He's a bit late. He's coming straight from Totley, where he went to pick up some stuff. I just wanted to grab a few words with you first, Sid.'

'Grab away.'

'George is in a foul mood. He says he's lost a Post-it note. Just imagine, after all we've been through, and he gets upset about a Post-it note.'

At that moment, George walks in through the double doors, a grim scowl on his face.

Sid notices how deeply wrinkled his father is around the eyes, like that old fisherman on the Adriatic; he looks as though he has caught the sun recently on the crown of his head, which looks oddly out of place in autumnal Sheffield. But he still holds himself upright, and his eyes, although superficially bloodshot, have a fiery blackness in their depths. He embraces Sid warmly, and Sid remembers, or maybe he's never really forgotten, how much he loves his father. Tears well up in his eyes and he tries to keep them from brimming over. Something weird has happened to him recently – he feels blubby nearly all the time.

'Hey, George! Good to see you!' croaks Angus from the bed, reaching out his hand to shake George's. 'How's the finger?' He doesn't seem to have any such blubby problems.

'Oh, it's better now.' George waves his revitalized finger. 'You look great, Angus.'

'Yes. I feel kind of great. Apart from my vital organs.'

'Don't worry about that. No one looks at your back. And you can live without one kidney.' George sits down on the other bedside chair, so he is facing Rosie across the bed. 'Rosie, light of my life, there was a Post-it note stuck on the monitor of my computer in Totley, which had an important code on it.'

'What code?'

'Well, if you must know, it was the password to my bank

account. The one with the winnings from the Kosovan State Lottery in it.'

She sniffs and bites her lower lip. 'I remember now. I put it in the pocket of my jeans.'

'So you must still have it?'

'They were the jeans I wore in Albania, when I was trying to rescue you from your idiocy!' Rosie's voice is raised but under control. 'They got soaked when I jumped off the boat into the sea.'

'Did I ask you to rescue me? Did I ask you to follow me to Albania? I was happy. I was in control of my life for once!' George's voice is querulous, whiney.

'You call that being in control of your life?' Rosie snaps. 'You were under the control of your libido and your greed. You're lucky you got off so lightly, thanks to me, George. Well, now you've come crashing down to earth. Welcome back to the real world.'

'But maybe the code survived?' There is a forlorn note of hope in his voice.

'Surely you must remember it yourself? Or are you getting senile, George?'

'No need to get nasty, Rosie. Haven't you still got it somewhere?'

'When I got back I had to put those jeans through the wash. They were filthy. They had splatters of blood on them.'

'Oh, Rosie! You didn't! How could you?' He buries his face in his hands.

'Don't be upset with *me*, George. I had no idea what it was. I thought it was a clue to where you'd vanished to. Well, it *was* a clue, in a way. Anyway, it was never really your money, was it? We don't need it.'

'But it was there in my account. I looked at it every day. It was my . . . my freedom, my dream, my escape route . . .' George's eyes have filled with tears.

'You don't need an escape route, George, you've got me,' she says in a cold voice. 'And besides, Sunil said you would never be able to withdraw that amount of money unless you could prove how you acquired it.'

George turns to Sid with a desperate look on his face. 'Can't you remember it, Sid? It was you that made it up. It was the first words of a sentence. Some letters in upper case, some in lower case, I can't remember which. I remember it included my name and a number, my age at the time. Seventy-nine. Or eighty.'

'Sorry, Dad.' Sid searches his memory and shrugs helplessly.

Just then there are sharp footsteps outside. The door to Angus's hospital side room flies open with a bang, and in stomps Brenda on a new pair of faux leopard-skin kitten heels, accompanied by a strong waft of flowery perfume. She is wearing dark glasses and a floaty faux leopard-skin scarf is wrapped around her neck. She embraces George, grips Rosie by the shoulders and pecks her cheeks, waving brightly varnished fingers at Sid. Then she leans over and kisses Angus carefully. Her dark glasses slide down her nose as she does so, and Sid notices she has a black eye, the bruise spreading downwards in streaks of yellow and purple on to her cheek. Rosie notices too.

'How are you, Angus pet?' Brenda asks.

'Rright as rrabbits in the rrain.' Angus rolls his 'r's perkily, as if to emphasize his Scottishness.

What a pillock, Sid thinks.

'What happened to your eye, Bren?' Rosie asks.

'Oh, you know what Sniffer's like. Very physical. Well, I've discovered I can be very physical too. You should have seen the shiner I gave him. We're back together, but he's not going to be in control any more. I've changed since we've been away.'

She goes off to fetch another chair from outside, which she carries with a self-confident bounciness that reminds Sid of the way she handled the gun, and sits down beside his mother, then blows a kiss across the bed to his father, who responds by wiggling his eyebrows.

His mother scowls. 'Where *is* Sniffer?' she asks.

'They wouldn't let him bring the dog in, so he started shouting at them. They called Security, who chucked him out. He's waiting in the car in the car park. Here, he bought you these, Angus.'

She pulls an enormous showy box of chocolates out of a Thornton's bag and hands it to Angus. There is a picture of a wild, unspoilt silver crescent beach, fringed by palm trees, on the lid, and it is tied around with two gold ribbons.

Rosie says, 'Come on, then, Brenda. Aren't you going to pass them around?'

'That's up to Angus. They're his chocolates. That beach picture on the box looks so nice. Like Paradise.' She chortles. 'If only they knew! Blood everywhere!'

'Please help yourselves,' Angus says, very politely.

Sid passes on the first round. He needs to watch his weight, and once he starts with chocolates, he finds it hard to stop until the box is all finished – unlike Jacquie, who can take them or leave them. No doubt that's why he has love handles, and she doesn't.

'Nice coat, Rosie,' says Brenda. 'Is it cashmere?'

'Mhm.'

'Must have cost a bob or two.'

His mother nods, lowers her head, and starts to rummage in both layers of the chocolates. No doubt she is looking for

Turkish delight, which is her absolute favourite. There are three: she sticks them in her mouth all at once, then passes the box across the bed to George.

'Come on, darling, I know you have a sweet tooth; they're wasted on Sid. He's so sensible when it comes to food.'

'Can't he speak for himself?' snaps Brenda.

'I must be off.' George sniffs the air, as if sensing trouble brewing between Rosie and Brenda, and not wanting to be there when it blows up, even though he is the probable cause. He helps himself to a chocolate and stands up. 'Got to look for that code. I must have written it down somewhere else before I put it on the Post-it note. Bye, Angus, hope you feel better soon. Bye, Sid. Take it easy, son.' He ambles out.

Brenda follows him with her eyes, then turns to Sid and asks, 'What code?'

While he is wondering what to say, Rosie interrupts, 'I've no idea. I think it's something to do with his computer.'

Brenda looks at Rosie and then at Sid, with a questioning arch of the eyebrows, as if she doesn't know about the lost bank password and the money George has in the bank – or if she does, she is not letting on. Her face, behind the dark glasses, is inscrutable.

Rosie takes another chocolate and passes Brenda the box. Brenda also takes one or two more. The top layer is all gone now, and neither Angus nor Sid have had a single one yet. The two women are both silent for a moment, their jaws moving meditatively, like cattle.

Then Brenda breaks the silence. She suddenly says to Rosie, 'I don't know what's got into your Cassie. She was out in your garden today shooting at a squirrel with a bow and arrows.'

'She's got it in for that squirrel,' says Rosie, picking absent-mindedly at the lower layer of chocolates.

Angus says in his hyper-Scottish drawl, 'She told me this morrrning she believes it's morrrally wrrrong to eat something you haven't killed yourself.'

'Really?' Brenda looks shocked. Discreetly she spits the chocolate in her mouth out into a tissue.

'I don't think that includes chocolate, Brenda. I mean, chocolate isn't alive, is it?' says Rosie.

'Well, it isn't dead,' says Brenda. 'She's got some funny ideas, your Cassie. I expect she gets them from Gwyneth Paltrow.'

'More likely, from Ivor,' says Rosie.

'Who's Ivor?' asks Angus.

'Oh, just a little jumped-up nobody that used to be Cassie's guru,' Sid replies.

Angus leans back on the pillows with a small satisfied smile.

SID: A bit of an arse

Cassie, who has been gone about twenty minutes, returns at last with a vase and a prim look on her face, as though she guesses they have been talking about her. 'Sorry, it took a while? There were loads of dead flowers left in the vases? So I had to go and find a compost heap?' she says.

Angus nods approvingly. Rosie fills the vase with water from Angus's bedside jug, arranges the dahlias and the white laurel in it, and puts it down on his bedside table. Brenda does not notice that the white laurel is from her garden.

After the visiting time is over, and the other three visitors have gone their separate ways – George back to Totley, Rosie back to Crookesmoor to finish measuring up for her make-over, Brenda to wander around the car park looking for Sniffer – Sid and Cassie slope off for a coffee. The hospital cafeteria seems to have soaked up so many people's anxiety and misery into its intestine-coloured walls over the years that it leaches into the bitter taste of the coffee. At the other tables, there are huddled groups of uniformed hospital workers, trying to snatch a few moments of calm before returning to the fray of distress, and hunched family groups talking in low voices about the member of their family who is causing them distress, who is not with them now but upstairs on a ward somewhere.

As soon as they have found seats facing each other, Cassie leans forward and says, 'Hey, Sid, I'm glad you're back? I need to talk to you? I don't know whether I should dump Ivor and marry Angus? What do you think?'

She doesn't usually ask Sid's advice about anything, so he gives it some thought.

'Mmm. Has he asked you?'

'Not yet. But I think he will?'

'Actually, I think they're quite alike. Angus and Ivor are both dominating types, they like to be in control,' he ventures, conscious that he is treading on dangerous ground.

But Cassie just smiles. 'Do you really think so?'

'Isn't it a bit obvious?'

'I know what you mean. But the main difference is Angus is a free agent, without any emotional baggage? And Ivor doesn't want babies, he says it would complicate things with Barbara? Dad says we can take over his flat in Totley, when he moves back in with Mum? And you and Jacquie are going to make me an auntie soon, so I'll get plenty of practice?'

Cassie goes on to complain that she has suffered all her childhood from inadequate parenting, which is why her life is such a mess, and a baby will help her get it together. Sid tries to switch off his listening, thinking that the trouble with Cassie is that she's a bit young for her age. She won't take responsibility for the things that happen to her. She always finds someone else to blame when things go wrong. Like when Mum nagged at her for still being single, with no serious boyfriend on the horizon apart from Ivor, she blamed Mum for putting pressure on her. Well, a baby won't put up with that, thinks Sid, though he does not say so.

He tries to suppress his irritation with his sister. She seems to think the whole Rosie–George Brexit break-up is just another family joke, on a par with their dad's red bobble hat and their mother's grandchildren obsession. But to him it seems like the inciting moment – the beginning of everything that went wrong afterwards, both in the country and in their family. And it will be up to them, to him and Cassie and their generation, or even maybe up to their own children and grandchildren, to heal the damage. This sombre thought brings a frown to his brow.

Cassie, true to form, doesn't notice. She brushes her hair back from her face and continues with a giggle. 'I remember that night so clearly, Sid, how Mum shouted at Dad and he just shrugged and held up his hands. Over breakfast next day Mum started to sing "Land of Hope and Glory" in an ironical high-pitched wail, waving her mug of tea around, and splashing it about.'

Listening to Cassie, Sid asks himself how things can ever be alright again after all that rage. Can all those angry buzzing insects be recaptured and put back inside Pandora's box? How is it possible that two adults who have lived together in relative harmony for so many years, and brought up their children to be industrious and mainly sober, have so totally lost control? What madness possessed them? And how can it ever be put together again after so much bitterness? Not just between his parents, but also between Rosie and Brenda, the 48 per cent and the 52 per cent?

It's the closeness of the result, it's the feeling of being cheated, it's the sense that the other side is being wilfully stupid and just doesn't understand the issues, that makes both sides so angry, he thinks.

It's as though the referendum has opened up a fissure in the country which was there all the time but that no one had spotted before, like in his parents' marriage. And at the same moment, the pressure that had built up over years came seething out, hot and furious, like molten lava. The morning after the referendum, when he went round to his family home, both his parents were in the kitchen, the floor was splashed with tea and littered with triangles of toast, and Rosie kept moaning at George, 'You idiot! You irresponsible bloody idiot! Think of our children! Do you want them to be impoverished?' His father's face was pale, his cheeks red and blotchy, his hair was sticking up with marmalade. His pupils were dilated, like he was high on something. Victory. He was high on victory. But at the same time he was scared. He didn't really know what would happen next.

'I've heard that babies can be very demanding, Cassie,' he says to her in his 'sensible older brother' voice. Since their parents have given up on parenting, and seem to have returned to adolescence once more, it's up to him to be the grown-up. 'They make unreasonable demands, and they think the only purpose of your existence is to keep them happy. The main thing is, you need a good partner; would *Angus* make *you* happy, sis?'

Cassie twirls a long strand of reddish hair around her finger as she speaks, and he notices she is wearing a blue paper flower-clip in her hair, instead of the faux ivory one. She sucks absently on her twirl of hair and replies, 'Do people ever make each other happy, Sid, or is happiness just something that's lurking there inside you all the time, waiting for the right moment to come out? Like worms in compost? I think Mum's never been really happy since she split up with Dad?'

'Nor has Dad. He thought a Ferrari would make him happy; then he fell for Afrodita. But in the end he got neither, and ended up back with Mum. Yet they both seem happy,' adds Sid.

'You've gone all philosophical, bro.' Cassie laughs, a merry uninhibited laugh, wrinkling her nose like she used to when she was a kid. 'What if it's up to us, the younger generation, to clear up the mess our parents have made?'

'Mmm. Or maybe it's not even us – it's our children, still to be born, who won't have any memory of all the bitterness,' he says. 'They'll inherit a changed world.'

'If there's any world left for them to inherit . . .' She pauses to wipe a finger around the rim of the coffee cup, and gives it a meditative lick.

Then he broaches the question that's been bugging him ever since Brenda let it slip. 'What's this about Mum's squirrel, Cassie?'

'Oh, that,' she shrugs. 'Ivor says it's morally wrong to eat anything you haven't killed yourself.'

'So did you eat it?'

'Ivor skinned it. There was hardly any meat on it. It was all sinew and bones, so we made it into a casserole.'

'Was it nice?'

'Not very. We gave it to Heidi. She finished it off.'

'So maybe you're better off with Angus. He'd never say a daft thing like that.'

'Ha ha. I think you're right. I'll have to marry Angus.' She grins, satisfied with her decision. 'I like talking to you, big bro. You're so sensible. How come I didn't turn out sensible like you? But I managed to learn some philosophy from them too, Mum and Dad? For example, do you remember how they went on about possessions not making you rich? And they were right, we didn't feel poor, did we? But now people believe you need possessions to show off who you are – your identity?'

'Is that what you believe?' Sid doesn't remember their parents going on about possessions or philosophy, just about sex.

'What Angus says about ivory is spot on? Men think elephant tusks will make them more virile. Well, we know that's not true? But it doesn't stop them, nor women wanting carved ivory trinkets – to show they can afford them? That's how we kill off the species. Bye bye, elephants?' She waves her slim white hands in the air. 'And we go everywhere by car or plane, because we're always in a hurry, so the earth heats up? Bye bye, polar bears? We fill up the oceans with plastic bottles, because we think we can't drink the tap water? Bye bye, whales? We modify crops to be resistant to weedkillers, so we poison ourselves with the weedkillers the plants are resistant to? Bye bye, butterflies. Bye bye, bees. We think we can't be bothered with composting? Bye bye, everybody?' More waving.

He realizes he finds it hard to take his sister seriously. When she pauses for breath he asks sardonically, 'Did Ivor tell you all that? Or was it Angus?'

'So what if he did?' she replies, not answering his question. 'Just because the person who says it is a bit of an arse, it doesn't make it wrong, does it?'

SID: Strange times

After he gets home from the hospital, Sid pours himself a beer (the sensible coffee-drinking resolution has been abandoned) and searches in the recesses of his memory for the sentence he made up on the spur of the moment to help his father create a new password. But so much has happened since then, it has vanished. He seems to remember it had his father's name and his age in it. Was he seventy-nine at the time or turning eighty? As always, when he can't remember something, he puts his brain into automatic by reaching for his guitar. What was that Ramonas' song with the great guitar riff? He cannot remember that either, but he can remember a strong surge of emotion. Was it courage?

Then the doorbell rings and there is his father on the doorstep, looking distressed and tired.

'I've remembered the sentence, Sid,' he stutters. '"I am George Pantis and I am seventy-nine years old." Or eighty. I can't remember which. And I've forgotten what was in upper case and what was in lower case. I was up half the night, trying out different combinations and permutations. Then I was locked out for too many failed attempts, so I'll have to try again later.'

'Keep a record of your attempts, Dad, on a scrap of paper. That way, you won't find yourself repeating the same errors.'

Sid thinks his father still does not understand the first thing about password security. He'll have to go over to Totley to give the old man a hand.

*

When he rings the doorbell in Totley next day, George shambles over in bare feet to open it. There is a sea of half-filled boxes and black bin bags in the hall, as his father empties the flat in preparation for moving out and for Angus and Cassie to move in.

He tells Sid that he's moving back in with Rosie, though Sid knew that already. George says with a rueful smile, 'You wouldn't believe how much stuff I've accumulated in just a couple of months, mainly poetry books and paper. I thought I was here forever. But things haven't turned out that way.'

George appears even more despondent than he seemed yesterday in the hospital; he seems to have aged ten years in a day. His head is drooping and his shoulders sag. It grieves Sid to see his father like this, but he only has himself to blame for everything that has gone wrong. He should never have given away his password. Still, don't we all sometimes do silly things we regret, and don't we all have just ourselves to blame? thinks Sid.

'What's with the password, Dad?'

'Look!'

George sits down heavily at the computer, which is on a desk in a corner of the sitting room, and stares at the screen. Looking over his shoulder, Sid watches his father's attempts to log into his bank account, trying various upper-and-lower-case combinations and permutations of iagpaia8oyo. He doesn't keep a record of his father's failed attempts, so neither of them can remember how he did it, when suddenly the bank's welcome screen flashes up. George selects a savings account. It opens. There is nothing at all in there. He rests his head in his hands. A look of incomprehension and despair falls like a shadow over his tired features.

He shakes his head in disbelief. 'Not even the original £4.50. I've been cleaned out. Where's it all gone?'

Sid cannot pretend he is not disappointed too. Even though he did not quite believe in the reality of the money from the Kosovan State Lottery that suddenly appeared in his father's account, he has built up some modest hopes for himself, Jacquie and the baby based on his father's assumed generosity. For instance, he thinks, it would be great to put a down-payment on a place of their own, and then pay off a mortgage instead of paying rent. It would be great to invest in some high-end baby gear, and a new cot, not like the one he slept in at Vohur. But he summons up some sensible words of comfort.

'Don't grieve over what might have been, Dad. Mum is right – you may never have been able to take the money out anyway. Whoever it belonged to, it wasn't you.' He reaches for his father's hand and gives it a squeeze.

'But it *was* mine. For a while.' George's voice is plaintive, almost childlike. It brings out the Mr Sensible who is still lurking inside Sid.

'Well, just think carefully – who else had the password, Dad? It may be a case for the police.'

'Rosie had it,' he retorts. 'She might have taken it out of the pocket before she washed her jeans, and is keeping it from me. She doesn't trust me. She might want her revenge, of course. Or she might just want the money. Rosie worries about having a secure future, while I believe in living life to the full in the present.'

Sometimes people say true things without realizing it, Sid thinks, and bites his lip, saying nothing. He wouldn't put it past his mother to have taken the password from his father's monitor and accessed the account. Maybe the new scarlet coat is a sign. But would she be able to keep a secret like that for long? His father rambles on, revealing that there are other possibilities.

'And Afrodita had it,' George confesses. 'She winkled it out of me in the end. Though she didn't write it down, she memorized it. But I don't suppose there's any banks or cashpoints within a hundred miles of Kashtanje, so she's bound to have forgotten it by the time she gets to one, isn't she?'

'You didn't tell anybody else? How about Brenda?'

George shakes his head glumly. 'I didn't even tell Brenda I'd won the money. She'd have been full of ideas for spending it quickly until it was all gone. Rosie knew, of course, because I blurted it out to her. She was worried I'd squander it. Typical Rosie. Doesn't trust me with money, you know, I don't know why.'

'Could Afrodita have told anybody?' Sid asks, looking his father squarely in the eye.

George squirms. A guilty look crosses his face, as if he knows he should not have told her. 'Only her mother. Or Kroçi. I couldn't remember whether the number was seventy-nine or eighty, so I told her to try both, but I doubt her mother would remember that. Of course, Pattie Smith and Kroçi were both after it, and Afrodita was their means of winkling it out of me.'

'Maybe we'll just have to accept that it will remain a mystery,' Sid says.

'Maybe Kroçi threatened or wheedled the number out of her, before she and her mother escaped on that boat with the chickens,' adds George. 'Or they may have been in league all the time.'

'What happened to Kroçi?' An image of the fraudster's merry grin as he stood on his doorstep flashes across Sid's mind, like a waking flashback to a remembered nightmare. He hopes he will never see him again.

George runs his hand over his stubbly chin and says, 'I don't know what happened to Kroçi. I think he was marooned at Kashtanje with Pattie and the gangsters. I can't imagine that he got away, and found a cashpoint, and remembered the password, and managed to guess the right combination of upper- and lower-case letters and numbers. It seems highly unlikely.'

'The whole thing seems highly unlikely, Dad.'

'But sometimes the unlikely happens. We live in strange times.'

SID: *Common purpose*

At about six thirty on Friday evening, Sid is at home in his terraced house watching the news on TV. It's dark outside, and an accumulation of large raindrops wriggle like transparent worms down the window. Inside, the TV screen flickers with grim fact piled upon grim fact. Yes, as his father said, we live in strange times. The news is unrelievedly gloomy, with politicians and positions everyone has got sick of hearing, so that most people, like Sid, only listen to the news out of habit – and no one, he thinks, knows what is real any more, and how ordinary people like him can affect anything. Is what is being said just to reassure the people, or to stir them up and to trigger certain predictable responses? Who is pulling those strings behind the scenes? Like he has no way of knowing whether his father's vanished money was ever real, or how it was whisked out of his account.

Suddenly the key turns in the lock and Jacquie bounces in with a cherubic smile on her face, her pregnant belly vast and round under her T-shirt.

'Good news, Sid. They've approved my transfer. I can start at the Hallamshire Hospital in Sheffield after my maternity leave.'

A touch of angel dust brushes his heart, and his throat fills up with honey, so he can't talk. Tears mist his eyes. Has Jacquie also noticed his new blubbiness? If so, it doesn't seem to bother her. Swallowing down the tears, he hugs and kisses her.

Elsewhere in the world, terrible things are happening. The

US presidential election seems to be going off the rails; the rich have commandeered the world's wealth and stashed it away in tax havens, just in case they need a new kidney or two; violence is tearing cities apart; millions are in flight from their homes to safer places; the planet is heating up; the NHS is being sold off; World War Three looms around the corner; The White Stripes have split up and music hasn't been the same since; the Blades lost to Bolton. His father's dream of riches has evaporated like dew. But here in the quiet home, with just him, Jacquie and the coming baby, all is heavenly calm and bright.

Jacquie sits down wearily beside him, puts her hand on his and says, 'Let's get married, Sid.'

His heartbeat speeds up a notch. Beads of sweat break out on his brow. This is what he's dreamed of for so long – ever since he met Jacquie, in fact. But it is a bit scary. And shouldn't it be him asking her? Will it turn out to be another beguiling fantasy, like all the others? A woozy feeling comes over him. He hesitates.

'But . . .'

'But what?'

'But do you really want to stay in this grey foreigner-fearing island?'

'Yes. I want to stay in England. I like working in the NHS. I like its sense of common purpose.'

'But do you really want to join our crazy family?'

'I've got used to you all – you and Cassie and your mum and dad, and Brenda. I expect with time I'll get used to Sniffer too. And you've changed, Sid, you've improved a lot. You're not so uptight as you were. And your music's better,' she laughs.

'Yes, I've changed. I saw at first hand that getting what you think you want doesn't always lead to happiness.' An image of a kidney slithering across a clinic floor pops into his mind. He pushes away the image, takes Jacquie's hand and kisses it.

He reflects on what he has learnt, after all, from both his parents, from watching their relationship disintegrate, then watching them grow together again, but differently.

'Do you want to feel our baby kicking?' she says.

She lays Sid's hand on her tummy, and he feels the tight skin of her bump and beneath his palm the thrusting movement, strong and confident, of a small person waiting to be born.

Acknowledgements

Many people have contributed to this book with their comments, suggestions, advice and encouragement, and I would like to thank all of them. I would especially like to thank the Nanyang Technological University, Singapore, who gave me time and space to get started, Michael Brown who gave me invaluable advice and information on cyber security, and the readers of the *Daily Mail Online* whose comments, often forcefully expressed, helped me to get to know their point of view. Thanks are also due to Donald Sassoon who read and commented on many drafts, to Bill Hamilton who sent me back to the drawing board again and again, to Juliet Annan and Assallah Tahir for their helpful suggestions in streamlining and polishing the story, and to Shân Morley Jones for her painstaking work in helping me to straighten out the timeline.

MARINA LEWYCKA

A SHORT HISTORY OF TRACTORS IN UKRAINIAN

'Two years after my mother died, my father fell in love with a glamorous blonde Ukrainian divorcee. He was eighty-four and she was thirty-six. She exploded into our lives like a fluffy pink grenade, churning up the murky water, bringing to the surface a sludge of sloughed-off memories, giving the family ghosts a kick up the backside.'

Sisters Vera and Nadezhda must put aside a lifetime of feuding to save their émigré engineer father from voluptuous gold-digger Valentina. With her proclivity for green satin underwear and boil-in-the-bag cuisine, she will stop at nothing in her pursuit of Western wealth.

But the sisters' campaign to oust Valentina unearths family secrets, uncovers fifty years of Europe's darkest history and sends them back to roots they'd much rather forget...

'Hugely enjoyable...yields a golden harvest of family truths' *Daily Telegraph*

'Thought-provoking, uproariously funny, a comic feast. A riotous oil painting of senility, lust and greed' *Economist*

'Delightful, funny, touching' *Spectator*

'Extremely funny' *The Times*

MARINA LEWYCKA

TWO CARAVANS

A field of strawberries in Kent, and sitting in it two caravans – one for the men and one for the women. The residents are from all over: minor's son Andriy is from the old Ukraine, while sexy young Irina is from the new: they eye each other warily. There are the Poles, Tomasz and Yola; two Chinese girls; and Emanuel from Malawi. They're all here to pick strawberries in England's green and pleasant land.

But these days England's not so pleasant for immigrants. Not with Russian gangster-wannabes like Vulk, who's taken a shine to Irina and thinks kidnapping is a wooing strategy. And so Andriy – who really doesn't fancy Irina, honest – must set off in search of that girl he's not in love with.

'A funny, charming, rollicking road trip' *Observer*

'Immensely appealing. All but sings with zest for life . . . could hardly be more engaging, shrewd and winningly perceptive' *Sunday Times*

'Hilarious and horrifying, *Two Caravans* is funny, clever and well-observed' *Guardian*

MARINA LEWYCKA

WE ARE ALL MADE OF GLUE

Georgie Sinclair's life is coming unstuck. Her husband's left her. Her son's obsessed with the End of the World. And now her elderly neighbour Mrs Shapiro has decided they are related.

Or so the hospital informs her when Mrs Shapiro has an accident and names Georgie next of kin. This, however, is not a case of a quick ward visit: Mrs Shapiro has a large rickety house full of stinky cats that needs looking after that a pair of estate agents seem intent on swindling from her. Plus there are the '   ' trying to repair it (uselessly). Then there's the social worker who   er in a nursing home. Not to mention some letters that point to a my   ful past.

As Georgie tries her best to put Mrs Shapiro's life back together somehow she must stop her own from falling apart . . .

'Vibrant dialogue, a family in meltdown, a clash of cultures and wonderful cast of expertly observed characters. Pure laugh-out-loud social comedy' *Daily Mail*

'Hilarious. A big-hearted confection of the comic and the poignant'
Literary Review

'A big, bustling novel, told with enthusiasm by a narrator who is warm, winningly disaster-prone and, crucially, believable' *Spectator*